MURDER, SWEET MURDER

MURDER, SWEET MURDER

Eleanor Kuhns

SEVERN
HOUSE

First world edition published in Great Britain in 2021 and the USA in 2022
by Severn House, an imprint of Canongate Books Ltd,
14 High Street, Edinburgh EH1 1TE.

Trade paperback edition first published in Great Britain and the USA in 2022
by Severn House, an imprint of Canongate Books Ltd.

severnhouse.com

British Library Cataloguing-in-Publication Data
A CIP catalogue record for this title is available from the British Library.

ISBN-13: 978-0-7278-5009-6 (cased)
ISBN-13: 978-1-4483-0733-3 (trade paper)
ISBN-13: 978-1-4483-0732-6 (e-book)

All Severn House titles are printed on acid-free paper.

MIX
Paper from
responsible sources
FSC
www.fsc.org   FSC® C013056

Typeset by Palimpsest Book Production Ltd.,
Falkirk, Stirlingshire, Scotland.
Printed and bound in Great Britain by
TJ Books, Padstow, Cornwall.

To all the readers who asked me for more about Lydia and her family.

ONE

Lydia brought the closely written letter to the window to read it in the bright light. Rees knew it was from his wife's sister, Cordelia. He had never met her, or any of her family, but he recognized the scent of roses. Cordelia's letters were permeated with it. He thought she must douse herself with the perfume for the scent to saturate the paper so thoroughly.

'I do wish Cordy would not write both ways,' Lydia said as she unfolded the paper. Rees nodded. His sister-in-law wrote horizontally as she moved from top to bottom and then turned the paper and wrote side to side, over her previous script. It made reading her news difficult at best. He didn't know why Lydia bothered. Her sister's news rarely included anything important, always more of a list of parties and new clothes than anything else. Lydia knew it too. That was why, although Thomas had brought the missive from the tavern the previous day, taking the opportunity to visit Annie at the same time, Lydia had not bothered to read the letter until breakfast today.

Rees helped himself to another cup of coffee and looked over at his family. The dame school had closed in early December in the hope it would stop the spread of smallpox. The school was still closed, and would be for the rest of January, but Jerusha refused to allow her siblings' schooling to end. She had taken everyone but the baby to the kitchen table where, one after another, they recited their lessons.

Rees sighed. The children were all growing up. Jerusha would be the next to fly the nest; she was already testing her wings. He glanced at Lydia. At least Sharon, Rees's youngest, would soon have a younger brother or sister in late April or early May. He was glad of it.

'Oh no,' Lydia said involuntarily, the blood draining from her cheeks.

'What now?' Rees asked in a resigned voice. 'Did your sister rip her best dress?'

'I wish that were so.' Lydia looked at Rees over the top of the sheet of paper. 'My father has been accused of murdering a young man last November.'

Rees stared at his wife for several horrified seconds. 'Murder? What happened?'

'I don't know.' She shook her head in mingled affection and exasperation. 'You know how she writes; every sentence is an exclamation. Her letter is even more disjointed than usual. I am having trouble making head or tail of it.'

'Maybe the "murder" is your sister's usual hyperbole.'

'Perhaps, but she says quite clearly a constable came to the house.'

'Does she tell you why he is accused?'

'Someone was shot.' Lydia examined the page. 'She wrote this almost two months ago. Who knows what has happened in the interim?'

'Well, is the accusation a serious one? Was your father jailed?'

'I don't know. Most of this,' and she rattled the paper, 'is assurances he is innocent.'

'No helpful information, then,' Rees said.

'None. But . . .' Lydia paused for so long Rees directed a suspicious look at her.

'What? What else?'

Lydia raised her eyes to his. She was wearing Rees's favorite dress, her dark indigo wool, and her eyes looked very blue. 'She wishes us to come to Boston and prove her father's innocence.'

'What? Boston? No.' Rees shook his head. 'Especially not now. Not in the middle of winter.' They were almost into the final week of January 1801. Congress was still fighting over who, Thomas Jefferson or Aaron Burr, had won the presidency.

'The weather is not terrible now—' Lydia began.

'We've already experienced several snowstorms,' Rees pointed out. Lydia bit her lip and looked down at the paper in her hand. With a guilty pang, Rees put his hand on his wife's arm. 'Of course, this is about your father. He is your father too, isn't he? Not just your sister's.'

'I would not be doing this for my father,' she said shortly. 'It is my sister's comfort and well-being I care about. As you know, the relationship between my father and myself has never been . . .' She paused abruptly as she searched for the right word. 'Affectionate? Respectful? He feels I am too outspoken and unfeminine. I feel he . . .' She stopped again. Rees waited. Finally, speaking very quickly, she admitted, 'I would not be surprised to hear he did murder someone.'

Rees stared at her, aghast. 'You can't believe that,' he said although he knew Lydia would not say it if she didn't believe it. Lydia's estrangement from her father was long standing. Rees himself had had contempt for his father, a cruel drunken bully. But suspecting someone of murder? That was an entirely different level of dislike.

Lydia regarded her husband for several seconds. Then she turned around and paced a few steps before turning back. 'I know you think I am speaking simply from some rancor toward my father. But he has not only been cruel – and *is* not – to me. I could tell you stories.'

'That does not mean he murdered someone,' Rees said. Lydia met his shocked gaze and sighed.

'I suppose not,' she said. 'I am only surprised that he is not the victim. I know there are many who wish to see him dead.'

Rees, only slightly less shocked by that statement, nodded to acknowledge he heard her. He did not trust himself to speak. Lydia was usually the most even-tempered of women. This detestation for her father stunned him. She turned and looked at him, eyeing his expression for several seconds.

'I perceive you find my lack of family feeling appalling,' she said at last. 'But you don't know him. And, without knowing him, you cannot possibly understand.' Her lips were trembling. Rees put his arms around her.

'I know you,' he said. 'And so, I must believe you.'

With a sob, Lydia leaned against his chest. He held her close while she struggled to compose herself.

This time, Rees thought, he had managed to express the most consoling words he could have found.

'What do you think we should do?' he asked. He hated to see her so unhappy. When Lydia did not speak, he continued. 'It is January, and the weather could turn at any second.' Lydia nodded and stepped away from him.

'And you are busy here,' she agreed, wiping her eyes.

'Not very,' Rees said. He could easily suspend his weaving for a week. 'If we don't go, you'll wonder for the rest of your life if your father was guilty.'

Lydia sniffed and took her handkerchief from her sleeve to wipe her eyes.

'I know,' she admitted. 'We parted on poor terms . . .'

Rees realized that for all her animus toward her father, a part of her still yearned for his approval. He understood. He had hated his father most of his life – but he had never suspected the old man of murder. And he had made some amends. Before he'd died, he'd told Rees he loved him. That had almost made up for the expectation a boy could work like a man, for the beatings, and for all the years that had come before.

Rees inspected his wife, noticing the violet shadows under her eyes. Maybe they should go to Boston, despite the threat of bad weather. She needed to resolve her feelings for her father. Besides, after the smallpox epidemic last fall and her falling out with her friend Ruth and then the murder at the Shaker community nearby, and her pregnancy, his wife had been unusually emotional. On a knife's edge. Visiting her family might serve to restore her.

Rees understood. His emotions were still raw after last fall's events.

'I think we should go,' he said now. 'We might be fortunate with the weather.'

'But there are the children,' Lydia said, meeting his gaze with anxious eyes.

'Annie and Jerusha will be staying here at the farm,' Rees said, understanding his wife needed to be persuaded. Lydia was nothing if not responsible. 'Annie is almost eighteen and Jerusha is fifteen. They can watch the younger children.' He stepped back so he could look into her face. 'You trust them, don't you?' Annie had recently left the Shaker community and was staying with them at the farm until she married. Jerusha, adopted with her siblings several years ago, had been caring for her brothers and sister alone since the age of nine. Rees felt they were capable.

When Lydia did not respond, Rees continued. 'Thomas will visit regularly to see Annie and we can ask Rouge to look in on them.'

Lydia hesitated for several seconds and when she spoke again it sounded as if she had changed topics.

'We should take Jerusha with us,' she said. 'I'd planned to visit Boston in the spring, after the birth of the new baby, so we could bring him as well as register Jerusha for Bingham's school. If she thought she would enjoy it, that is.'

Rees, who had heard nothing of these plans, blinked. But he rallied. 'We will take her now,' he said. 'The dame school is not open. And if Miss Francine does open, she can manage without Jerusha for a few days.' The smallpox that had swept through town had died down and the school was supposed to open in a week. 'But do you think the children will be too much for Annie?'

'We'll bring Sharon too.' Lydia smiled. 'That will leave only the three older kids. And Cordy has been pressing me to bring her to Boston so they could meet her.'

'How does your sister even know we've successfully investigated other murders?' Rees asked, already sure he knew the answer.

'I may have mentioned it a few times,' Lydia admitted, ducking her head self-consciously.

Rees nodded without speaking. He knew the sisters had corresponded but now realized it had been more often than he'd guessed. 'We should make our arrangements quickly and leave while the weather is fair. For now, although it is cold, it is clear. With any luck, this weather will continue.'

'I will write back immediately,' Lydia said, her voice lifting. 'You can deliver the letter to the tavern and Constable Rouge can put it on the coach for Boston.'

'Very well,' Rees agreed. The sooner, the better.

TWO

R ees spent some time pondering their mode of travel. Since the roads were snow-covered, a sleigh might be the most practical. But that conveyance would not be useful on Boston's cobbled streets. He had decided to use his own wagon, with Hannibal pulling it, when Lydia threw his plans into disorder.

'Instead of tiring our own horse, we should book seats in the coach,' she said. 'That way, we will travel inside. And the coach, with its team, will be faster than our own wagon and a single horse.'

'But we will be gone for a week or more,' Rees objected.

Lydia smiled. 'Probably for longer than that,' she said.

Rees shook his head, stiff with reluctance. He hated the thought of losing the freedom to leave at a moment's notice. Especially considering his wife's feelings about her father.

'I am certain Thomas will gladly return Hannibal and the wagon to the farm,' Lydia continued. 'He will take the opportunity to visit Annie, your wagon will be safe, and Hannibal will be back in his accustomed stall.'

'That is fine,' Rees said. 'But . . .' His voice trailed away. How could he explain he did not want to be trapped in her father's house?

Lydia regarded him for several seconds and then reached out and put a hand on his.

'I know you prefer the comfort of your own transportation,' she said. 'But remember, Boston is a city. We will be able to walk everywhere.' She paused for a moment. When he said nothing and she could see his worried expression did not change, she added, 'Boston is also a city of taverns and inns. If we elect to remove ourselves from my father's house, we will have other options. And I still have friends who might be willing to put us up.'

'I will consider it,' Rees said at last. Every time he thought of staying in Boston without his wagon and his own horse, he broke out in a cold sweat. Finally, he went to town and met with Simon Rouge, inn-keeper and constable. To Rees's surprise, the other man agreed with Lydia. Taking the coach was the most practical solution.

'After all,' Rouge said, 'if the visit is as terrible as you fear, you can always take the coach home from Boston to Maine.' And when Rees still hesitated, the constable said briskly, 'Make the sensible decision for once. Taking your own vehicle will ensure the journey is uncomfortable and exhausting – for you and your horse.'

Somewhat reassured, Rees booked four seats for Tuesday next. Now his primary concern was the weather. He prayed the clear skies would hold.

Three days later, Rees, preparations made, drove to town at first light. Snow had fallen during the night, leaving a thin coating over the dirty older accumulation. But the gilding of the treetops by the rising sun predicted a sunny, although cold, day. Rees had packed the wagon with their luggage the previous evening and covered it with a sheet of canvas. Both Sharon and Jerusha were clad in their Sunday best and the older girl wore a new redingote of blue wool.

Lydia wore her second-best dress, woolen with a high waist and an embroidered ribbon under the bust. Even Rees, who eschewed fancy clothing, wore his second-best breeches, and an embroidered waist-coat – something he saved for formal dress. He had put aside his favorite tricorn, a hat he had worn for more than twenty years, for a wide-brimmed black wool hat trimmed with beaver. He knew he did not cut a fashionable figure, but he did not care. In his opinion, a focus on fashion was a form of vanity.

They arrived at the tavern early, before the coach had even arrived. Since of the four, only Sharon had eaten breakfast (Jerusha had been too excited and both Lydia and Rees too anxious), they decided to eat something while they waited. But Rees, although he drank the coffee, found eating difficult. Now that the flurry of preparation was done, he had begun to fret about the upcoming meeting with his in-laws. Lydia watched him move the eggs around on his plate.

'Are you nervous?' she asked in a low voice.

'What if your family doesn't like me?' Rees said. Lydia put her gloved hand on his wrist.

'Oh, Will, you are a good man,' she said. 'Both my stepmother and Cordy will like you. Isabeau raised me, you know, and they will be happy if I am happy.'

'I want them to think you chose well,' he said, his voice rough. He knew she came from wealth, not a poor farming family like he had.

'I do not care what they think,' Lydia said. 'As for my father, he does not like his own daughter. If he dislikes you, you should take it as a compliment.'

Rees tried to smile but he was not reassured.

They arrived in Boston just after mid-afternoon. Rees, who knew they would have reached Boston earlier if he had taken his wagon instead of the coach, wished he had gone with his instincts. But Lydia – and Rouge too – had persuaded him to leave Hannibal home.

For the first time, Rees wondered how they would travel from the coach stop to the Farrell family home. Now, if he had taken his own vehicle . . . Lydia's thoughts must have been traveling in the same direction. 'I hope my stepmother received my letter,' she murmured softly. Rees glanced at her. 'If so, they will be waiting for us.' She smiled at him, her eyes worried.

'Do they know at which inn the coach will stop?' Rees asked.

'We will disembark at the Warren Tavern,' Lydia said. 'I told them so in my letter.'

Rees nodded, realizing with an uncomfortable sense that they were now entering a world Lydia knew well and he did not. He would be the outsider and must rely upon his wife to direct him. That was not an emotion he enjoyed feeling. What was worse, he anticipated feeling this discomfort several times during the visit as Lydia demonstrated her familiarity with this other world. Rees would make mistakes and that would prove to her family that he did not deserve her.

'We will be there soon,' Lydia murmured, clutching Sharon to her. The toddler had been whiny and fractious most of the journey.

'I wish you had told me more about your past,' Rees said now. 'Why you left home and became a Shaker.' Not knowing left him at a serious disadvantage.

'I should have, I suppose, but I never thought I would return to Boston. Telling you would have served no purpose.' She glanced at him from under the brim of her bonnet and nodded at the two girls. 'I'll try to describe my past as we go. Now is not the time.'

The coach drove along narrow streets hemmed in by brick build-ings on either side until it approached a large structure built on a corner. The stables and inn yard were positioned behind the inn and that was where the coach finally drew to a stop. Rees climbed out, a trifle stiffly, and turned back to assist his wife.

She had no sooner climbed down than a whirlwind in human form descended upon her screaming, 'Lydia.' Rees could smell the scent of roses from across the yard.

Lydia, nonplussed, stood there while the young woman flung her arms around her. 'I am so glad you have come.'

Rees helped Jerusha down the coach step and picked up the still drowsy Sharon.

'Cordelia Farrell. Stop behaving like a hoyden right now.' The sharp reproof came from an older woman mincing across the inn yard. She spoke with the trace of an accent. Rees thought it might be French, but her speech bore more of a musical inflection than any French he'd heard before. She was clad in the height of fashion, a dark burgundy pelisse that flattered her fair complexion. High pattens protected her delicate leather slippers from the dirt and muck on the ground. Since the young female clutching at Lydia and screaming in excitement closely resembled the woman, Rees guessed she was Lydia's stepmother.

Cordelia's hair was not the spun gold of her mother's, but more reddish, and she was of a sturdier build. She shared only her small retroussé nose and full lips with Lydia. Still, the resemblance was so close they could almost be twins. Beautiful twins. Rees tried not to conclude these women were frivolous empty-headed fashion plates.

'You received my letter, then,' Lydia said in a strained voice.

'Yesterday,' Mrs Farrell replied.

'We've been so busy preparing for you,' Cordelia squealed.

'Cordelia,' said her mother reprovingly. 'A lady never uses that tone. You sound like a barnyard animal.'

'Permit me to introduce my family,' Lydia said as she gently pushed her sister away. 'My stepmother, Isabeau Farrell, and my sister Cordelia.' She gestured to Rees. 'My husband, William.' Two pairs of identical light blue eyes regarded him, inspecting him until he felt like a side of beef hanging from a hook.

'Delighted,' Mrs Farrell said, extending her gloved fingers.

'Mrs Farrell,' Rees said politely, taking her hand.

'Oh, please call me Isabeau,' she said, almost flirtatiously. Rees nodded uncomfortably and took a step back.

'My daughters, Jerusha and Sharon,' Lydia continued, gesturing to her daughters.

'I'm Cordelia,' said Lydia's sister, throwing herself into Jerusha's arms. 'You may call me Cordy. I am quite convinced we shall become bosom companions.' Rees smiled to see Jerusha's terrified expression.

Cordelia was probably two to three years older than fifteen-year-old Jerusha. Both girls had fair hair, but there the resemblance ended. Jerusha's hair had darkened through the years and she was both taller and more robust than the other girl. Both wore green, but Jerusha's dark wool resembled one of the hardy Maine pines. Cordelia's soft sage-green pelisse was both feminine and youthful and it exactly matched the be-ribboned bonnet she wore.

'The baby is yours?' Mrs Farrell asked, her gaze passing over Jerusha without interest to rest upon Sharon. 'It is unfortunate about the red hair. But I dare say she will grow up to become a beauty.'

Rees opened his mouth and then closed it again. Should he say thank you? Mrs Farrell had not really complimented his little girl. And the offensive snub she had offered Jerusha infuriated him.

Linking arms with Lydia and Jerusha, Cordelia chattered on. 'We've brought the carriage. It will be such fun to take you to the shops. We will soon have you rivaling the most fashionable ladies in town. I promise you that.'

'Oh, we expect to be far too busy to spend all our time shopping and at the dressmaker's,' Lydia said in a quelling tone.

'Surely, while you are here, you will want to acquire some new things,' Cordelia said, her voice rising into a disappointed wail.

'Jerusha, is it?' murmured Mrs Farrell, looking at the girl for the first time. 'If you are planning to attend school here in Boston, you will not want to appear the poor country cousin. Of course you must purchase some new things.'

Although Rees could not see either Lydia's or Jerusha's expressions, he could imagine them from the stiff set of Lydia's shoulders. She was furious. As for himself, he already wished they had not come.

THREE

The carriage proved to be a grand vehicle with a coachman in the box and a tiger at the back. Although the doors were plain, without an insignia, the dark mahogany was polished to a glossy sheen and the inside was lush with blue velvet seats and silk curtains. Four perfectly matched horses, chestnuts with black manes and tails, were harnessed to the coach. Rees eyed them, thinking that although they bore a superficial resemblance to Hannibal in coloring, the differences were more significant. These were aristocrats. Hannibal looked exactly like what he was: a no-nonsense work horse from a farm.

But Rees wished he were driving Hannibal now instead of climbing into a carriage so luxurious it made him wonder if his breeches were sufficiently clean for the seats.

'Your father is at his office,' Mrs Farrell was saying to Lydia. 'He expects to join us for dinner.'

Dinner? Noon was long past. Then Rees realized that, unlike farmers who took their main meal at midday, the city dwellers followed the new fashion of dinner in the evening.

'But Cordy said in her letter . . .' Lydia began.

'Oh yes, that bit of unpleasantness.' Mrs Farrell smiled slightly. 'The sheriff was quite willing to believe Marcus had nothing to do with the unfortunate demise of the other man.'

'You mean he bribed him,' Lydia put in drily.

'You always did have a regrettable bluntness,' Mrs Farrell said.

'Then why did Cordy ask us to come?' Lydia asked, even more drily.

'Well, people do talk, don't they?' Mrs Farrell began. Cordy interrupted her.

'That is not all they do.'

'There's already been one scandal,' Mrs Farrell said, frowning at her daughter. 'And now, with Cordy approaching a marriageable age . . .' Her words trailed to a stop. Rees was not quite sure what she meant but Lydia nodded as if it was all perfectly clear.

'So, all of the invitations to parties and balls and other social events are no longer offered?' she said.

'Not entirely,' Mrs Farrell said. 'But—'

'Some of the invitations were rescinded.' Cordelia interrupted her mother once again. 'They tried to dress it up by saying there was an illness or something just as foolish. I knew the ball still went on. I heard about it.' Her mouth drooped. Lydia and Rees glanced at one another. No doubt other young women, girls not so pretty as Cordelia, were more than happy to tell her about the parties from which she was now excluded.

'And some of the young men to whom Cordy is now being introduced are not . . . top drawer.' Isabeau grimaced at her use of the slang. 'In the past most of them were the sons of other wealthy merchants. Mr Bartlett is certainly acceptable on that score. But now? I fear some of them are interested in my darling child only because of her father's wealth. And even at that—'

'I had friends,' Cordelia assured her sister. She did not seem to realize she had interrupted her mother. 'I was popular. And there were several young men who were interested in me and one in

particular who . . . well, no matter. But I have heard he has now
been forbidden my company. His father threatened to stop his
allowance. It is the scandal, you see.' She looked around at the
others, her eyes swimming with tears. 'It was a very dull Christmas
Season.'

Lydia and Rees both nodded. Even though this was not Cordelia's
scandal but her father's, it tarnished her reputation and made her
almost unmarriageable. Rees's gaze went to Jerusha. Although
some rumors could affect her, a baby out of wedlock for example,
the necessity to make a 'good' – i.e., wealthy and important –
marriage was not so important. His hope for her, as for Annie and
Sharon, was that they found good men and were happy.

Lydia leaned forward and clasped Cordelia's hand. 'We will do
our best to unravel the knot. Please understand, though, that an
investigation of this kind always uncovers secrets, some of them
unpleasant.'

Rees thought his wife had spoken almost too diplomatically.
Sometimes those secrets were not just unpleasant, but deadly. It
was up to him to articulate the danger they might be putting
themselves in.

'We will have to ask some probing questions, some uncomfortable questions. Are you prepared for that?' he asked.

'Of course we are,' Cordelia said immediately. But her mother
said nothing for several seconds. Instead she examined the gloved
hands clasped in her lap. Finally, she spoke.

'Cordy is a young girl. She is still an innocent. But others, no
matter how blameless they appear, might have made mistakes in
their pasts. Mistakes they would prefer no one else know.' She
looked up, her eyes boring into Lydia's. 'This is for Cordy's future.
So, I must rely on your family feeling to keep whatever you discover
to yourself.'

Rees wondered if Mrs Farrell was really asking them to keep
unfortunate information secret. What did she fear they would
discover? 'If it has no bearing on the murder,' he said. And then,
feeling he had to ask, he added, 'Is it possible that Mr Farrell is
guilty of the murder?'

'Of course not,' Cordelia said vehemently.

'He would never do such a thing,' Mrs Farrell declared. 'He
would not. He is too much a gentleman. And if you believe him

guilty and are setting out to prove it, then you can turn right around and return to the District of Maine.'

'We do not believe it,' Lydia said, untruthfully as Rees knew.

'But one must always be aware of the possibility,' he put in. 'And that is the kind of difficult question we might ask.'

Mrs Farrell glared at him. 'It sounds as though you have already made up your mind,' she said. Rees, who thought she was over-reacting, did not know what to say.

'Be assured, you may rely on our discretion,' Lydia said into the uncomfortable silence.

They drove for some time through crowded streets and over a bridge, and then through even more congested streets. Most were narrow meandering thoroughfares with buildings almost to the curbs. Some of these narrow lanes, barely more than alleys, were so constricted that when the carriage squeezed through, it left scarcely enough room for a pedestrian on either side.

Rees breathed a sigh of relief when they emerged on a wider street thronged with other carriages and many wagons.

Cordelia, who had been chattering animatedly all the while, laughed at his expression. 'Did you think we would get stuck?'

'It is said that many of these streets were once cow paths,' Mrs Farrell said. 'Several have already been widened—'

'And new houses are being built,' Cordelia interrupted.

'Cordelia,' scolded her mother. 'Please. You must curb your habit of interrupting.'

The coach was ascending State Street. As they passed a fine three-story house Mrs Farrell said, 'That is the State House.'

'And this one is ours,' Cordelia announced, pointing to an elegant brick manse with two floors and a widow walk on the roof nearby. A stone wall separated the residence from the sidewalk in the front. A garden was laid out inside the wall. Now the tree was bare and the shrubs brown and dead-looking but Rees could imagine how beguiling this spot would be in the summer.

The tiger jumped down and opened the gate. The coach paused just inside so the passengers could disembark. As the coach continued through to the mews behind the house, an older gentleman with curly white hair and dark skin opened the door.

FOUR

He waited while Rees and Lydia walked up the path to the front door before speaking. 'Welcome, Miss Lydia,' he said, sounding as if he had just seen her at breakfast. He spoke in the same lilting English spoken by his mistress.

'Thank you, Morris. How are you? And your family?'

'Very well, thank you.'

'This is part of my family,' Lydia said. 'My husband, William Rees. My two daughters, Jerusha and Sharon.'

Rees hesitated. Did one shake hands with servants? Finally, he extended his hand. Morris looked at it in surprise before giving it two quick shakes. So, no, Rees guessed, one did not.

'You said part of your family?' Morris asked, turning his attention back to Lydia.

'I have another daughter, three sons, and a stepson.'

'My goodness,' said Morris, his eyes widening, 'that is a large family.'

'Stop chatting with the servants and come inside,' Cordelia said, taking Lydia's arm and drawing her forward.

'You must be tired and hungry,' Mrs Farrell said as she handed her outer garments to Morris. Rees glanced at the gown she wore underneath and quickly looked away. The burgundy dress was cut very low, almost to the gold ribbon underneath the bosom. He felt heat rise into his cheeks. 'A maid will show you to your rooms—'

'You will sleep in your old bedchamber,' Cordelia told Lydia in excitement. 'Mr Rees will have the room next door.'

'The box room?' Lydia said incredulously.

'Oh, it isn't for storage now. It has been fitted up as a bedroom. And the door between the two rooms will be unlocked.'

'I am to sleep separately from my wife?' Rees asked in amazement.

Mrs Farrell smiled at him. 'Of course.' She glanced at Lydia and said derisively, 'You have adopted some rustic habits, I see.'

'And you,' Cordelia said as she turned to Jerusha, 'will share my room. I am quite looking forward to it. We will have such fun.' She sounded extremely pleased with herself. Jerusha tried to smile.

'Sharon will go into the nursery,' Mrs Farrell added. She nodded at the young maid who had quietly appeared at her elbow. She, like Morris, appeared to be mixed race.

'Oh dear,' Lydia said. 'She is not used to being apart from us.'

'It is high time she learned, then,' Mrs Farrell said unsympathetically.

Rees and Lydia exchanged glances, both vowing to visit their child in the nursery as often as possible.

'Come with me,' Cordelia said, pulling Jerusha toward the stairs. 'My room is just across the hall from Lydia's. Your mother's. My,' she added, giggling, 'that is a funny thing to say.'

'When you are ready, come downstairs to the breakfast room,' Mrs Farrell said to Lydia. 'Cook will set out a cold collation for you.' She looked at the maid. 'Take them upstairs, please, and show them their rooms.'

'Yes, ma'am,' the maid said so softly Rees could barely hear her. She could not be older than fourteen or so. She was an uncommonly pretty girl with black hair and bright brown eyes fringed with thick black lashes.

'You're new,' Lydia said to the child as they moved toward the stairs. 'What is your name?'

'Bridget.'

'I'm Mrs Rees. Lydia. This is my husband, Will.'

The girl managed a slight nod, her expression frightened. Lydia sighed.

Rees and Lydia looked at the nursery first, a large room at the top of the house. A dormered window on one side and another that led to a small veranda on the other let in light from both sides of the house. Positioned against one wall was a small bed with a ruffled coverlet, and a rocking chair.

'Most of these are my old toys,' Lydia said, gesturing to a large doll house and a porcelain-headed baby in a cradle. A rocking horse attracted Sharon's attention and with a squeal, and a funny little shuffle of excitement, she ran to it and, climbing on, she began rocking furiously.

The maid looked at the child and then at the adults she had been charged with showing to their rooms and began to bite her lip. Faced with an impossible decision, she looked quite desperate.

'Please, don't worry,' Lydia said. 'We will find our own rooms.' She nodded at Rees and he followed her from the nursery and down to the second floor. 'Cordy's room is this way,' Lydia said, pointing left. Rees knew that; he could hear Cordy's squeals of excitement. Lydia pointed right, down a longer hall to a double door at the end. 'My parents occupy separate rooms with a sitting room between them.' She led Rees through a door opposite the stairs and into a large room that looked out upon the street. A small desk and chair had been placed before the windows. The bed had been pushed in front of the wall. Two chairs flanked a small table in front of the fireplace. The furniture in here was from an earlier time, the middle of the last century, Rees thought, but it had been well cared for. Lydia went to her small writing desk and stroked the top fondly. 'I spent many hours here,' she said. 'In school we were required to write in a journal every night.'

'Is that my room?' Rees asked, gesturing to a small door adjacent to the desk.

'I suppose so,' Lydia said, throwing it open.

The one miniature window overlooked the drive to the mews. A small bed, more like a cot, had been placed against the wall. Rees thought it looked about as comfortable as sleeping on the floor. A clothes press occupied one corner and a ewer and stand the other.

'My sister and I used to store out-of-season items here,' Lydia said. 'Skates for the Mill Pond and all. When Cordy was younger, we played hide and seek around the boxes and baskets.'

'Hum,' Rees said. 'I guess I know where I stand in your family's estimation.'

Lydia turned and stood on tiptoe to kiss his cheek. 'This room will be a fine place for our clothing. You will sleep with me in this large room, of course.'

'Aren't you afraid your family will mock us for such plebeian behavior?'

'Let them,' Lydia said. 'Why should we care? We came at their invitation, to help them – and I don't expect to return very soon, if ever.'

Rees nodded. But he wondered if Lydia, despite her show of indifference, was really as unconcerned as she appeared. This was her family. Surely she wanted to shine in their eyes.

He rarely considered how he appeared to others. He knew his strengths, as well as his weaknesses, and he'd always taken comfort in knowing he'd made a success of his life. But now? He wasn't at all sure how this visit would go. He yearned for Lydia's family to like him and think she had chosen her husband well. He was terribly afraid they would find her choice of a weaver and part-time farmer disappointing.

FIVE

B y the time Rees and Lydia washed and brushed the dirt of travel from their clothing, the sky outside was darkening. When he looked at his pocket watch, Rees saw it was almost five. If they were at home, Lydia would be preparing supper and the children coming in from doing chores.

Rees's heart began to pound as they descended the stairs. He could not help his gasp of relief when he saw no one was inside the small room to the side.

Cold meats, bread, some kind of fish and a large cake adorned the circular table. Two large pots, one of tea and one of coffee, reposed at the side. 'Don't eat your fill,' Lydia warned as she inspected the offerings. 'Dinner will be served at eight o'clock.'

'I won't,' Rees said as he took bread and meat. Lydia took a sliver of meat, all that would fit on her plate next to a large slice of cake. After a few bites, Lydia rose and poured coffee for her husband and tea for herself. In Rees's opinion the cups were too small, but the sugar had already been broken into pieces.

'I hope everything is to your liking.' Mrs Farrell stood at the door. She had put a patterned shawl over her shoulders that exactly matched the blue of her eyes. In the flickering candlelight she looked the same age as her daughter.

'Yes, thank you,' Lydia said, putting down her cup with a clink. Rees, his mouth full, tried to swallow and choked. Lydia patted him on the back while Mrs Farrell waited politely. Her expression said this was exactly the kind of provincial behavior she expected.

'May I join you?' she asked when Rees could breathe again.

'Of course,' Lydia said.

Mrs Farrell sat down near the fire and arranged her skirts about her. Rees suspected she was trying to marshal her words. 'Marcus,' she said at last, 'is not in favor of any kind of an investigation. He feels the scandal will blow over.' She glanced at Lydia as if to say, 'You know your father.'

'I suppose the disgrace is not affecting him directly,' Lydia said angrily. Startled by her tone, Rees turned to look at her.

'No. Very little anyway. But it is shattering for Cordelia.'

'And for you too, I would imagine,' Lydia said.

Mrs Farrell nodded and Rees saw her mouth tremble. 'Indeed. Friends I've known for years . . .' She stopped, quickly gaining control of herself. 'But I am not a young woman preparing to enter the world. Several of Cordy's bosom companions have cut her off without a word.' Mrs Farrell forced a shaky smile. 'That is why she is so very excited by Jerusha's arrival. Although your daughter looks like quite a different sort of girl. Almost a bluestocking, I would guess. Anyway,' she continued, oblivious to Lydia's annoyed expression, 'there were several young men who were interested in her. Not courting her, since she is still too young, but their attention might have evolved in the next year or so. Every one of them has disappeared, gone as quickly as ice in spring. Including Edward Bartlett, who, up to now, has been her most devoted suitor.'

'Cordy must be devastated,' Lydia said soberly.

'That is why she is so eager for you to identify the murderer.' Mrs Farrell shook her head. 'The foolish child believes Eddy will marry her, if only he has permission.'

Lydia eyed her stepmother sharply. 'That sounds as though you do not wish her to marry Mr Bartlett.'

'Of course, she is far too young to consider wedding anyone.' A slight smile touched Isabeau's lips.

'She is certain of her father's innocence then,' Rees said, uninterested in Cordelia's marriage prospects.

'Of that, my daughter has no doubt.' Mrs Farrell smiled once again, but not as though the situation presented any humor. Regret, cynicism and a deep unhappiness were all expressed by her upturned lips. Rees suspected that Mrs Farrell, for all her expressed belief in her husband, was afraid he might have murdered the other man. Marcus Farrell's guilt would certainly explain his lack of support for an investigation;

he would not want to be exposed. 'Cordy idolizes her father. In her eyes, he can do no wrong,' Mrs Farrell continued.

Rees glanced at his wife. Her eyebrows had risen almost to her hair line and she looked aghast. 'I can scarcely credit that,' Lydia said.

'I know you and your father were frequently at loggerheads,' Mrs Farrell said to Lydia. 'But Cordelia sees no faults. She is like him in many ways. I often think that, if she had been born a boy, she would have been the son he wanted. More so than James.'

'My older brother,' Lydia said to Rees's questioning glance. He had not known she had an older brother. 'But James has proven himself as a ship's captain, hasn't he?' she asked, turning back to her stepmother.

'He sailed on the runs to Barbados and Jamaica. He does not sail to Africa. Your father feels he is not tough enough as a negotiator.'

'Sailed?' Lydia asked, glancing quickly at Rees. 'He does so no more?'

'He and your father argued. I am not sure what transpired . . .' Mrs Farrell allowed her words to trail off.

'When did James last come home?' Lydia asked. Rees glanced at her in concern. Despite the innocuous words, she was trembling with emotion.

'He rested between voyages last fall. But we saw little of him. He stayed with your Uncle Julian.' Drawing her shawl about her shoulders, Mrs Farrell prepared to rise from the chair. 'I just wanted to explain why Cordy . . . I implore you not to be swept away by her enthusiasm. Although I pray you find the murderer and clear my husband's name, please be aware that my daughter is young and does not understand the nuances of an investigation such as yours.' She bestowed an insincere smile upon both Rees and Lydia and flitted from the room.

Lydia picked up her teacup. Her hand was trembling so much tea splashed over the side. Rees took the fragile china cup from her and put it on the table. 'Why are you so upset?' he asked.

'Do you know the story *Cendrillon ou la petite pantoufle de verre*?' she asked.

'No,' Rees said, translating the French in his head. '*Cinderella, or the little glass slipper*? That does not sound like something I would know.'

'It is about a young girl and her stepmother.' Lydia forced a smile. 'I was eight, almost nine, when my father brought Isabeau Jarre home. They married within the week. My stepmother, she had me call her by her given name rather than Mother, was not cruel to me. I think Isabeau enjoyed dressing a little girl. Of course, that all changed when Cordy was born. But I was never mistreated. And I was happy to attend school. My brother James was fourteen, almost fifteen, when Isabeau came into our lives. He resented her and she returned his feelings tenfold.' Lydia smiled slightly. 'I see now it was not James, per se, but his role as eldest son and heir that she resented. But, as it turned out, that didn't matter. Cordy was the only one of my stepmother's children who lived. So James would have become the heir anyway.'

'What happened to James?' Rees asked.

'The relationship between them grew so terrible even my father noticed, and he is not an observant man. He shipped James out on one of his sailing vessels when he was just nineteen. Isabeau has spent all these years denigrating James, belittling him and implying he does not deserve his position. I do not wonder James chose to stop with my uncle Julian.'

Rees put a hand over hers and squeezed it comfortingly. His feelings for his father were complicated, but he was beginning to think Lydia's family had been a more challenging household in which to grow up.

'She spoke in such obtuse terms about your sister's enthusiasm and lack of understanding that I am not quite sure what she meant,' he said now. 'Was she suggesting we abandon the investigation and go home?'

Lydia shook her head. 'No,' she said slowly. 'I don't think that is what she wants. The gossip, and I'm sure she's heard it, must be hurtful. For all her talk about protecting Cordy, I suspect Isabeau is concerned about herself. You saw that, didn't you?'

Rees recalled Mrs Farrell's moist eyes and nodded. 'I did. Although, to her credit, she seemed more worried with her daughter's well-being. Does she believe, then, that her husband, your father, might be the murderer? Or is she just worried that we might discover and reveal family secrets?'

Lydia hesitated. 'Both, probably,' she said at last. 'I certainly know my father has a past. I've heard snippets . . .' For a moment they sat in silence.

Rees knew there were few secrets in his family. All the problems had been obvious, laid bare for all in the community to see.

'We should probably retire upstairs—' Lydia began.

'Daughter.' Marcus Farrell stood in the doorway. Although he'd addressed Lydia, his gaze was fixed on Rees.

'So, this is the man my daughter chose to marry,' he said, his quiet voice thick with disdain. His eyes rested upon Rees's jacket, his second best, but old and well-worn and certainly not stylish. 'Well, at least you took her away from that unpleasant religion; I suppose I should thank you for that.'

Rees opened his mouth to reply but could not think of anything to say. He already disliked the man. With such negative feelings, Rees would have to work hard to keep an open mind and not just assume Farrell was the murderer on the basis of his sentiments.

Marcus Farrell was shorter than Rees by about eight inches. Lydia had inherited her dark blue eyes and red hair from him, although her father's hair was beginning to fade to a sandy color. He was elegantly dressed in white breeches with gold buttons at the knees, and polished buskins. His black linen jacket and simply tied cravat appeared simple but Rees recognized the quality of the cloth. No doubt Mr Farrell used the best, and therefore the most expensive, tailor as well.

But it was his waistcoat that caught the eye and held it. Of creamy silk, the front was heavily embroidered with colorful peacocks of different sizes.

Even though Rees was wearing his second-best coat and breeches, he suddenly felt as poorly dressed as one of the homeless men who wandered the roads.

SIX

After regarding Rees for several seconds, Mr Farrell extended his hand. Rees grasped it, painfully conscious of his rough hand, calloused by both farm work and weaving. 'Please attend me in my office,' Mr Farrell said. 'We are expecting a few guests for dinner tonight so we will have little time to talk then.'

Turning, he strode away. Rees started to follow but, realizing that Lydia was not by his side, he turned back. She stood hesitantly by the table, her hands tightly clenched together. Rees glared at Mr Farrell's back and then, reaching out, he pulled one of her hands through his elbow. Together they followed her father into his office.

As Farrell moved a stack of papers from the center of the desk to one side, Rees looked around. A large globe on a stand stood to the right of Farrell's desk and one chair had been drawn up to the front. A seating area, with additional chairs, was arranged by the window that looked out upon the front garden. A table in the center held an intricately carved tray with a crystal decanter and several glasses. Shelves of books lined the wall behind and adjacent to the desk, on Rees's right.

The room was chilly although the fire was burning. Newly laid, it had been lighted, no doubt by some anonymous servant.

Farrell looked up and his eyes rested on Lydia in surprise. Rees felt his wife shrink back, intimidated. He was not going to stand for that. He pulled a chair from the window grouping and placed it in front of the desk. She hesitated for a few seconds and then, lifting her chin defiantly, she sat down. Once she was seated, Rees lowered himself into the opposite chair. After one final dismissive glance at his daughter, Farrell looked at Rees.

'So, you are a weaver.'

'That is so,' Rees said, adding politely, 'I understand you are a merchant.'

Farrell smiled. 'I see your wife has told you very little about me or my profession.' Since responding in the affirmative seemed somehow disloyal to Lydia, Rees said nothing.

Farrell took a box from his desk drawer and opened it to extract a cigar. 'Would you like a smoke?'

'No thank you,' Rees said.

'Or a glass of rum? Or whiskey if that is your tipple.' When Rees declined again, Farrell put away the cigars and walked to the fire-place to light a splint. The end of the cigar glowed red and the acrid scent of burning tobacco filled the room. Puffing, Farrell returned to his seat. 'I suppose one could say I was a merchant. But I do so much more. I own a plantation as well as a fleet of ships that sail between Boston, the West Indies and Africa. In Jamaica they take on sugar and molasses which are brought to Boston. Some of it is transformed into rum in my distillery. I export the liquor overseas, both to England and to Africa, where the proceeds are used to purchase slaves.'

Sick to his stomach, Rees glanced at Lydia. She was staring at her hands, her face flaming with shame. Although she had alluded to her father's profession, she had not told him the half of it. She had not told him of her father's pride in it. Rees understood why she hadn't.

'Most of the slaves are brought to the sugar plantation,' Farrell continued, seemingly oblivious to his daughter's distress, 'but some are sold in the Southern states. And you needn't look so shocked. Why, that upstart Republican with his radical ideas, Mr Jefferson, owns slaves. And he may be the next President. I suppose you voted for him.'

Rees did not respond immediately. Although many of Mr Jefferson's ideas were appealing, Rees had found in the end that he could not vote for a slave-holder. Instead, he had voted for Mr Adams. But that gentleman had not placed; the election was a tie between Thomas Jefferson and Aaron Burr. Sent to the House for resolution, Jefferson had won by one vote. 'No,' Rees said carefully, keeping his voice level with an effort, 'I voted for his opponent.'

'Well, that makes us kin then. Although you will meet a few slaves here in Boston, in this very house.' He grinned and Rees thought of Morris and Bridget with their tinted skin. 'But few, very few. Neither the Africans nor the Spanish Indians adapt well to this northern climate and they quickly die.' This was said with indifference as though he spoke of a broken chair.

Farrell flicked a glance at his daughter and smiled. With a surge of anger, Rees realized that Farrell fully understood the effect his speech would have on her and was enjoying her misery. Rees gathered himself to rise from his chair. Lydia reached out and grasped his sleeve.

'This is for Cordy,' she whispered. Rees sat down again, his body stiff.

'But you did not come to listen to me natter on about my profession,' Farrell said, watching the byplay with interest. 'Shall we discuss that ridiculous murder, the one of which I was accused?'

Rees looked into Lydia's beseeching eyes and after a few seconds he relaxed into his seat. God forgive him, a part of him hoped Marcus Farrell was guilty.

'Go on,' Rees said coldly. Marcus smiled.

'Permit me to save you both time and effort,' he said. 'I did not kill that boy.'

'Then why do people think you did?' Rees asked. Puffing furiously, and clearly unwilling to reply, Farrell took a turn around the room.

'Did you know him?' Lydia asked, her voice low and clear. 'This boy?'

Farrell stood up so abruptly his chair almost tipped over. 'Yes, I knew him.' He glanced at Rees. 'We were seen, Roark and I, arguing down at Long Wharf.'

'Arguing about what?' Rees asked.

'It is not important. He was a nobody.' Farrell glared at Rees, daring him to persist. Rees waited, never removing his gaze from the other man. Sometimes silence made the best hammer. Finally, Farrell said angrily, 'He wanted a rise in his wages. I said no. He disagreed. That was all there was to it.'

Rees glanced at Lydia and found her staring at him. He knew, and he suspected she did too, that her father had just lied to them.

'Well, if you were home that evening,' Rees said in a reasonable tone, 'your wife and the servants can most certainly attest to your presence.'

'I wasn't home,' Farrell said. 'Of course I wasn't and you must know that. I was at the counting house until late.'

'What time did you arrive home, then?' Lydia asked. 'Perhaps Isabeau . . .'

'She had retired by the time I returned. In fact, I let myself in and slept here, in my office, so as not to disturb her or anyone else. I left again before breakfast.'

'Did anyone see you?'

'No. I left before anyone else had risen. Including the maids.'

Rees stared at his father-in-law. Farrell must know that his explanation was so poor as to be worthless. He *claimed* he'd come home, but too late for anyone to see him, and then he'd left again the following morning early. There were no witnesses or any possible way to confirm his story.

'If you were at the counting house for all of that time,' Lydia said, not troubling to disguise her disbelief, 'how did you hear about the murder?'

'My wife sent a messenger to me. Of course, I was horrified. But, at that point, I didn't see how it had anything to do with me. Little Africa is a dangerous place. Every day someone is stabbed there.'

'Did Roark live in Little Africa?' Rees asked.

'I don't know. Why would I care?' Farrell snapped.

'And was Roark stabbed?' Rees persisted.

'Well, no. He was shot.'

'I'd like to see the body,' Rees said. He was beginning to think he couldn't believe a word his father-in-law said. Farrell shook his head.

'Roark was buried almost immediately. And in a pauper's grave, so there will be no stone or anything else to mark his resting place. Not even a wooden cross.' Farrell smiled at the dismay on Rees's face. 'He was a nobody. The son of a man I once knew. I did what I could for Roark out of respect for his father.'

'What is Roark's full name?' Rees asked.

'Why do you want to know?'

'Is his name a secret?' Lydia asked, calm but scornful. Her father glared at her.

'You never did know when to keep silent,' he said. 'The boy's name was Roark Bustamonte. Are you happy now?' He threw his cigar into the fire and said in a clipped tone, 'I am pleased that my daughter has come home for a short visit. It comforts me to meet her husband and to know she is happy and provided for. I never thought to see her wed. But please, do not trouble yourself to search out Roark's killer. Any attempt to uncover the murderer's identity is doomed to failure and I suggest you abandon any hope of doing so. Cordelia's fears to the contrary, I believe the scandal will disappear like the wind when some new *on dit* appears. Besides, she need have no fear she will not marry. I have a gentleman in mind for her. A sober, well-set-up fellow who, I think, will serve very well as Cordelia's husband. You will meet him at dinner tonight. Questioning our neighbors and friends, as well as my business associates, will only keep the rumors flying. None of us want that.

'So, enjoy yourselves while you are here. Lydia, I hope you visit the shops. I would like to see you attired in clothing befitting your station.' Glancing at Rees, he added, 'A weaver should be more cognizant of the latest fashions, don't you agree?' Rees gaped at

Farrell, stunned by the slight. Smiling, Farrell's glance moved to his daughter. 'And now, we should all go upstairs and dress for dinner.'

'Oh, I do not believe we should join—' Lydia began.

'Come now. I won't take no for an answer.' Farrell walked around his desk and almost lifted her from her chair. With one hand firmly clutching her elbow, he escorted her to the door. Rees hurried after them. Without quite knowing how it happened, he and Lydia found themselves in the hall. 'I know you will wish to meet the man I have chosen for your sister,' Farrell said. 'I look forward to seeing you at dinner tonight.' He closed his office door firmly behind them.

Rees and Lydia stared at one another. 'I am so sorry . . .' she began.

'This is not your fault,' Rees said. He wondered if she would be willing to return home now, after their unceremonious ejection from her father's office.

SEVEN

Rees and Lydia did not speak again until they were in Lydia's bedchamber with the door firmly shut behind them. 'Well, if the object was to learn something useful from the conversation with your father, we failed,' Rees said. 'I don't understand what his purpose was.'

Lydia turned. 'To confuse us. To let us know he is the one in authority. And to tell us to drop the investigation.'

'Why would an innocent man not wish his name cleared?' Rees asked rhetorically.

'Exactly. I think we can both be certain that my father was lying to us.'

Rees exhaled in relief. He had not wanted to accuse Mr Farrell of lying to Lydia. He should have realized she was too clear-eyed to ignore the truth. 'Yes, he was,' he agreed. 'He knows far more about that Roark Bustamonte's death than he wants to admit.'

'And I don't believe for one second that they were arguing over wages,' Lydia said, taking an angry spin about the room. 'He was attempting to put us off.'

Rees nodded. 'Yes. And that makes me believe he has something to hide.'

'I am more determined than ever to see this through,' Lydia said resolutely. Rees's heart sank.

'This will be a very difficult investigation,' he cautioned her. 'We will not have much, if any, assistance.' He stopped, suddenly realizing how much he'd always relied on his friends and the people he knew. Even Rouge, the constable of Durham, could be an asset and his standing as constable lent Rees's inquisitiveness a legitimacy that he would not have here in Boston. 'Especially not from your family,' he continued more slowly. 'Both your father and your stepmother have advised us against questioning their friends and colleagues.'

'Huh,' Lydia said scornfully. 'I will anyway. Subtly. Tactfully. But I will not be deflected.'

'So, who do we approach?' Rees said, putting his arms around her. Her refusal to back down was one of the things he loved most about her; even now, where she was clearly frightened of her father.

'I'll talk to the servants,' Lydia said. 'Most of the older ones know me and although Morris might be reluctant to speak, I expect I can glean some information from Cook and some of the maids.'

'But the shooting took place somewhere else,' Rees objected. 'And what is this Little Africa he mentioned?'

'Boston is the center of the abolitionist movement,' Lydia said. 'Little Africa is the area where many free blacks – and probably a good number of fugitive slaves as well – live.'

'How will I find out where Roark lived, or anyone else who might know something?'

'I have an idea about that,' Lydia said. 'Tomorrow we will visit Uncle Julian. Both of us. He will surely know something about the scandal and may be able to give us some ideas.' She paused and then added, 'My father won't like it but no one will think it unusual if I choose to call upon my uncle.'

'Why? Is he afraid your uncle will share family secrets?'

'My father is estranged from his brother as well as from his eldest son,' Lydia said, adding scathingly, 'that's my father.'

A sudden tap on the door heralded the arrival of Mrs Farrell. She entered so soon after her knock that Lydia and Rees did not have time to break apart. She stared at them, aghast.

'Whatever are you doing?' She looked at Rees sternly. 'You should be in your room changing for dinner.'

Chastened, Rees released his wife and stepped back. Mrs Farrell looked over her shoulder and gestured at the maid who stood behind her. The woman's arms were filled with gowns.

'I brought a few things here for you to try on,' Mrs Farrell said to Lydia.

'I have gowns of my own,' Lydia replied, her mouth pinched.

'Yes, I've seen them,' Mrs Farrell said disdainfully. 'We can't have you appearing dowdy and unfashionable tonight; some people you know will be in attendance. You will attend, won't you?'

'I will,' Lydia said to Rees's surprise. 'You know Father plans to marry Cordy off to one of his business associates? You said she was too young.'

'Tonight's dinner is only to determine if he will serve,' Mrs Farrell said equably. 'If Cordy does not like him, then the matter is settled.'

'That is not what my father said to me,' Lydia said, her expression hardening. 'It sounded as though my father has already made up his mind.'

Her stepmother laughed. 'Please, do not worry. As I said, Cordy is still too young.'

'I want to meet this man,' Lydia said. 'Show me what you have.'

'I think one of these may serve until we've purchased some new things for you.' Mrs Farrell glared at Rees. He cast a sympathetic glance at Lydia, wondering why she was now so determined to attend this dinner party. She had been unwilling just a little while before. He withdrew into his own small chamber, shutting the door behind him. His preparations would be quick; he planned to change his coat and waistcoat. He suspected Lydia would not experience such an easy time.

When Lydia stepped out of her bedchamber, Rees caught his breath. She looked like a different person. Her auburn hair was caught up into a bun at the back and held there with combs. She wore a garnet gown with a design of gold squares and she'd borrowed a garnet and gold necklace that complemented her white neck and shoulders. The bosom was cut very low, but she wore a gold silk shawl over all.

She was quite beautiful.

'Ah good, you're ready,' Cordelia said as she and Jerusha came out of the room across the hall. Cordelia, dressed in white with the embroidered ribbon under her bust the only color, resembled a sprite more than ever.

Jerusha was also clad in a new dress, one of Cordelia's Rees guessed by the shortness of the hem. But the pale blue color was flattering even if Rees found the short sleeves that bared her arms and the low neckline were rather more revealing than he would have liked. Her hair had been dressed into curls over each ear – Rees smelled burnt hair – and she kept pulling at the bunches as if they annoyed her.

Together they descended the stairs to the hall. The sound of voices emanated from the drawing room. The polished wooden door had been thrown open. 'Ready,' Rees murmured to Lydia. She nodded, her face pale. Cordelia, linking her arm through Jerusha's, drew her into the room.

This chamber occupied fully a quarter of the ground floor, its windows overlooking the garden to the side. Mrs Farrell had recently re-furnished the drawing room but not in the plain furniture Rees preferred. In here, the walnut chairs and the couch all had curved arms, cabriole legs and upholstered seats in a pale sage green. The back wall featured trompe l'œil panels. Rees guessed the wallpaper had been imported at great expense, probably from Great Britain. When Rees looked around at the furniture, all English imports, the Eastern carpet and the gold silk drapes upon the windows, he caught his breath. He'd known Lydia came from money but had never really considered the details. He glanced at her quickly. She'd turned her back on all this luxury when she joined the Shakers.

Despite Mrs Farrell's promises to re-introduce Lydia to people she knew, only one guest joined the family gathered before the fire. He was a tall man wearing a tight black coat with spotless linen underneath. One of the elaborately tied cravats that were becoming so fashionable covered his neck in a waterfall of lace and, like Mr Farrell, his waistcoat was a marvel of embroidery on silk. But he hadn't ceded his black breeches, caught at the knees with glittering buckles, or his snowy hose to trousers.

'Cordelia dear,' said Mrs Farrell. 'Come and greet Mr Hutchinson.' Cordelia obeyed, curtsying, as she would for any of her parents' friends.

Lydia and Rees joined Mr and Mrs Farrell by the fire. 'My daughter, Lydia Rees. Oh, and her husband,' Mr Farrell said. 'Mr Hutchinson.' Although Rees did not know if Farrell had meant his discourtesy as a slight, he felt it keenly, nonetheless.

Mr Hutchinson turned at Rees's approach and held out his hand. He was only slightly younger than Rees himself; silver threaded his dark locks. And, to Rees's surprise, Mr Hutchinson's face and hands were lightly tanned, an unusual sight for a Massachusetts January.

'Mr Rees,' Hutchinson said with a firm handshake. 'And Mrs Rees.'

'Mr Hutchinson is your father's associate,' Mrs Farrell said, adding with a smile, 'He returned from the West Indies little more than three months ago.'

Ah, Rees thought, that explained Mr Hutchinson's brown skin.

'And what is it you did there?' Lydia asked politely.

'I managed some of Mr Farrell's business interests,' Hutchinson said. 'I went to Jamaica many years ago to make my fortune. Having done so, I am now in search of a wife.' His gaze drifted toward Cordelia, who was leaning forward as she whispered to Jerusha and laughing.

Rees and Lydia exchanged glances of shocked dismay.

'Cordelia?' Lydia said, horrified.

'Mr Hutchinson is an estimable man and will provide a steadying influence upon her,' said Mr Farrell sternly.

'Does Cordy know?'

'Not yet. We will inform her tonight,' said Mr Farrell.

Neither Rees nor Lydia could think of anything to say that would not sound critical and the silence rapidly became awkward. 'As I told you, I was born in Saint-Domingue,' Mrs Farrell said, turning to Mr Hutchinson and speaking quickly. 'I lived in Jamaica for several years before my marriage. How I miss those warm breezes.' Chattering gaily, she drew both Mr Hutchinson and her husband away.

'Mr Hutchinson must not know of the scandal surrounding the family,' Rees murmured. 'Or he doesn't care.'

'He's old enough to be her father,' Lydia muttered under her breath. 'This is disgraceful. I vow I will do my utmost to prevent this disaster.'

EIGHT

Afterwards, Rees could never describe what the Farrells served for dinner. He was tense to begin with and, after his long day, hazy with fatigue. He had already encountered several shocks, and the surprises did not cease. When they went into the dining room, the table was laid for twelve. Rees glanced around and silently counted. There were only seven people here.

Mr Farrell's cheeks flushed with anger and humiliation.

'Some of our guests had other commitments,' Mrs Farrell murmured self-consciously.

'They chose not to come,' Lydia said to Rees in an undertone. 'This is a terrible snub.'

'I suppose the scandal is not disappearing, as your father thought it would,' Rees muttered drily.

He and Lydia were separated, placed on opposite sides of the table. Lydia, who was seated on one side of Mr Hutchinson, tried to engage him in conversation. But although Mr Hutchinson's gaze drifted to Cordelia a few times, he seemed more interested in conversing with Mrs Farrell.

Cordelia, for her part, spoke to no one but Jerusha, especially after Mr Farrell suggested Cordy might wish to know Mr Hutchinson better. When she understood what he was saying, she flushed red and then paled. She refused to look at her parents again.

Conscious of Mrs Farrell's gaze upon him, Rees could barely eat. By the time coffee and dessert were served, he was so tired he felt as though he were watching a play through a pane of glass. Still, even as exhausted as he was, he could see this dinner party had been a catastrophe.

The coffee succeeded in energizing him somewhat. When Mr Hutchinson took his leave, and Rees made his way upstairs, he realized he was famished. Lydia and the two girls had disappeared, so he climbed to the second floor alone. He glanced into Lydia's bedchamber but, although the candles were lit and the counterpane turned down, the room was empty. Glumly, he retreated to the small space allotted to him.

He had just taken off his coat when he heard footsteps and soft laughter in the hall outside. A few seconds later, the door between the box room and Lydia's bedchamber opened.

'Are you hungry?' Lydia asked, holding up the candelabra.

'Starving,' he replied.

'You'd better come in here, then.'

When he entered her room, he saw that Cordelia and Jerusha had thrown a cloth over the writing desk and were laying out a substantial repast. Rees stared at the bread and butter, the cold meat, and the cake.

'Do visitors to your father's household frequently leave hungry?' he asked.

'This dinner was worse than most,' Lydia admitted. 'First, half the guests did not come. That was uncomfortable for everyone. Then my father inflicted Mr Hutchinson upon us all.'

'My father didn't even warn me,' Cordy said angrily. 'I don't want to marry my father's assistant.'

'When Mr Farrell did not speak to me, I thought he was annoyed because I had the temerity to wed his daughter,' Rees said.

'Quite the contrary,' Lydia said. 'He is . . . grateful to you and he doesn't enjoy the feeling. I've been a trial to him all my life. Too outspoken, you know.' She grimaced.

Rees shook his head. He did not understand how Marcus Farrell could not appreciate his smart and loving daughter. 'He is a fool then,' he said. Lydia threw her husband a smile.

'And you are the better man,' she said.

Turning to Cordelia, Rees said, 'So, are felicitations in order? Will you marry that young man?'

'Don't tease her,' Lydia rebuked him in a low voice.

'No,' Cordelia said shortly. 'And he is not a young man, he is an old man. One of my father's business associates.'

'He is at least twenty years Cordy's senior,' Lydia said, frowning. 'Probably more.'

'My father told me I could learn to love Mr Hutchinson,' Cordelia said, slapping meat on the bread and taking a large furious bite. 'I don't believe it. I wish I had your courage, Lyddie. I would run away.'

'Oh, Cordy,' Lydia said. 'That is not the answer.'

'Will your father force you to marry Mr Hutchinson?' Jerusha asked Cordelia sympathetically.

'He told me he wouldn't,' Rees said.

'I wish I believed that,' Cordelia said mournfully. 'I don't want to marry someone so old and then live far, far away. I want to marry someone my age. And live here, in Boston. I believe it is always hot in the West Indies and they never see snow.'

'You can say no,' Lydia suggested.

'I suppose.' Cordelia heaved a sigh. 'But Father will be so disappointed in me.'

'I know how that feels,' Lydia murmured.

Jerusha looked at Rees. 'You will never force me to marry a man I don't love, will you?'

Rees shook his head. 'Never,' he promised her. 'But we are farming folk. Not wealthy merchants.'

For a moment everyone was silent as they ate their informal meal. Then Cordelia wiped her mouth on the edge of the cloth. 'Well, I'll bid you all goodnight.' She leaned forward to kiss her sister. 'And, oh, Lydia, it is so wonderful to have you home again.'

Jerusha rose as well and followed Cordelia. As they closed the door behind them, Rees said to his wife, 'Was that what happened to you? Your father tried to marry you to one of his associates?'

'Yes. But it was a little different in my case from Cordy. Micah was closer to my age, for one thing. And I fancied myself in love with him.' She offered Rees a dry smile. 'He threw me over for one of my best friends. My father blamed me, of course, and accused me of a lack of femininity.'

Rees nodded. Now that he had met Mr Farrell, he could well believe his father-in-law capable of such hurtful comments. 'Well, that is Micah's loss and my gain,' he said, taking her hand. 'Shall we look for other accommodations? Is it too difficult to stay here, in your father's house?'

She shook her head. 'No. All of that is in the past. It doesn't hurt me anymore.' Rees did not believe her; she was still anxious around her father. Looking into his face, she smiled. 'You have nothing to fear.' Standing on her tiptoes to kiss him, she continued. 'I was a silly young girl then and Micah was a handsome man. I've learned to value character more highly.'

Rees returned her kiss. 'Are you saying I am not handsome?'

She laughed and freed herself from his embrace. 'Of course not. You are easily the most handsome man of my acquaintance.'

Now Rees chuckled as well. 'Flatterer.'

Lydia grinned at him. 'We'd better retire for the night,' she said, her smile fading. 'I want to leave early, as early as possible, tomorrow morning. My stepmother plans on taking me and Jerusha shopping and I want to be gone when she arises.'

'Your stepmother is formidable. She is not the sort of woman who surrenders easily,' Rees said. 'You will not be able to fob her off for very long.'

'I know. But perhaps we can visit the shops in the afternoon; after you and I have spoken to my uncle Julian. He is an early riser. Well, he has to be, to start work at the distillery.'

'I'm anxious to meet him,' Rees said. 'I hope he can help us. And that he doesn't try to persuade us to drop our investigation into the murder.'

NINE

D espite his fatigue and although he fell asleep quickly, Rees awoke very early the following morning. Carefully sliding out of the bed so as not to awaken Lydia, he went to the windows. He pushed aside the curtains and, leaning upon the sill, he looked out upon the street. Already, in the gray dawn, wagons were trundling past the house. He could see gentlemen outside the State House on the opposite corner. The open space of Boston Commons was just visible behind the State House.

He could see nothing of the harbor, although he knew it lay to the east.

'What's the matter?' Lydia asked.

'Nothing,' Rees said, turning from the window and allowing the curtain to drop.

Lydia rubbed her eyes. 'We'd better dress. I want to leave early.'

'Not before breakfast,' Rees said. He was very hungry this morning.

'After we've breakfasted, then.'

'Will the coach be ready?' Rees asked, moving back to the bed. 'Yes. I spoke to Morris last night.' Lydia covered her yawn with her hand. In the silence they both could hear the rattle of crockery outside their room. Rees looked down at the body linen that provided his only cover and fled into the small room next door. He dressed quickly and was almost done when a soft knock at his door heralded a young man with a tray. Rees looked at the cup of hot chocolate and sent the tray away.

He followed the man out and down the stairs. He was very glad to see an army of people laying out food in the breakfast room. Rees stopped the young girl he'd met the previous day – Bridget – and asked if there was coffee.

'Of course, sir,' she whispered with a curtsey. 'Right away.' Her deference inspired such discomfort in Rees he almost offered to fetch the coffee himself. But that would not serve; Bridget might be punished, and Rees could well imagine the furor if he lumbered into the kitchen. He wondered if it would do any good if he told the girl he had sprung from farming folk.

He had just begun filling his plate when Lydia arrived. She had put off the borrowed gown of the previous night and was clad once more in one of her own dresses. She would have to let out the waist again; Rees could see the cloth stretching tightly over her expanding belly.

He offered her his full plate and when she accepted it helped himself to more food. As she poured tea from the flowered teapot upon the table, Rees filled a second plate. He sat down and began to eat rapidly.

'There is no need to eat quite so fast, Will,' Lydia said in amusement. 'The carriage won't be ready until eight thirty.'

'I thought you wanted to make an early start,' Rees said as soon as he'd swallowed. 'Aren't you worried your stepmother will come downstairs and drag you off to the shops?'

'She never leaves her bed until after ten – at the earliest. I expect it will be closer to eleven,' Lydia said. She put down her fork with a clink. 'Although, in fact, I would prefer to be home by noon. I doubt either you or I will want to answer too many questions about our whereabouts, especially since we've been urged to suspend our investigation.'

'Your stepmother is bound to hear about our excursion,' Rees pointed out.

'If Isabeau asks about the carriage, I will simply say we went for a drive.'

'And what about your uncle? Won't he mention our visit to your father?'

'I'll ask him not to. Anyway, they speak rarely. Unless his feelings have softened, my uncle despises my father and speaks to him as little as possible.'

Rees did not argue; he did not yet understand this family. They all seemed to be at each other's throats. He did wonder if Julian Farrell's anger extended to betraying his brother. After all, Rees and Lydia were investigating Marcus Farrell for murder.

The vehicle that waited outside when Rees and Lydia left the house was not the large grand carriage of the day before. Instead, it was a much smaller landau with only two horses between the traces. The hood was folded back despite the chilly air and when Rees settled himself into the seat he understood why. The leather top smelled disagreeably of oil and blacking.

The coachman pulled out of the drive and turned left, toward the wharves and the harbor.

Despite the narrow, crowded streets and the crisp air, it was a pleasing drive. The briny scent of the ocean intensified as they approached the water, but it was not unpleasant. The docks were already busy, noisy with loud voices in several languages, and congested with men hauling bales and barrels from one side to the other. The coachman plunged on through, forcing the laborers to move aside.

Rees smelled the distillery before he saw it, the scent of molasses combined with a faint suggestion of yeast and the hint of ocean salt. As they approached, the molasses-y aroma intensified, taking on a smoky smell, with an alcoholic tang. The distillery was not positioned on the wharf, it was set back from it – but it was very close. A wagon carrying barrels was drawn up to the connecting warehouse. As Rees watched, one of the barrels tipped off the back of the wagon and crashed to the ground. The lid broke and a small but steady stream of a thick brown liquid began to leak out. Molasses. Cursing, several of the men quickly got the barrel upright once again and into the warehouse.

The carriage driver swerved around them and kept going, turning toward a building at the back. He pulled to a stop and jumped down to assist Lydia. Rees climbed down on the other side. Lydia slipped her hand into his elbow and they walked to the building.

Before they reached the door, it popped open and a man hurried through. 'Lydia! How long has it been?'

'Uncle Julian,' Lydia said, her voice muffled as she was folded into his embrace.

Julian was taller and leaner than his brother. Instead of red hair, his was – or had once been – brown but it was now almost entirely gray. When he released his niece, he looked at Rees.

'And who might this be?' His eyes were a lighter blue than Marcus's and flecked with shades of green and gold.

'This is my husband, Will Rees.'

Julian immediately extended his hand. 'I am very glad to meet the man who captured Lydia's heart.'

'I am happy to meet you, sir,' Rees said. 'My wife has spoken of you.'

'Has she? That is a surprise. When she left, I assumed she would not think of us, and certainly never speak of us, again. You've met my brother, I expect.'

'I had the pleasure yesterday,' Rees said.

'And what a pleasure it was too,' Julian said sarcastically. Almost immediately he apologized. 'Forgive me. Now that you've met Marcus, I'm sure you understand.'

'It is so wonderful to see you,' Lydia broke in diplomatically.

'I am glad you made the journey,' Julian said. 'But I suspect you did not come to Boston to visit your Uncle Julian. Why are you really here?'

'In truth, we came because of Cordy,' Lydia said. 'She wrote me—'

'And told you all about her father's trouble,' Julian said, nodding his head.

'As you might expect, the scandal is seriously damaging her ability to make a good marriage,' Lydia said.

'Of course it is,' Julian agreed. 'But my brother has always been a selfish—' He stopped short when he saw Lydia watching him. 'But you know him as well as I do.'

'We, Will and I that is, have had some success in looking into crimes such as murder,' Lydia continued. 'That is why Cordelia begged us to come to Boston. She thought, if we came, we could look into the accusation and clear her father's name.'

'Thereby improving her chances in the marriage market,' Julian said with a nod.

'He warned us off,' Rees put in. 'Your brother, I mean. And his wife too, although not so obviously. He lied about where he was the night of the murder. And he says he does not want us to bother his friends and business partners. For fear of gossip. Even though he assured Cordelia and us, that the scandal would disappear.'

'As if any of that would matter now,' Julian cut in to say. 'It is far too late to worry about gossip. Everyone in town has heard about it already. Besides, he has no friends.'

'So I thought—' Lydia began.

'You thought I might know something,' Julian said, completing her sentence for her.

'More than we do presently,' Lydia said.

'You do realize he might be guilty,' Julian said. 'Marcus may have murdered that young man.' Rees glanced at his wife's pained expression. 'Surely you have thought of it,' Julian said.

'We are aware that is a possibility,' Rees said. 'But we can't know anything for sure until we collect the facts. We need the names of people to speak to. Directions to Little Africa and the place where Roark was shot.'

'What all the gossip is saying as well,' Lydia added.

'You don't ask for much, do you?' Julian asked with a grin. 'All right, I'll tell you what I know. You'd better come into my office.'

TEN

The aroma was even more pungent inside the distillery than outside.

'Don't worry,' Julian said to Rees, catching his grimace. 'You'll get used to it. By the time you leave, you won't notice it at all. I promise.'

The ground floor was a hive of activity as men in their shirt sleeves scurried around the large vats in the center. Molasses barrels, some full, some partially used and some entirely empty, were ranged around the walls.

'Where are the stills?' Rees asked, looking about him.

'In the chamber behind,' Julian said. 'This is where we begin making the wort.'

Rees pretended he knew what that meant.

Julian led Rees and Lydia to a flight of stairs that led to a second level. It was more of a gallery with windows overlooking the floor below. Flinging open the door, Julian gestured them inside. Although a stack of ledgers occupied one side of his desk and several invoices made an untidy pile, the room was relatively neat. He too owned a large globe and the greasy fingermarks smeared across the orb spoke of many hours spinning it. Artifacts from his sea career, strange carvings, a necklace of wooden beads, a small piece of logwood were jumbled together on a shelf.

'Would you like a drink,' Julian said, waving a glass of amber liquid at Rees. He shook his head. 'This is the good stuff from Jamaica and Barbados. Not our product, which is barely fit to give a pig.'

'Why distill it, then?' Rees asked.

'We export it to Great Britain and to Africa. It's like currency there.' Julian took a swig and thumped the glass down. By the look of the blistered wood, he had done exactly that many times a day for many days. 'Ask your questions.'

'Do you know what happened?' Lydia asked.

'Only what I heard.' Julian eyed Lydia's belly and waved at a chair. 'Sit down, please, Lydia.'

'Your brother told us the young man was shot,' Rees said.

'Yes. There seems to be no dispute about that.'

'Did anyone witness it?' Rees asked.

'No.'

'Do you know where in Little Africa the victim was shot?' Rees asked.

Julian threw a glance at him. 'I don't know what my brother told you, but Roark was not murdered in Little Africa. He was murdered in the alley behind a tavern, the Painted Pig, on this side of town. Not far from here, actually.'

'A tavern frequented by sailors?' Rees asked, recalling his experiences in Salem a few years previously.

'No. There are plenty of grogshops nearer the wharves.'

'Does my father frequent the Painted Pig?' Lydia asked.

'No. As far as I know, until he met Roark there, Marcus had

never set foot inside. It is a tavern patronized by tradesmen.' Julian offered Lydia a stiff smile. 'Not your father's kind of establishment at all.'

'So, how would either Mr Farrell or Mr Bustamonte have heard of this tavern?' Rees asked. Julian shrugged; he didn't know.

'What exactly happened?' Lydia asked from her position in the chair. Rees pulled another seat up beside her and sat down as well.

'No one is quite sure. The shooting occurred very early in the morning, just after midnight, and after the tavern had closed. The tavern-keeper was still awake. He rushed outside and saw the body.'

'I cannot imagine my father visiting a tavern frequented by working men, especially so late at night,' Lydia said, her forehead wrinkling.

'That sounded odd to me as well,' Julian admitted. 'But . . .' He stopped short, scowling self-consciously.

'But what?' Rees asked.

'Well, who would be out and about at that time?' Julian said. Rees, who was convinced that Julian had changed his response at the last moment, eyed the other man thoughtfully but decided not to pursue Julian's evasion right now.

'Did anyone see the shooter?' he asked instead. Julian shook his head.

'Not that I know of. Most people would have been in bed and anyway, it would have been dark, and I can't imagine there would be much to see. Marcus is smart like that.'

Rees regarded Julian. 'That sounds as though you believe your brother might be guilty.'

Julian heaved a sigh. 'Of course I don't,' he said unconvincingly. 'But they were heard arguing, Marcus and Roark, earlier that afternoon.'

'Yes, he told us that,' Lydia said.

'He told us they were arguing about Roark's wages,' Rees said.

'It was certainly not about wages,' Julian said with a chuckle. 'Mr Bustamonte does not work for my brother.'

'Are you sure?' Rees asked. Julian nodded.

'He was looking for work, I believe.'

'Do you know what they were quarreling about, then?' Lydia asked.

'How could I? I wasn't there.' Julian's gaze slid away from Lydia's.

'But you know who Roark Bustamonte is?' Lydia said, leaning forward. 'Who is he? And how do you and my father know him?'

'Well, um. I don't really *know* him,' Julian replied, flustered. 'I never met him. Mr Bustamonte is from, um, he has some connection with the sugar plantation owned by your father.'

Rees stared at the other man. Julian was a poor liar.

'What connection is that?' Rees asked.

'I don't know,' Julian said. He could not look at either Rees or Lydia.

'How old was Mr Bustamonte?' Lydia asked.

'I don't know. Young. Eighteen or nineteen maybe?'

Lydia turned to look at her husband to see if he'd heard what she had. How did Julian know Roark's age when he claimed not to know him? Julian caught Lydia's glance and added quickly, 'I don't really know. I assume so.'

'That raises another question,' Rees said. 'How did Mr Bustamonte find his way from the West Indies to Boston?'

Looking genuinely surprised, Julian shook his head.

'I don't know. By ship, I would imagine.'

'Do you know any of my father's friends to whom we might talk?' Lydia asked.

'He has no friends,' Julian said. 'He has business associates. That is all.'

'Could one of them have shot Mr Bustamonte?'

Julian stared into space for a few seconds. 'I suppose that is possible. My brother's dealings have ruined a few men. Financially, I mean. But why would one of them shoot a young man just recently arrived in Boston? If Marcus had been found murdered, well now, that would be a different story.'

Since Lydia had said something of the same sort, Rees nodded. 'I know I am probably grasping at straws here, but if we could have the names?'

'I'll make you a list,' Julian promised.

Rees glanced at Lydia. He was ready to leave. Despite Julian's assurance Rees would grow accustomed to the smell, he hadn't and in fact had developed a punishing headache.

'Anything else?' Julian asked.

Lydia clasped her hands together, separated them, and joined them once again.

'James?' she asked. 'How is he?'

'He's fine. I know he would like to see you.'

'I understand he stopped with you the last time he docked.'

'He did,' Julian said, looking at her in some surprise. 'He stayed home until there were problems with your father. James is still here, in Boston, you know.'

'He is? But Isabeau told me . . .' Lydia's voice ran down. She stared at her uncle in anguish.

'We assumed James had shipped out once again,' Rees said.

'No, no. He won't be leaving again until spring.' Julian threw a sympathetic glance at his niece. 'And maybe not even then.'

'What do you mean?' Lydia asked.

Julian hesitated. 'That is his story to tell,' he said at last.

'He doesn't want to see me?' Lydia asked, her voice breaking.

'I'm certain he will wish to. Once he knows you are visiting,' he added with a smile at his niece. 'It is just that . . .' His voice trailed away, and he shook his head. 'Well, no matter. We will arrange a meeting. I'll send around a note.' His gaze moved to Rees. 'And I'll include the list of men ruined by my brother as well.'

'Why can't he call on me at home?' Lydia asked in surprise.

'Your father told James never to return,' Julian replied. 'It would be . . . awkward.'

'Do you know where Roark Bustamonte was living?' Rees asked as Lydia rose from her chair.

'I believe I have his direction somewhere,' Julian said, moving papers around on his desk. 'Yes, here it is.' He tore the address from a larger piece and brandished it in front of Rees. 'Please, take it. I don't expect to ever need it again.'

Rees glanced at it and tucked it in his pocket.

Julian embraced Lydia. 'Please return for another visit,' he said as he hugged her tightly. 'You left Boston barely more than a girl, but you've grown into a fine woman.' He stepped back to allow Lydia to precede him to the door. As she moved away, he caught Rees's arm and said in a portentous voice, 'I do hope I see you again soon.' He winked meaningfully.

'Of course,' Rees responded politely, momentarily puzzled by Julian's strange behavior.

They quickly crossed the distillery floor, not speaking until they stepped outside into the pale sunshine. Then Lydia said, 'My father lied about my brother. James is still in Boston.'

'I know,' Rees said. 'And your uncle lied to us about Mr Bustamonte.'

'Yes. He knows more than he is willing to tell.'

'Much more. Your uncle Julian claimed he did not know that young man. But he gave us Roark's name before we mentioned it, told us his age, and also quickly produced the young man's address. I suspect Julian knew Mr Bustamonte and knew him well.' Rees thought of Julian's strange contortions. 'He may be willing to tell me more, if you are not in our company,' he said to Lydia with a grin. 'I suspect he is trying to protect your delicate sensibilities.'

'What nonsense!' Lydia said in annoyance.

Rees, spotting the coachman on the other side of the wharf, raised his hand. 'Go on without me. The distillery is not a great distance from your father's house. After I speak to Julian, I'll walk back.'

'Very well.' She looked up at the overcast sky. 'It is still early. I will have time to stop in the nursery and visit with Sharon.' Dropping her gaze to Rees, she continued, 'My stepmother and Cordy will most likely carry me off after luncheon. Me and Jerusha. Be sure you are home by then so you can eat with us. Otherwise, we will find ourselves spending this evening fielding uncomfortable questions about your absence.'

'I will,' Rees promised. He had hoped to stop at the Painted Pig as well, but he feared he would not have the time before the meal. Still, there was nothing stopping him from walking back toward the docks after luncheon.

ELEVEN

Once Rees had helped Lydia into the landau and waved her off, he turned around and re-entered the distillery. He knew his supposition had been correct when he found Julian Farrell waiting for him.

'I wondered if you would understand me,' Julian said. 'I know Lydia, and she would want to stay and listen.'

Rees nodded but said, 'I think you underestimate your niece. She is more worldly than you believe.'

'But what I have to tell you is about her father,' Julian said inarguably. 'For one thing, I suspect I know exactly where he was when Roark was murdered – if he wasn't the murderer, that is. Marcus has a mistress.'

Rees was shocked but then wondered why he should be. Many men of Marcus Farrell's standing maintained a separate household. 'Do you know her name?' Julian shook his head. 'Or where she lives?' Another shake. Rees rolled this new information around in his mind. 'Could it be possible Roark was Marcus's son?'

Julian's eyes widened and he vehemently shook his head. 'No. As I think I told you, Roark arrived very recently from the West Indies. Of course, my brother might have children with his mistress, but I don't know that.'

'I am puzzled by the connection between Roark and your brother,' Rees said. 'Why would your brother murder this young man who had just arrived in Boston?'

Julian shook his head, frowning. Rees had the distinct impression Julian had hoped Rees would just accept the salacious gossip about Marcus Farrell without asking other difficult questions.

'Could Mr Bustamonte know something about your brother? Could the young man have been attempting to extort money from Marcus?'

'Roark was just recently arrived,' Julian said shortly. 'There is nothing he could know about my brother, save what everyone else knows.'

Rees regarded the other man for a few seconds. 'You, yourself, told me your brother and Mr Bustamonte were heard arguing before the murder. Do you have any idea what the disagreement was about?'

Julian shook his head. 'No. As I told you, I was not there.' After a pause, he added, 'But I thought you should know about the mistress.'

Rees thanked Julian and departed. But as he left the distillery behind, he wondered why Julian expected Rees to believe him. He had given no information about a possible mistress that would help;

only a bit of so far unprovable gossip. And why had he tried to distract Rees's investigation from Roark Bustamonte, the victim?

After a brisk walk through the streets of Boston, Rees arrived at the house breathless and quite warm. When he handed his greatcoat to Morris, he asked about Lydia's whereabouts.

'Miss Lydia is in the nursery,' Morris said, his polite response touched with the faintest whiff of condescension. Rees nodded and took the stairs two at a time to the third floor.

Lydia was not the only family member in the nursery with Sharon. Jerusha was there as well, sitting on the floor playing dolls with her younger sister. 'I am surprised to see you here,' he said to the older girl. She looked up, her eyes heavy with fatigue.

'This is . . .' She paused and bit her lip. 'It is a relief,' she said at last. 'You don't know what it is like. Cordy never stops talking.' She glanced at her mother. 'I would not be able to stay here and go to school as well. I couldn't study.'

'We will find another solution if it continues,' Lydia promised, as she crossed the floor. Turning to Rees, she asked, 'How did your talk with Julian go?'

Rees glanced at his daughters and then at Bridget, the young maid who was clearing away Sharon's dirty plates. No one appeared to be listening or paying him any attention at all. 'Julian says your father has a mistress.'

Lydia's face registered surprise. 'That does not sound like him,' she said. 'As far as I know, he has never . . . But what daughter truly knows her father?'

'The putative mistress may not even exist,' Rees said. 'Julian had no name or address. In fact, he had nothing helpful. And when I asked him about Mr Bustamonte, he claimed to know nothing.'

'He knows Roark well enough to have his address,' Lydia said tartly. 'There is some mystery surrounding that young man that my uncle does not wish us to know. Tomorrow we will have to visit the address my uncle gave us.'

'Tomorrow,' Jerusha said, who had apparently been listening more carefully than they'd realized, 'you promised we would visit the school.'

'And we will,' Lydia said.

'You'll do what?' Cordelia asked, pushing the nursery door open.

'Take Jerusha to Mr Bingham's school,' Lydia said.

'But we need to call upon the dressmaker,' Cordelia wailed in disappointment. 'She still has to be fitted . . .'

'That may have to wait, Cordy,' Lydia said briskly. 'We have an appointment tomorrow morning.' She glanced from Rees to Jerusha and back again. 'All three of us.' She smiled at her sister. 'Maybe you can arrange for the dressmaker to come here. Late afternoon would be best.' The sulky curve to Cordelia's lips disappeared and she was all smiles once again.

'Oh, what fun that will be.' She clapped her hands together and added, 'Jerusha especially needs some new gowns. Something light, not those mournful dark colors she wears.'

Rees caught Jerusha's expression, a mix of fury and humiliation. She quickly wiped away the tears that rolled down her cheeks.

'Oh no, now you're angry,' Cordy cried, hurrying to Jerusha's side. 'I didn't mean to offend you. We are like sisters, you and I. I just want to offer you some town bronze. Please, say you've forgiven me.' She held out her arms. Jerusha reluctantly rose to her feet and submitted to Cordelia's embrace.

'Why did you come up here, to the nursery, Cordy?' Lydia asked, casting Jerusha a sympathetic glance.

'Oh. I forgot. I've been looking all over the house for you.' Cordy turned and made a sheepish moue. 'My mother sent me to remind everyone luncheon will be served at one o'clock.'

Rees took out his pocket watch. 'It is almost that now,' he said in alarm.

Cordelia linked her arm through Jerusha's and pulled her to the door. 'Then we must hurry.'

Lydia hastily kissed Sharon and, leaving her in Bridget's care, joined her husband. They all hurried down the stairs, so rapidly Jerusha tripped and would have fallen but for her father's quick grab.

Luncheon was served in the formal dining room instead of in the smaller and more welcoming breakfast room. Rees did not care to eat in this dark paneled room and he really disliked the soft movement of the servants behind him. He was perfectly capable of fetching his own food instead of sitting in the chair with his hands in his lap waiting. Of course, his friend Rouge the tavern-keeper, and his employees, served Rees and his family frequently but it was a different experience. They chatted back and forth and it was not unusual for one of them to join Rees at the table.

He would never dream of inviting any of these very superior servants to join him at a meal. Not one would accept. And every single one, from the lowliest footman to Morris the butler, would sneer at Rees for even advancing an invitation.

Mr Hutchinson joined them again. Mr and Mrs Farrell were clearly quite eager to affiance their daughter to him. But Cordelia acknowledged him with only the barest minimum of courtesy and ignored him from then on. Mrs Farrell was left to converse with their guest once again. Marcus Farrell scowled at his daughter throughout the meal.

The thick tension at the table did not foster a good appetite and anyway Rees was aware of Mrs Farrell's gaze. It was as though she was checking his table manners. Rees rose from the table almost as hungry as when he'd sat down.

TWELVE

Rees waved away the carriage holding the women with a sense of relief. Once Mr Hutchinson had left, Cordelia and her mother had spent the remaining time at luncheon discussing dressmakers and other purveyors of fashion. They, at least, were looking forward to the outing. Lydia and Jerusha exchanged glances of desperation and then looked at Rees hopefully. He knew without a doubt that they would much rather join him on his visit to the Painted Pig but he could think of no excuses to offer. He was just glad no one expected him to visit the shops with Isabeau and Cordelia Farrell.

Because he hadn't thought to ask Julian where the Painted Pig was located, Rees had to ask around. One of the stablehands was able to give clear and concise directions. As soon as the carriage turned the corner and disappeared into the noisy congestion beyond, Rees set off walking. He was heading toward the wharves again, but the Painted Pig was not located that far east. Instead, Rees made a few turns and ultimately found himself in a much less wealthy neighborhood.

Here were the tradesmen: the wheelwrights, the brickmakers and stonemasons. Rees easily found the tavern, the sign with a garish smiling pig swinging outside. He went inside and almost instantly felt at home. Although there were a few sailors seated at the tables, most of the occupants here were the men who operated the nearby shops.

Rees picked a shadowed corner and sat with his back against the outside wall. The tavern was not very busy now. The crowd who came for the midday meal had mostly departed and the men who would arrive for dinner and after would not turn up for another few hours.

'I'll take a glass of ale,' Rees said when the girl approached his table. She was a skinny little thing with a band of freckles across her nose and cheeks. He guessed she was no more than fourteen, just a bit younger than Jerusha. Despite working in a tavern, she did not appear well fed. 'Is the kitchen still open?' She nodded.

'There's a stew,' she said. 'And some bread, baked fresh this morning.'

'I'll take a bowl of the stew and some bread,' Rees said.

She flitted away, exchanging some banter with a group of regulars at a table as she passed.

Rees looked around. The windows that looked out upon the street outside were placed in the wall to his left. To his right stood the bar with a few tables and chairs next to it. Two small grimy windows on the north wall brought in some light. He could not tell if they looked into the alley where Roark's body was found or not.

When the young girl brought his food and tankard of ale, Rees said, 'Were you here when the body was found?'

'Yes, I was.' She sighed. 'Everyone wants to know about it and keeps asking.'

Rees nodded. 'Can you answer some questions for me?' He took two pennies from his pocket and held them out. She eyed them for a moment, biting her lip in concentration, and then she nodded.

'We're quiet now for a bit.'

He gave her one penny. 'The other when you've answered all my questions,' he said.

She slid the penny under her apron and made it disappear.

'What do you want to know?'

'Will you tell me what happened?'

She grinned. 'Of course. We'd closed for the night and I was in my room. My parents were downstairs. My father heard the shot. But when he ran out, he didn't see nothing. Not at first, anyway.'

Rees nodded. He had the sudden sensation that he was being watched, a crawling tingle between his shoulder blades. But when he looked around, he saw nothing suspicious. No one nearby – neither the three men at the table or the lone gentleman at the bar – appeared to be paying him any attention. He looked back at the young maid. 'The man who was killed. Did either you or your parents know him? Did they recognize him? Did you see him?'

The young girl stared over Rees's head for several seconds and shuddered, as though she were remembering something terrible. 'They wouldn't allow me to see him,' she said. 'I did, when the dead wagon came for him. When I looked through my bedchamber window, he was pointed straight up at me.' She shivered again but Rees thought she was trembling as much from excitement as well as horror. 'But I couldn't see his face. They'd covered it.'

'Do you know if he was one of your customers? Did he frequent the tavern?'

'My father said no. He said he didn't recognize him.'

'And no one saw the shooting,' Rees muttered. The killer had chosen his time well.

'No.' She hesitated and then said, 'I can show you where he was found. If you like? It's quiet now.'

Rees scraped up the last of the stew with his spoon and jumped up. 'Let's go,' he said.

He followed the young woman through the front door and around to the right. A narrow lane led to a small enclosure in the back. It was dirty and smelly and full of refuse, all filmed with a thin coat of icy snow. Rees distinctly saw a rat scurry from one pile of rubbish to another.

A door, propped open to the air, allowed entry to the kitchen. He could hear the clatter of crockery and the low murmur of voices.

To the left side of the tavern was another alley, this one so narrow, the opening so tight, Rees could see he would have a difficult time squeezing through.

In the yard, directly in front of the alley, lay a large canvas sheet half-frozen into the snow. The discarded cloth was scattered with old rubbish – but it was the large brownish stain in the center that attracted Rees's attention. He stared at it. Up to now, the murder had seemed abstract. All his focus had been on Marcus Farrell and the question of his guilt or innocence. But as Rees gazed at the blood, the reality of the murder came into sharp relief. A young man had died here, alone in a yard full of rubbish.

It suddenly became less important to prove Farrell's innocence than to find the murderer of this young man, whoever he might be, and bring him to justice.

Rees stepped around the stained canvas and stared down the alley. He could see the street beyond. He turned to survey this small and grimy space. It was quite private. None of the tavern's windows looked out upon the yard and if the back door was closed and the proprietors safely tucked in bed, there could be no witnesses to the murder.

If Mr Bustamonte had chosen this meeting space, he had chosen poorly. After the shooting, the killer had easily escaped through the alley, disappearing into the streets that surrounded this tavern.

'He was shot here,' the maid said impatiently, gesturing at the canvas. Rees looked at her. She was hugging herself against the cold.

'Yes, I see the blood,' Rees said, trying to imagine the position of the body. 'Do you know how he fell? Where his head was?'

'My father would know,' she said. 'Let me fetch him.' She disappeared through the tavern door.

Rees heard a male voice exclaim, 'What were you doing outside?'

As the low murmur of conversation continued, Rees looked around once more, trying to visualize the scene.

The reed-thin alley was almost directly behind him. Roark's killer had probably been standing within an arm's length of the victim. No one, no matter how unpracticed with a pistol, could miss at that range. When Roark dropped to the ground, his murderer had slipped through the alley and fled.

'What do you want to know?' the proprietor asked warily from behind Rees. He turned.

The tavern-keeper was almost as tall as Rees, maybe within six inches or so, but they could not have looked more different. While Rees was muscular, broad-shouldered and solid, the other man was round. His white shirt strained across his belly. His balding head was a ball and his eyes were large blue marbles. He looked, Rees thought, like a porcelain doll made flesh.

'He wants to know—' his daughter began. The inn-keeper shushed her.

'Why are you asking?' he asked Rees suspiciously.

'Marcus Farrell hired me to prove his innocence,' Rees said. It wasn't entirely a falsehood. 'How did the victim's body fall? Where was his head?'

The other man eyed Rees for a few seconds and then moved forward. 'He fell here,' he said, gesturing to the dirty canvas. 'With his feet pointing at the alley.'

Rees looked at the other man without really seeing him. In his mind's eye, Rees pictured the young man facing his murderer, the shot, and then the escape of the killer through the alley. 'Did you look at the body?' Rees asked.

'No. Not after the first glance.' The tavern-keeper shuddered.

'Did you see where the bullet hit him?'

'It caught him here,' the tavern-keeper said, pointing to the side of his neck. 'Just above the shoulder.' He paused and added in a low voice, 'His life's blood was pouring out like a flood.'

Rees swallowed. Injuries to that area of the body almost always resulted in death. 'Did you recognize the victim?'

The tavern-keeper shook his head. 'No. I admit I didn't look, not once I saw the blood.'

Rees understood. The sight of the blood would have consumed the other man's attention. He would not have wanted to examine the body further. Most people would feel the same. Rees darted a glance at the young girl. Her father had not told the truth when he claimed the victim was not a patron of this establishment. He could be; the inn-keeper had not looked at the body long enough to know.

'Did you see the murderer?' Rees asked the other man.

'No.' The proprietor hesitated several seconds. Rees eyed him sternly.

'If you know anything else . . .'

'The poor man's murderer was looking for something. The victim's coat was open and his shirt disordered.'

'You frightened him away,' Rees guessed.

'I must have done.' Heaving a sigh, the proprietor said mournfully, 'I just wasn't quick enough to catch sight of him.'

'This isn't your fault,' Rees said. He glanced over his shoulder. 'The villain who did this would have fled down this alley as soon as he heard your back door opening.'

'And I could not have followed,' the tavern-keeper said, placing his hands on his round belly.

'No,' Rees agreed.

'Anything else?' the other man asked. Rees shook his head. Wiping his hands on the front of his breeches, the tavern proprietor withdrew into his establishment. 'Come inside,' he said to his daughter.

'Coming,' she said over her shoulder. Rees handed her the final penny he'd promised. Instead of retreating into the tavern, she paused, looking at him almost as though she wished to speak. But she said nothing and with one final glance at Rees, she disappeared through the tavern door.

Rees remained in the cold yard, thinking. What had compelled Roark to come to a shuttered tavern in the middle of the night? He must have known he was putting himself in harm's way. And what had his killer been searching for?

No answers presented themselves and after a few seconds, Rees turned and left.

THIRTEEN

He had not gone very far when he became aware of soft footsteps behind him. Nervously, he spun around. A heavyset woman with a basket over her arm brushed by him. There were several other people on the street as well, but when he studied them, not one was looking at him. They all seemed like working people. The sun would set in an hour and they were hurrying to their homes and warm fires. Rees turned and continued on. But now, alarmed, he kept glancing around him. Although he saw nothing suspicious, he remained convinced someone was following him.

The narrow streets offered few spaces to hide and appeared gloomy even during daylight. Now, with dusk fast approaching, and long shadows stretching across the alleys, they were growing dark. Rees turned a corner and saw his chance. As quickly as he could he darted into a sliver of space between two buildings and pressed his back against the wall. A young man in buff breeches and a bright yellow jacket hurried around the corner and ran past the opening. Rees peered after him. The stripling – he was barely out of his teens – had paused at the corner and was looking desperately from side to side. Rees tiptoed out of the fetid alley and crept up behind the fellow. Grasping him by the arm, Rees growled, 'Why are you following me?'

The young man jumped with a scream. But he recovered quickly enough and turned with a defiant glare. 'Why are you asking about Roark Bustamonte?' he demanded. Pale blue eyes stared at Rees from a tanned face. He had dark curly hair. Rees realized this man had been the lone customer at the bar in the Painted Pig.

'Why do you want to know?' Rees demanded.

'None of your business.'

'Are you Roark's brother?'

Without replying, the young man suddenly pulled backwards, twisting his body so that the fabric of his jacket jerked from Rees's grasp. He ran into the crowd and almost instantly disappeared.

Cursing under his breath Rees walked up and down the street several times, peering down the alleys and around corners. He saw no sign of that bright yellow jacket. Finally, he gave up and trudged back to the main street. From there he made his way back to the Farrell house.

Dusk had fallen. Rees was quite tired, and his feet hurt. The narrow twisty streets of this town were hard to follow, and he'd gotten lost more than once. He gave his coat to Morris and walked through the foyer. Voices from the drawing room drew him to the door. When he looked inside, he found Lydia, Jerusha and Cordelia gathered around the table in front of a recently lit fire. One plate of sandwiches and another of cake rested on the table in front of him. A large teapot beckoned to him, although tea was usually a beverage he scorned. Rees realized he was both thirsty and famished. When Lydia gestured to him, he entered gladly and sat down. Lydia passed him a plate and a cup and saucer.

'I guess the shopping trip was a success,' he said, looking around at the smiling faces.

'I purchased the loveliest pink sarsenet,' Cordy said enthusiastically. 'And a pale lavender handkerchief cotton with several yards of embroidered ribbon to match.'

Rees filled his plate with sandwiches. 'Did you purchase

anything?' he asked Jerusha. He hoped Lydia had kept a close eye on the budget. Jerusha nodded enthusiastically.

'A length of pale green cotton. And one of blue linen. And Cordy is giving me some of her older gowns to make over,' Jerusha said, turning a wide smile upon the other girl.

'Pish,' Cordy said dismissively. 'I will enjoy seeing them upon you. And you will need more clothes when you attend school here in Boston.'

'I will love them the more because they came from you,' Jerusha said warmly, reaching out to squeeze Cordelia's hand. She added, glancing at her parents, 'Don't forget, we are visiting the school tomorrow.'

'We haven't forgotten,' Lydia said with a smile.

Rees stared at them. He could not imagine a sharper contrast to the murder scene he'd just witnessed, with its sad bloody snow, and these smiling girls chatting about dresses.

He turned a stunned look on Lydia. She smiled at him and took up the teapot to pour the hot brew into his cup. 'The dressmaker comes on Friday to begin fitting us.'

'I wish she'd been already,' Jerusha said vehemently.

'Us?' Rees asked his wife as he closed his cold hands around the hot cup to warm them.

'I purchased several yards of dark blue wool,' she replied.

'I could not persuade my sister to accept any of the cottons,' Cordelia said, mock-frowning at Lydia.

'I am an old married lady,' Lydia said comfortably. 'That new style of diaphanous shorter gowns is not for me. And Jerusha,' she added, turning to look at her daughter, 'I know Cordy is pressing you to adopt the new fashion of lower-cut decolletages. You are too young, and it is not appropriate.'

'You do not need to worry on that score,' Jerusha assured her, a faint pink rising into her cheeks. 'I would not be at all comfortable exposing so much of myself.'

'Do you want to see what we bought?' Cordy asked Rees, leaning forward as she spoke.

Rees nodded and opened his mouth but before he could reply, Morris came into the room. He looked directly at Lydia.

'Forgive me for intruding.'

'Not at all, Morris,' Lydia said.

'There is a young woman who wishes to know if you are receiving callers.'

'A young woman?' Lydia repeated in mystification. 'What is her name?'

'Mrs Sarah Fitzpatrick.' For the first time Morris unbent slightly. 'She said to tell you her maiden name was Giroux.'

'Giroux? Sally Giroux? She's here now?'

'In the hall,' Morris affirmed.

'Of course I am at home,' Lydia said. 'You must remember her, Morris. She was my greatest friend. I shall greatly enjoy seeing her again. Please show her in immediately.'

'Very good, madam. And this arrived a little while ago for you.' Morris held out a small silver tray with a rather grubby paper upon it. It had been sealed shut with an untidy blob of wax.

'Thank you,' Lydia said, taking the note from the tray. She slid the paper up her sleeve.

As Morris withdrew, Rees asked, 'How long has it been since you've seen your friend?'

'Seven years,' Lydia replied. 'It feels like a lifetime.'

'Lyddie,' shrieked the young woman as she appeared in the doorway. Rushing forward, she threw her arms around her friend. Laughing, Lydia returned the embrace.

FOURTEEN

Sally Fitzpatrick was dressed in the height of fashion: a filmy gown of pale yellow more suited to May than to January. Fortunately, she had an embroidered shawl wrapped around her shoulders. She was quite plump, rather too curvy for the current uncorseted style. Brown curls peeped from underneath a yellow turban. A style usually adopted by older ladies, the turban had the effect of making Sally appear younger than she was, as though she were dressing up in someone else's clothes.

'Permit me to introduce you to my husband, William,' Lydia said. Rees found himself the object of a pair of curious dark brown eyes.

'I believe you know my sister Cordelia. And this is my daughter Jerusha.'

'Your daughter?' Sally looked confused. 'But you would have been a mere child . . .'

'I'm adopted,' Jerusha said, her voice too loud and abrupt.

'But no less loved, for all of that,' Lydia said quickly. She knew Jerusha resented being treated as less important because she was adopted.

'I am very happy to meet you both,' Sally said, holding out her hand to Rees. He took it and gave it a slight shake before dropping it. Surely, he thought, she did not expect him to kiss it.

'Pleased to meet you,' Jerusha said, barely polite. Sally looked at her and smiled.

'Don't be cross,' she said, leaning forward and placing one plump hand on Jerusha's arm. 'Cry friends with me. Your mother was as close as a sister and I would like to think of you as family.' Jerusha blinked but, under Sally's warmth, she couldn't help but return the other's smile.

'Let's all sit down,' Lydia said as she moved forward into the drawing room.

Lydia and Rees sat upon the couch, with Jerusha, while Cordelia and Sally chose two of the four chairs nearby. Against the green walls, Sally looked like a flower in her yellow gown.

'Are you the oldest?' Sally asked, leaning toward Jerusha. She opened her mouth to reply and then, flummoxed, she looked at Lydia.

'I have a stepson who is the eldest,' Lydia replied. 'We brought Jerusha with us to look at the schools in Boston. She wishes to become a teacher.'

'How admirable,' Sally said, sounding genuinely impressed. 'Your mother will tell you how poorly I did in school. I am sure she is quite proud of you. I hope you are enjoying your visit to Boston.'

'It has been interesting,' Jerusha said politely.

Lydia glanced at her daughter and then at Cordelia.

'You girls can go on upstairs,' Lydia told them sympathetically. As Jerusha and Cordy quickly escaped, Lydia added, 'The two girls have become great friends.'

'How many children do you have?' Sally asked.

'Six.' Lydia smiled as Sally gasped. 'The baby of the family is upstairs napping in the nursery. And another is on the way.' Lydia put her hand on her belly. 'But you must have children of your own.'

'Three,' Sally said. 'Two girls, one six and one a little over four. My son just turned one. The sweetest little angel.' She waxed sentimental for several seconds about her little angels. Rees wondered if all the ladies in Boston talked without drawing breath.

'They sound delightful.' Lydia finally interrupted her friend. 'And they all sound so sweet-natured. Did you marry your Quentin?'

'Yes.' A blush suffused Sally's cheeks. 'My parents weren't happy but finally agreed.' She paused as a maid brought in another teacup and a second plate of small cakes. Rees, who found it difficult to eat under the gaze of Mrs Farrell – he suspected she was judging his table manners despite her smiles – was very hungry. In unison, he and Sally reached for the plate. Laughing, he offered it to her. While she spent a few seconds inspecting them before choosing two, Rees helped himself to the two remaining sandwiches. Lydia poured for herself and her friend before speaking once again.

'I am happy they saw reason.'

'He has been able to provide for me. And when the children began coming, they turned sweet.' She bent forward and took Lydia's hand. 'I was so worried about you when you left. I feared you would never marry. Now, to see you so happy . . .' Tears filled her eyes. Lydia squeezed Sally's hand.

'Everything turned out for the best.'

'I should say,' Sally agreed. 'Micah married Chloe Adams, you know.'

Rees, who had been planning to make his excuses as soon as he finished the sandwiches, since he did not want to sit through an hour of women's talk, settled back into the seat. It appeared he might learn something about Lydia's past.

'Yes, my sister wrote me,' Lydia said. She glanced at her husband but did not suggest he leave.

'Well, he has led her a merry dance. It is no secret he has taken any number of mistresses, he takes no trouble to hide them, so you can add indiscretion to his sins.'

'How humiliating for her,' Lydia said, but not as though she meant it. Sally smiled.

'Yes. Poetic justice, to be sure. I haven't seen Chloe for an age.

She took the children and moved somewhere in the country outside of Boston. I daresay she couldn't face any of us anymore.'

'Why, Sally,' Mrs Farrell said from the doorway, 'I did not know you were here. How lovely to see you again.'

Sally and Lydia exchanged a look and Sally rose to her feet. 'How are you faring, Mrs Farrell?'

'Well, thank you. And the children?'

'Growing like weeds, thank you.'

Mrs Farrell glanced at Lydia and Rees before moving on. Sally sat back down with a thump. 'I see she has not changed,' she whispered to Lydia.

'What do you mean?' Rees asked.

'She used to listen in on all our conversations when I was a girl,' Lydia said.

'Always creeping about listening at keyholes,' Sally said with a shudder. 'We met at my house as often as possible.' As she eyed the last remaining cakes on the plate, Rees offered it to the ladies. Lydia took one and Sally the other.

'We must meet again,' Lydia said with a glance at the door. 'Perhaps at one of the coffee shops . . .'

'Oh my, I almost forgot,' Sally said. 'I thought you and your husband might wish to come for dinner tomorrow night. You can meet the children. And I know Quentin would be delighted to see you again. As well as meet your husband,' she added with a quick smile at Rees.

Lydia glanced at Rees and then turned back to her friend. 'We would be happy to accept.'

'Wonderful,' Sally cried, clapping her hands together. 'Quentin usually arrives home around six. Shall we say six thirty? We don't keep fashionable hours, so we eat by seven.'

'Excellent,' Rees said. Accustomed to eating his main meal at noon, he was finding it difficult to adapt to eating late at night and then retiring. The food settled in his stomach like a cannonball.

FIFTEEN

Although Rees had several matters he wanted to discuss with Lydia, only one was uppermost in his mind.

'Tell me about Micah.'

'He was a partner of my father's. You probably guessed, we were engaged to be married.'

'But you didn't marry him,' Rees said.

Lydia shook her head. 'It was probably the most shaming day of my life. I walked in on him and Chloe kissing. Her clothing was all disordered.' She glanced at Rees. 'I don't know what she expected. But *he* thought we would still marry. He was quite annoyed when I told him the wedding was off and I wouldn't marry him if he were the only man in the world.'

'My God!' Rees said, at a loss for words.

'You know what my father said?' Lydia managed a bitter smile. 'That many men took mistresses and I should learn to live with it.' She looked across the drawing room at the wallpaper scene on the back wall but Rees knew that, instead of seeing it, she was lost in a memory. 'I went to visit my aunt in the District of Maine and shortly after I joined the Zion Shaker community.' Another bitter smile. 'A celibate sect seemed the perfect answer to me.'

Rees nodded. He had met her in Zion. Celibacy had not proven to be her answer. A secret marriage had led to a pregnancy and she had been expelled.

'I cut off all ties to my family, except for Cordy,' Lydia added. 'Not that they missed me. Neither Isabeau nor my father ever made an attempt to find me.' She turned and added seriously, 'Now you know why I am so opposed to Mr Hutchinson. My father chose Micah for me and thought his lack of fidelity was just a peccadillo. Although Mr Hutchinson may not possess that particular tendency if he is connected with my father, he is corrupt. There can be no other determination.'

'I'm very glad Micah proved to be a scoundrel,' Rees said. 'We might never have met otherwise. And as Sally said, Chloe has certainly paid a price for her poor judgement.'

Lydia nodded and, leaning forward, she said, 'I forgot to tell you. I met Edward Bartlett.'

'Cordelia's Edward Bartlett?'

'Yes. We bumped into him outside the draper's. A very well-mannered young man and uncommonly handsome. I can see why a young girl such as Cordy would be smitten.'

'Is he as taken with your sister as she is with him?' Rees asked.

Lydia hesitated. 'Perhaps. He is older than I expected, closer to my age than hers, and I think she amuses him. But more in the sense of a charming child.'

'Why do you think so?' Rees asked. He understood; he found Cordelia charming, as he would any lively child, but he would be as likely to court her as sprout wings and fly.

'I am not sure. In any case, Isabeau sent Cordy and me to the carriage while she reprimanded him for accosting us on the street.'

'I thought she liked young Bartlett,' Rees said in surprise. Lydia smiled.

'I believe she does. Just not for her baby girl. I suspect she would view royalty with suspicion.'

'But she is willing to entertain Mr Hutchinson's suit,' Rees remarked.

'Perhaps. We do not know what she says to my father in private.' As Lydia stood and adjusted her clothing, both she and her husband heard the crinkle of paper.

'Oh, I forgot I received this,' She pulled out the letter. 'It is from Julian.'

'Ah. The list of the men ruined by your father.'

Lydia broke the seal and quickly glanced at the contents. 'My brother will meet us Saturday at the Green Dragon at ten. Good,' she added, darting a quick look at Rees. 'It is early enough that there will be no awkward questions about our whereabouts.' Rees frowned. He was rapidly growing tired of dancing around Mr and Mrs Farrell's sensibilities. 'And here,' she pulled out a second sheet, 'is the list of names you requested.'

Rees took it from her. There were only three names, with the addresses appended, on the paper. 'Surely there must be more victims than this,' he muttered.

'Probably,' Lydia agreed. 'Let's bring the list to Sally and ask her. She lives here. I wouldn't be surprised if she knows all the latest gossip and scandal. And if she doesn't know the names, her husband will.'

'Will he be willing to confide what he knows?' Rees asked a little doubtfully.

'Oh yes,' Lydia said with a nod. 'Don't worry. He is not a snob. Sally's parents wanted her to marry someone else, a man with a higher social standing. Quentin is a silversmith. You'll like him.' She smiled teasingly. 'He is a craftsman just like you.'

Rees, who had not realized how anxious he had been about the dinner with Lydia's friend, felt himself relax. At least he could hope Sally and her husband would not watch him eat with contempt in their eyes.

It was barely five o'clock but the drawing room was already in shadow. 'The servants will soon come around to light the candles,' Lydia said. Rees nodded; why use candles when it was unnecessary? He followed Lydia from the room and was unsurprised to find Mrs Farrell standing just outside the door. He wondered if she had been eavesdropping and how much she had overheard. Lydia must have been wondering as well. She smiled stiffly at her stepmother.

'It was delightful seeing Sally again,' Mrs Farrell said. 'Of course, she made a rather unfortunate marriage.' She flicked a glance at Rees.

'Sally is very happy,' Lydia said. 'Besides, Quentin seems an estimable man, not like some.'

'I don't know what you mean,' Mrs Farrell said. Rees couldn't be sure whether she was truly bewildered or if she was just a good actor.

'I am referring to Micah, of course,' Lydia said.

Mrs Farrell frowned. 'That was a long time ago,' she said.

'Sally has invited us to dinner tomorrow night,' Lydia said. 'We will not be dining with you and my father.'

'Very well,' Mrs Farrell said. 'I will inform Cook.' She smiled at Lydia and said, 'What a pity your new gowns are not ready yet. But I suppose it doesn't matter; it is only your good friend Sally. She will not be critical.'

Lydia blinked but clearly could think of no rejoinder.

As they walked to the stairs, Cordelia shouted down from above, 'Oh good, you are finally coming. I'll tell Jerusha.'

'Really, Cordy,' Mrs Farrell said in dismay.

'Don't worry,' Lydia said quietly to Rees as they climbed the stairs, 'we did not spend a great deal. I know there will be school fees for Jerusha.' She paused a moment. 'Cordy and Isabeau spent a great deal, however. And Cordy already owns more gowns than she can easily wear.'

'That explains her gifts to Jerusha,' Rees said.

'I expect most of Cordy's gifts will be from last year,' Lydia said a trifle drily. 'She is not so generous she will give away her newest gowns.' Worried lines settled into her forehead. 'I hope whatever she does pass on to Jerusha is made with extra fabric. Without it, the dresses can't be made over to fit. Jerusha is so much taller and plumper.'

'How many gowns did Cordy give Jerusha?' Rees asked.

'Five or six.'

'Good. Do you think Cook will send up more sandwiches?'

'Really, Will? We will be dining in only a few hours,' Lydia said disapprovingly.

'I walked all over Boston today,' he said, adding, 'I stopped at the Painted Pig.'

'Did you learn anything?' she asked, leaning forward.

He nodded. 'A young maid, who is beside herself with the turmoil, showed me the spot where the murder occurred.'

'And?'

'It is very private. No one saw, or could have seen, anything. The murderer shot Mr Bustamonte from scarcely an arm's length away before fleeing.'

'Could the murderer have been my father?' Lydia asked in a low voice.

'I don't know.' Rees took her hand and squeezed it. 'Possibly. But probably unlikely. Mr Bustamonte obviously did not fear for his safety. Would he have been so trusting if he were meeting your father?'

'Hmmm,' Lydia said with a nod. 'That is true. And that raises some other questions. Why would Mr Bustamonte even agree to this meeting? In an alley? Behind a closed tavern? And in the middle of the night? What could be so important?'

'Exactly my question,' Rees agreed. 'The tavern-keeper said it looked as though Bustamonte's jacket had been searched.'

'Searched? For what?'

'I don't know.'

'And the tavern-keeper saw nothing?' Lydia paused on the landing.

'No. Bustamonte was shot after the tavern closed. There were no witnesses.'

'What about his wife?' Lydia asked. 'Was she awake?'

'The entire family was, I believe. The proprietor and his wife were cleaning up. The daughter was already in bed.'

'Did you question the daughter?'

'She saw nothing,' Rees said in surprise, wondering why his wife would ask that when he just said there were no witnesses.

Lydia frowned. 'Did she say she saw nothing?'

'Well, no. But she just saw the body as it was being removed. That is what she said.'

'Hmm. I will join you when you return to the tavern and quiz her myself,' she said.

'Of course. But listen, something even more interesting happened after my visit. A young man followed me from the tavern.'

Lydia went pale. 'Do you think he is the murderer?'

Rees stared at her. 'I didn't consider that. Maybe. But he made no attempt at all to harm me.' He paused, recalling the interchange. 'He asked me what my interest in Roark Bustamonte was. When I tried to question him further, he pulled away from me and ran.' He hesitated once again, thinking. 'I doubt he is the murderer although, of course, I could be wrong. But he knows something, I am convinced of that. And I suspect he knew the victim. We need to find him.'

SIXTEEN

When Rees descended to the breakfast room early the following morning, he found Jerusha already there. Although she had drunk some of her tea, the bread in front of her was untouched. 'Do I look all right?' she asked as Rees entered. He inspected her. She had put on her Sunday best, an indigo-dyed wool that flattered her coloring.

'You look very well,' he said.

'This is not cut in the current fashion,' she said, plucking at the skirt unhappily. 'Oh, how I wish there'd been time to make over at least one of Cordy's frocks.'

'I doubt the pedagogues will care,' Rees said matter-of-factly. 'They will be more interested in your commitment to learning.'

'And that's another thing,' Jerusha wailed. 'I don't know any Latin. Miss Francine's dame school did not offer it.'

'I don't know if it will be offered here at this school either,' Lydia said as she entered the breakfast room. 'When I attended Mr Bingham's school, it was privately run. Mr Bingham offered a number of unusual subjects. But he closed the school a few years later and took the position of Headmaster of one of the new public schools for girls; he's retired now. So I expect Latin may not even be offered.'

Jerusha's mouth drooped in disappointment.

'What will Jerusha be learning?' Rees asked. He could not suppress a flicker of hope that his daughter would not need to leave home.

'More than penmanship and embroidery,' Lydia said.

'I must change my dress,' Jerusha said, pushing herself from the table and hurrying away. Lydia and Rees exchanged a glance.

'This is very important to her,' Lydia explained.

'I see that,' Rees said.

'I think,' Lydia said as she helped herself to tea, 'that after we visit the school, we should also call at Mr Bustamonte's address. We will have the landau . . .'

Rees nodded in agreement. What Lydia had not said was that, since they would be out anyway, there would be no need to justify leaving the house to her parents. Without discussing it, Rees and Lydia had tacitly agreed to keep all details of their investigation between themselves. Still, he didn't see why Lydia was so worried about crossing them when she was an adult herself.

Rees was finding this visit with Lydia's family difficult. He tried to be careful around Mr Farrell, who bullied and intimidated his daughter. And then there was Mrs Farrell, condescending and flirtatious by turns. Rees did not know how to respond when her 'how did you sleep' was freighted with innuendo. He wished he had insisted they stay at an inn, but hesitated admitting this to his wife.

Rees filled his plate. Breakfast was the one meal where he could eat until satisfied without feeling the scornful eyes of Mrs Farrell watching him; she never came downstairs for breakfast. As he sat down and tucked in, Jerusha returned to the breakfast room. She had changed into the dark green wool. With a desperate question in her eyes, she looked at her mother.

'You look lovely,' Lydia said. 'Very appropriate.'

Jerusha sat down and nibbled at a corner of her cold toast. But after only one bite, she jumped to her feet and hurried from the room.

Rees raised his eyebrows and glanced at his wife. 'She is nervous,' Lydia said. 'Much more nervous than necessary.'

'What if she doesn't like the school?' Rees asked.

'There are other schools,' Lydia said easily. 'I know of a private girls' school in Litchfield, Connecticut. Jerusha would have to board there and the fees would be greater. But they do offer Latin and, I think, Greek.'

Rees, who had never had any desire to learn either of those languages, shook his head in amazement. He found it difficult to align the ragged girl he had found in a dilapidated shack with this young woman who was so bent on becoming a scholar. The Jerusha of a few years ago and the Jerusha now seemed like two different people.

When she returned to the table, she was once again clad in her dark blue wool. Rees wisely made no comment.

When Rees helped Jerusha step down from the landau, he felt her trembling beneath his hand. He squeezed her arm encouragingly. She managed a shaky smile before stepping down to the ground.

Rees looked over his shoulder at the brick building behind him. It was several stories high and the brick looked new but otherwise it was not a grand structure.

'You'll be fine,' Lydia said as she drew her daughter's arm through hers.

A woman with iron-gray hair and pince-nez spectacles waited for them just inside the door. She announced her name as Miss Cheney. As Rees introduced himself and his family, Miss Cheney inspected the new pupil. Although the teacher did not smile, she nodded approvingly at Jerusha's plain dark costume. 'The head-master is waiting for you,' she said, preceding them down the long hall and into a room with paneled walls. A scarlet turkey carpet covered the floor. A large desk backed by bookcases occupied one wall and behind the desk sat a man in a white wig. Rees stared. Although he remembered the style from his youth, such wigs had gone out of fashion years ago. And this gentleman's wig was askew, as though he'd reached underneath to scratch his head.

While Rees reflected on the wig, the headmaster cleaned the ink from his pen with his fingers, put the pen down, and wiped his ink-stained fingers on his head underneath the wig.

Rees inadvertently caught Lydia's eye and almost burst out laughing. She changed her chuckle into a cough.

'Mr Tileston,' said Miss Cheney. 'The Rees family are here.'

'Good, good. Please sit down,' said the headmaster, gesturing to the chairs ranged in front of his desk.

'So, you want this young lady to attend school?' Mr Tileston said, fixing Jerusha with his mild eyes. She nodded.

'She has already attended the local dame school for several years,' Lydia said.

'And she has begun teaching the younger students,' Rees added.

'Hmm.' Mr Tileston was not impressed. 'We have a rather more difficult curriculum here,' he said. 'We teach writing, arithmetic, reading, spelling and English grammar. No embroidery or painting or any of that.'

'Latin?' Jerusha asked in a small voice. 'Greek?'

Mr Tileston stared at her, dumbfounded. 'In all my years, I have never heard a young lady ask for such challenging subjects. No, no. You don't really wish to study such demanding fields, do you? Totally unnecessary. As an educated lady, you would succeed in making an advantageous marriage. But no man wishes to wed a bluestocking.'

As he spoke, Jerusha's eyes grew wider and wider. Since Rees could see her struggling to hold on to her temper, he spoke first.

'My daughter wishes to teach,' he said in a quelling voice. 'My wife and I desire to educate her to that goal.'

Mr Tileston regarded Rees solemnly. 'I see you are a very progressive father; very progressive. Well, Miss Cheney will show you around. We would be delighted to admit your daughter to the school.' He looked down at his desk. Rees and Lydia remained seated for a few more seconds, not realizing the interview had concluded.

'Come this way,' Miss Cheney said from the door.

They followed Miss Cheney down the hall to a classroom on the right and looked into a room filled with girls. Rees thought they were all younger than Jerusha, maybe eleven or twelve. The young woman at the front was teaching English grammar; the eyes of most of her pupils were glazed with boredom.

Miss Cheney moved on to another classroom. The students here were older, almost young ladies soon to graduate. This class was not a lecture but a discussion of something. When Jerusha peeked inside, they turned to glance at her curiously. Her cheeks flushing, she backed away.

'*The Tempest*,' Lydia remarked to Miss Cheney. 'That seems advanced.'

Miss Cheney smiled. 'We pride ourselves on fully educating the mothers of tomorrow.'

'This is quite a large school,' Rees commented.

'There are other Reading Schools in Boston,' Miss Cheney said with quiet pride. 'When Mr Bingham first established his school for girls, he attracted the daughters of the finest families. Since the school has become a public school, we now also educate the children of tradesmen.' She flicked a glance at Rees.

Did he look that much like a tradesman? He wondered if the word weaver was inscribed across his forehead.

They spent a few more minutes touring the school before taking their leave. Rees wasn't sure what he had expected but it wasn't this large brick structure. Lydia was frowning slightly. And Jerusha, as soon as they started down the steps, burst into noisy sobs.

'What is the matter?' Rees asked.

'My clothes!' Jerusha wept. 'They are all wrong.'

Rees stared at her in shock. Until they arrived in Boston, he would have said she cared nothing for such fripperies. Lydia put her arm around Jerusha's shoulders.

'Come now. Dry your tears. By the time you attend this school, you will have many new gowns and other items,' Lydia said reassuringly. 'You know that. Why, the dressmaker is coming first thing tomorrow to fit you.'

Still weeping, Jerusha nodded.

'I don't understand,' Rees said in puzzlement. 'I think she looks lovely.'

Lydia threw him a glance as she urged her daughter toward the landau. 'All of the young ladies were wearing newer, more fashionable gowns,' she said. 'Similar to those worn by Cordy. All pastels. And all cut in the new style.'

'I see,' Rees said. 'I noticed they all wore shawls.' He had paid scant attention to the girls, and now his focus was already moving forward to his next plan. 'Did you remember to bring Mr Bustamonte's address?'

'I believe so.' Lydia pulled a ragged paper from her reticule and handed it to him.

SEVENTEEN

After the landau carried Jerusha home, Rees gave Mr Bustamonte's address to the coachman. He looked surprised but did not ask any questions. Rees understood the coachman's concern when they arrived at the victim's lodging.

He resided close to the wharves, in a poorer section of Boston where the buildings leaned over the narrow cobbled lanes and shaded them from any illumination by the sun. Although it was almost midday, the steps leading up to Roark's home were almost invisible in the deep shadow.

The landlady, an enormously fat woman, directed them to the top floor and the garret on the right. She displayed no curiosity at all, and she did not ask any questions about their intent. When Rees pointed out they would not be able to enter, she handed them the key. Rees and Lydia began the long climb. The flights of stairs grew narrower and ever more rickety as they ascended and by the time they reached the top landing both of them were panting.

There were only two rooms here, one on either side of the stairs. The key afforded them access to the large room although Rees thought he could have probably pushed the flimsy door open with brute strength.

There was no fireplace to warm the space and it was very cold. A large bed and one broken chair equaled the sum total of the furniture. On one side, two clean shirts and a cloak were hung over the window. A welter of clothing took up the floor on the other half.

'Two people are staying here,' Lydia said as she looked around.

'How do you figure?' Rees asked.

'One,' she said, pointing to the window, 'is neat. The other,' and she pointed at the pile of clothing on the rough wooden boards, 'is not.'

'I see,' Rees said. The difference was obvious now that Lydia had pointed it out.

'Wasn't Mr Bustamonte from the West Indies?' Not waiting for Rees to respond, she went on. 'Look at the clothing. Most of it is older, well-worn, and more appropriate for a warm climate. But the cloak is new.'

Rees looked in at the clothing on the floor and then at the cloak and saw that she was right. Very gingerly, Lydia began picking up the clothes and examining them. 'Mr Bustamonte's companion was another young man.'

'I wonder if he is the one who followed me from the Painted Pig,' Rees said.

'I wouldn't be surprised,' Lydia replied as she lifted a shirt between two gloved fingers.

'Is he still staying here? Roark's roommate, I mean.'

'Probably.'

While Lydia finished sorting the clothing, Rees searched the rest of the room. Other than the apparel, and a set of wooden rosary beads draped across the chair back, there was nothing personal in here at all.

Roark, it appeared, had been murdered so soon after his arrival that he had not made an impression on his surroundings.

Rees and Lydia finally concluded there was nothing more to find. Locking the door behind them, they descended the stairs. Since the landlady was nowhere to be found, they left the key on the bottom step and went outside.

The landau parked in front had attracted attention and was surrounded by a crowd of mostly young boys. The coachman stood by the horses, shouting at the children to keep them away. And the tiger, a fairly young boy himself, had descended from his perch and was strutting around the vehicle. Guarding it, but also proudly displaying his position. When he saw Rees and Lydia come out, he quickly jumped up on the back. The coachman hurried around and opened the door. As Rees and Lydia crossed to the vehicle, and he offered her a hand to assist her inside, he looked around him. Behind the throng of young boys, and heading straight toward Rees, was the young man in the yellow jacket and buff breeches. Rees stared into the face of his pursuer from the night before.

Dropping Lydia's hand, Rees pushed his way through the throng. But the young man, who saw Rees coming for him, turned and fled in the direction from which he'd come. Rees gave chase, hearing the hoots and hollers of the kids behind him.

Rees managed to keep the bright yellow coat in sight for several blocks, even as the fellow made a number of turns. But he was younger than Rees by far and he knew this neighborhood. Rees pursued him down an alley that opened onto a busy main street and realized, as he searched the mob around him, that the yellow jacket had disappeared. Rees walked up and down for several minutes, peering down one narrow street after another, but he could not find his quarry.

Rees looked around. He had arrived in a square near the waterfront and was standing in front of a very large building. He had no idea where he was. But this area was crowded with people, both men and women, passing in and out of the building in front of him. Rees knew Lydia's family home was located near the State House; surely he could find someone to ask how to make his way back. He did not think he was too far away.

As he prepared to walk inside of the building, he heard someone calling his name. And when he turned, there was Lydia, waving at him from the landau. He hurried across the square to meet her.

'What happened to you?' she asked, at the same time flicking a glance at the coachman. Rees nodded slightly to show he understood.

'I thought I saw someone I knew,' he said vaguely. 'How did you find me?'

'Oh, we thought it was a safe bet you would end up here, at Faneuil Hall,' Lydia said. 'If your friend went inside, you would never have found him. It is a large market . . .'

Rees nodded. He was still breathless and, despite the cold, sweating like a running horse. When he finally caught up with that young man, who was quite clearly Roark's roommate, he would have some choice words to say.

They arrived home just before one. Rees had barely enough time to wash his face and hands before descending to the dining room for the meal.

'Where were you,' Cordelia demanded of Lydia and Rees when they met on the stairs.

'You know we went to the school—' Lydia began.

'Yes, and you deposited Jerusha on the doorstep like an unwanted baby,' Cordelia said. 'Where did you go, that you did not even want her with you?'

Rees hesitated as they reached the ground floor. Mrs Farrell was waiting for them and he did not want to discuss their investigation in her presence.

'We took a drive past the residence of the murder victim,' Lydia said.

'Roark Bustamonte?' Mrs Farrell asked. As Rees had feared, she was curious.

'Yes,' Lydia admitted.

'What did you find?' Cordelia asked eagerly.

'Not a thing,' Lydia said, shading the truth a little.

'Did you find any connection to my father?' Cordy persisted.

'No,' Lydia said. 'That is still a mystery.'

'Or anything that might direct you to Roark's true murderer?'

'Cordelia,' Mrs Farrell murmured reprovingly.

Rees nodded. He also thought the girl was displaying an unhealthy relish for the seamier side of this investigation.

'Nothing, as I told you,' Lydia replied, turning a stern eye upon her sister.

'We will have no more of this subject,' Mrs Farrell said as they entered the dark-paneled dining room. 'It is not a fitting topic for conversation in polite company and certainly not when one is eating.'

Cordelia went silent but the mutinous curve to her lips and her quick glance at Rees and her sister told them she would not let the matter rest.

Quietly they took their places at the table. After saying grace, Mrs Farrell began the luncheon conversation with an approved topic – the weather, by remarking on how cold it had been. Lydia made some innocuous response about the temperatures in Maine. Rees allowed his thoughts to drift. He had to speak to the young man in the yellow coat. That fellow knew something, of that Rees was certain. But it would be difficult to find him again. He might not return to his room, now that he had seen Rees and Lydia there. And if he changed his coat from the bright lemon to something more sober, Rees suspected he would not be able to pick the young man out of a crowd.

Tracking someone down in a town as large as Boston would be much more difficult than in a village in Maine, especially one in which Rees knew almost everyone.

But he did know someone here, he realized. The proprietor of the Painted Pig. That fellow might know something further. Or his wife. Or the little maid who'd been so helpful. Rees realized now that Lydia's probing questions were niggling at him, prompting him to ponder some follow-up queries.

He was drawn out of his reverie by a sudden quiet. Returning to his surroundings, he realized Mrs Farrell and Lydia were staring at one another. Mrs Farrell looked angry and suspicious and Lydia's tight lips and cool expression betrayed her stony defiance. He glanced at Cordelia. 'My mother—' she began.

'I wish to know how you obtained Roark's address,' Mrs Farrell said. 'Surely it is not a secret?'

'Is Mr Bustamonte's address a secret?' Rees asked, raising his eyebrows at Mrs Farrell.

'Well, no, but we asked you not to approach our friends.'

'And we didn't,' Rees said. 'Would any of them have known it anyway?'

'We went to Uncle Julian,' Lydia said. 'As a member of the family, he is already involved.'

'Did you suggest that?' Mrs Farrell asked, turning on her daughter.

'No, she did not. I thought of Uncle Julian,' Lydia said. 'I wanted to see him . . .'

'He is not welcome in this house,' Mrs Farrell said. 'And neither is your brother, James. I had hoped not to address this with you. But their behavior has been so offensive I felt I had to forbid them from calling on us. I am very distressed that you felt it necessary to visit him. I ask that you not do so again.'

Lydia said nothing. But Rees knew, if Mrs Farrell expected her step-daughter to obey, she was mistaken in Lydia's character.

The remainder of the meal passed in an uncomfortable silence.

EIGHTEEN

After the meal ended, Rees and Lydia convened with Jerusha and Cordelia in the nursery. Sharon was asleep, napping in her little bed. While Bridget put away toys and gathered the little girl's dirty dishes, the others squeezed around the small table in the center of the room.

'So, you spoke to Uncle Julian,' Cordy said.

'Yes,' Lydia said. 'We had to. No one else would tell us anything.'

'And he gave you Mr Bustamonte's address?'

'Yes.' Lydia exchanged a glance with Rees.

'I didn't realize he knew Mr Bustamonte,' Cordy said thoughtfully.

'Now I am more interested in the animus between your mother and Julian,' Lydia said.

'Mother and Father's animus,' Cordy corrected. 'Well, you know Julian and my father have not been friendly for years. I'm not sure why. Another family story they keep from me,' she added in a sulky voice.

'What happened with James?' Lydia brought her sister back to the topic.

'I don't know,' Cordelia said. 'Mother and Father kept the arguments out of my hearing. When he came home last time, they were all shouting at one another. I could certainly hear that. But they wouldn't tell me what the quarreling was about. They treat me like a baby.'

'Can you guess?' Rees asked.

'Something to do with his shipping.' Cordelia tossed her head in annoyance. 'Everything is about my father's business.'

'We don't need to concern ourselves with that now,' Lydia said, putting her hand on Cordy's arm. 'Perhaps, if I speak to your mother, she will confide the whole.'

'I thought you would have discovered the murderer by now,' Cordelia said angrily. 'You are not even trying.'

As Rees stared at the girl in exasperation, Lydia said, 'Be patient, Cordy. We only just arrived on Tuesday. These things take time.'

'I think Roark's friend, the one he traveled from the West Indies with, is the guilty man,' Cordy said. 'Did you ask Uncle Julian about him?'

'We didn't know he existed then,' Rees said, wondering why Julian had not mentioned the connection.

'But we will,' Lydia promised. She glanced at Rees. 'When we visit him again.'

As they left the nursery, Rees looked at the empty afternoon before him. The prospect of chatting with Mrs Farrell did not appeal. Turning to his wife, he asked, 'What are you planning to do until dinner?'

She waited until they gained the privacy of Lydia's bedroom until speaking. 'Talk to Cook and the other servants,' Lydia said. 'You?'

'I think I'll walk down to the Painted Pig again,' Rees said. 'I hope to find someone who recognizes the description of either your father or Roark.'

'I'll accompany you,' Lydia said, instantly changing her mind. 'I want to see the tavern and the people there for myself.'

It was half-past three when they left the house and just after four when they reached the tavern. By then, the sun was setting, and the streets were dim with shadows. When Rees stepped inside the taproom, it was half full. Mostly men, but a few women sitting with their husbands. The proprietor stood behind the bar. He nodded in greeting, his china-blue eyes flicking toward Lydia before returning to Rees.

'Back again,' the tavern-keeper said as Rees approached him.

'I'm looking for two men,' he said. 'I'm wondering if you know either one.'

The barkeep eyed Rees. 'I didn't look at the fellow that was shot. I told you that.'

'I was wondering about an older man, probably older than you by ten years or so. Slim, reddish hair. Expensively dressed.'

Rees knew even before he finished speaking that the other man did not recognize the description.

'Doesn't sound familiar. He's probably not a regular. And if he were well-dressed, he'd stick out like a sore thumb. Look around you.'

Rees glanced about. Every man in here was a working man,

exactly as Julian had said. Bricklayers filmed with brick dust, a carpenter still in his leather apron, a minor clerk with grubby cuffs, even a few seamen.

'What about a younger man?' Lydia asked, leaning forward. 'Yellow coat?'

The barkeep pondered. 'I do remember seeing a yellow jacket. Tanned? Spanish-looking?'

'Yes,' Rees said. 'He looks as though he might have some Spanish blood.'

'Maybe,' the tavern-keeper said slowly. 'Wait a minute.' He called over his wife and daughter. They closely resembled one another; both with dark hair and a slight build. Lydia quickly repeated the description.

'Maybe,' the wife said. 'I do not recall a yellow jacket.'

'He has blue eyes,' Rees added.

Now the woman shook her head. 'No, he does not sound like a regular.'

But the daughter, the young maid Rees had first met, blushed scarlet and nodded.

'He's been in a few times,' she admitted, blushing more furiously still. 'He was nice.' Her parents stared at her, aghast. Rees guessed she had found the young man attractive.

'Did you speak with him?' Lydia asked.

'Some.'

'Did he tell you anything about himself?'

Sighing, the young woman shook her head. 'No.' She clearly wished he had.

'Thank you,' Rees said to parents and daughter alike. Turning away from the bar, he accosted a few additional customers. None of them remembered seeing either Marcus Farrell or the young man with blue eyes.

Finally, Rees gave up. He had learned all that he could. Looking around for Lydia, he spotted her in a corner speaking with the tavern maid. 'Are you ready?' he asked.

Lydia threw him an angry glance. 'Please, Will,' she said. But it was too late. The young girl hurried away.

'What?' Rees said guiltily.

'She told me she was awake when Mr Bustamonte was shot,' Lydia said. 'And she saw a young man running away.'

'A young man?' Rees repeated. Why hadn't the young woman told him that? 'Young does not describe your father.'

'No. But it was dark and the man she saw carried only a lantern so we can't be certain. He wore white breeches . . . I know there is more to that child's story.' Biting her lip, Lydia stared after the young girl. 'What else did she see that night?'

NINETEEN

When they returned to the Farrell house, Lydia took the opportunity to request a private meeting with Morris. Rees, understanding that the servant would not speak freely in front of him, continued up the stairs. Instead of entering the tiny room allotted to him, Rees went into Lydia's bedchamber. The fire was blazing, and the room was pleasantly warm. Rees made himself comfortable in one of the chairs and prepared to wait.

His thoughts drifted to the Painted Pig and the interviews he had conducted there. Since the tavern-keeper and his wife had not identified the young man who had followed Rees, and he knew for a fact that the young man had been in the tavern, wasn't it possible that Roark Bustamonte himself had frequented that tavern? Maybe he, without a bright yellow coat and the blue eyes possessed by the other young man, had not made an impression on the proprietors.

That realization inspired another thought. Maybe Marcus Farrell had visited the tavern but in disguise? Wearing rougher clothing and wearing a cap, he would not have stood out in any way. He would not have been memorable. Possible, Rees decided although he could not imagine his father-in-law wearing anything but his fashionable and costly clothing.

Lastly, his attention turned to the young woman. What had she been able to see in the dark of a winter's night? And why hadn't she mentioned it when he spoke to her first? She'd been beyond alarmed and excited by this unusual disturbance and he would have expected her to tell him that first.

The door opened with a slight click and Lydia entered. 'I asked for hot tea, coffee for you, and cake to be brought up,' she said. 'I'm famished.'

'Did you learn anything from the servants?'

'A little. They are all concerned about their positions, of course. And I could not persuade Morris to speak to me at all. He told me that his employer's comings and goings were not his business.' She grimaced. 'He's even more afraid of my father than I am.'

'That is not helpful,' Rees agreed. Lydia nodded.

'Cook was somewhat more forthcoming. She said my father had not been home the night of the murder—'

'He admitted he had not seen anyone—'

'And she'd prepared no food for him. If he came home and ate, someone else served him. They also cleaned up after his meal; there were no dirty dishes. And, as far as she could see, no missing food either.'

Seeing her expression, Rees said consolingly, 'We knew he lied to us. That does not mean he is the murderer. Julian could be correct, you know. Your father could have been visiting his mistress.'

'I don't know if that's any better,' Lydia said miserably.

'Of course it is better,' Rees said. 'Having a mistress is unfortunately common; it does not make him admirable but at least he would not be a murderer. Besides, we don't even know if your father *has* a mistress. Only Julian made that claim.'

'That's true. But why would my uncle lie?'

'I don't know.' Rees sat up. 'To protect him perhaps. Although they are estranged, Julian probably still loves his brother.'

Lydia took her handkerchief from her sleeve and angrily dashed away her tears. 'Even if my father is not a murderer, we know he was out of the house. None of this would have happened if he had been home, where he should have been all along.'

'Don't fret. We'll untangle this knot,' Rees said, rising to his feet to put his arms around her.

'I know we will. I just feel that my entire family, with the exception of my sister, is arrayed against us. Everyone has lied to us. And that includes my Uncle Julian.'

'I think you are right,' Rees agreed with a nod. He kissed the top of her head. 'We need to visit Julian again. This time I will press him for more information, and I will not take no for an answer.'

As a knock sounded on the door, Lydia freed herself from his embrace.

'Come in,' she said. A maid with a large tray came inside. She glanced at Rees and hurried to the table to distribute the refreshments. As soon as she'd gone, both Rees and Lydia sat down. As he dropped in sugar and poured cream into his coffee, Lydia took a small cake.

'Did Cook say anything further?' Rees asked, returning to the more immediate topic.

'She corroborated Isabeau's story about the quarrel with James,' she said. 'Cook said she could hear the shouting all over the house. She isn't sure what they were arguing about, but she thinks it has to do with the business. Finally, James stamped out in a temper. He has returned a few times but only to retrieve his possessions from his bedroom.'

'She doesn't know where he went?' Rees asked.

Lydia shook her head. 'No one knows, apparently. Not even my father. James wouldn't tell him.'

'Hmmm.' Rees took a cake and chewed it meditatively. 'I wonder if James knows something about Roark Bustamonte's death.'

'Perhaps,' Lydia said doubtfully. 'To be sure, if my father were the murderer, I would want to talk to my brother immediately. Him and Julian.' She heaved a sigh. 'Cook also suggested speaking with Isabeau's maid. She might know something.'

'Will you?'

'I don't know. I suppose I'll try. But Morris has known me since I was a child and he wouldn't tell me anything. Why would my stepmother's maid?'

'We are facing a wall of silence,' Rees said, taking another cake. 'It is damned frustrating.'

'Language,' Lydia said. But Rees noticed she did not disagree.

Two hours later, they left the bedchamber, dressed for dinner. The servants had cleaned and brushed Rees's jacket and starched his shirt so he made a finer appearance than he had previously. But he was groggy. The warmth of the fire as well as the hot drink and the cakes had conspired to put him to sleep. Lydia had awakened him in time to dress but he still felt dazed.

They met Jerusha and Cordelia on the stairs and descended together. Mr Hutchinson had just arrived and was at the front door divesting himself of his outer clothing. Cordelia stared at him, her mouth drooping.

'I thought to invite Mr Hutchinson to join us,' Mrs Farrell explained as she crossed the hall. 'Otherwise, with Lydia and Mr Rees dining elsewhere, and poor Marcus ill, it would be a small sad group.'

'He closed the office early,' Mr Hutchinson said. 'He began shivering and complaining of a fever.'

'He has suffered from the ague since his first visit to Jamaica,' Mrs Farrell said. 'Although he is on the bark, it does not always seem to help him.'

Rees nodded in understanding. Quinine was a powerful drug. Some men thought the nausea and other side effects worse than the malaria itself.

'I remember,' Lydia said. 'He endured this illness when I was a child.'

'It comes and goes,' Mrs Farrell said with a nod that set the curls over her ears trembling. 'Comes and goes. As far as I can see, there is no rhyme or reason to it. It just happens. But I am quite certain he will be completely recovered in a few days.'

'I hope so,' Mr Hutchinson said. Turning to Cordelia, he asked politely, 'I thought we might take a drive soon, if the weather is fair.'

'Of course,' she replied unenthusiastically.

'What a kind invitation,' Mrs Farrell said warmly, frowning at her daughter at the same time. 'I'm certain Cordelia will enjoy the diversion. I hope to join you as well.' She and Mr Hutchinson exchanged a smile.

'I expect you remember we will be dining with the Fitzpatricks,' Lydia said.

Isabeau nodded. 'I do.'

Jerusha shot her parents a 'please don't leave me here' glance. Rees knew she wished them to invite her along to their dinner out and smiled at her sympathetically.

'We won't return late,' Lydia assured her daughter. Jerusha's mouth drooped in disappointment.

TWENTY

The Fitzpatricks lived in a pleasant neighborhood not far from the State House. Their house fronted on the street with all of the garden behind. It was immediately apparent that this dwelling was neither so large nor so imposing as the Farrells' home.

They were greeted at the door by a young woman who collected their outer clothing and showed them into a parlor. She did not behave with any of the deference of the servants at the Farrell household, and eyed them with lively curiosity.

Three blond children waited with their parents to greet them, flanked by a short older woman. She was quite stout and the face under the mob cap was rosy. 'It isn't – surely this isn't Nurse Gertrude,' Lydia said in surprise.

'Indeed it is, lovey, and how wonderful it is to see you,' the woman said, stepping forward to catch Lydia in an embrace.

Rees glanced at Sally in confusion. 'Gertrude was my old nurse,' she said, laughing. 'When I married, she came over to my household to help out.'

'I said when I knew you was coming that I had to pay my respects,' Gertrude said. 'And this is your husband?' She looked Rees up and down, her inspection embarrassingly frank. 'Well, he is a tall one, isn't he? Red hair, and a temper to go with it, I'll be bound.'

Rees could feel himself blushing.

'Now, come and meet the little ones.'

Lydia greeted the children and oohed over their beauty. Rees thought his wife would not have been able to compliment the parents on the children's manners. Although the six-year-old curtsied, the four-year-old began bawling and the baby, a boy despite the long skirts, tried to crawl away. Gertrude snatched him up before he traveled too far.

'You've met the guests, now,' Gertrude said to the children. 'Time to go to the nursery.'

As she bundled them from the room, Sally turned to her guests and said apologetically, 'I'm sorry. We rarely have guests and they were so excited . . .'

'It is quite all right,' Lydia said warmly. 'I have children of my own; I am well used to them.'

'Come and sit down. We still have a little time before dinner is served.'

'I'm Quentin,' said the tall man standing by Sally's side. 'Quentin Fitzpatrick.'

'Oh dear,' Sally said remorsefully. 'Where are my manners? I completely forgot to introduce you.'

'Will Rees,' he said, extending his hand.

Quentin was almost as tall as Rees but far thinner. He was younger too; Rees thought the other man could not be much above thirty. Quentin's hand was calloused and scarred from his years of working with molten silver.

'Sally tells me you are a weaver,' he said, gesturing Rees to a seat by the fire. Rees admitted that was so and for a few minutes they discussed their crafts.

Then Sally interrupted. 'You remember, Quent, I told you that Mr Farrell had been accused of murder?'

'I remember. But nothing came of it.'

'No. But Lydia and her husband are looking into it. And Lydia heard from her uncle – here, you tell the story.' Sally gestured at Lydia.

'My uncle suggested that my father was visiting his mistress the night of the murder,' Lydia said.

Quentin must have known of Lydia's propensity for speaking forthrightly from the past for he did not even blink. 'I doubt your father has a mistress,' he said, just as bluntly. 'None of the gossip has ever mentioned him in connection with another woman. I think your uncle might be misinformed.'

'So, what has gossip ascribed to Mr Farrell?' Rees asked, feeling emboldened to speak as openly as everyone else.

'Besides his worship of lucre,' Lydia put in with a touch of bitterness.

Quentin shuffled his feet. 'Well now—'

'Oh, go on and tell them,' Sally said. 'Whatever he is faulted for, it can't be any worse than supporting a mistress.'

Quentin half-nodded but still did not speak for several seconds.

Rees recognized Mr Fitzpatrick as the type of man who was accustomed to keeping his own counsel. Quentin did not feel comfortable sharing rumor and hearsay.

'My father cannot account for his whereabouts the night of the murder,' Lydia said, breaking the silence. 'I confess, I would much prefer he was in the arms of a mistress than cold-bloodedly shooting an unarmed young man.'

'You're sure he wasn't home?'

'He said he was,' Lydia said.

'He gave us some story that was clearly a tissue of lies from beginning to end,' Rees added.

'Well, when you describe it like that. Your father,' Quentin said, looking at Lydia, 'is widely believed to be a gambler.'

'A gambler,' Lydia repeated in surprise. 'That does not sound so terrible.'

'It is if you are in danger of losing everything,' Quentin replied drily. 'I heard a few months ago that the totality of one of his cargos was already owed to the men who held his chits.'

'My goodness,' Lydia said involuntarily.

'Where does he gamble?' Rees asked. He did not believe there were too many places; gambling was much frowned upon as a serious vice.

'I don't know,' Quentin admitted.

'You don't gamble yourself?'

'I work too hard to throw my money away on the turn of a card or the roll of the dice,' Quentin said. 'But . . .' His voice trailed away and he stared at the ceiling for a few seconds. 'I can probably ask around. Someone is bound to know.'

'Thank you,' Rees said gratefully. He would barely know where to begin in this unfamiliar place. It was humbling to realize how dependent he was on his friends. Even Rouge, for all that the constable annoyed him. 'I'll appreciate the assistance.'

'Once I obtain the name, I'll pass it along,' Quentin said.

'Fair enough,' Rees said.

'I wonder if you could look at these names,' Lydia said, extracting the grubby note from her uncle from her reticule.

Sally took the paper and glanced at the inscriptions before passing the paper to her husband. 'Why? Are they important?'

'According to my uncle,' Lydia said, darting a quick glance at

Rees, 'these are men who were ruined by my father and who might still bear him some animus.'

'There are many more names than this,' Quentin said with a grin. 'But why?' He looked up and stared at Rees. 'Do you think one of them is trying to ruin Mr Farrell?'

'Something like that,' Rees agreed.

'Well, Mr Wendell is dead,' Sally said. 'The smallpox, I believe.' Quentin nodded in agreement.

'I think you might find the other two in their offices near the wharves,' he said. 'One of them – Mr Bartlett – recovered and is again wealthy so he probably does not loathe Mr Farrell as much as he once did.' As he handed the note to Lydia, she and her husband exchanged startled glances. But there was no time for further questions; a young girl appeared at the door and announced that dinner was served. Rees and Lydia followed their hosts into a small room with west-facing windows. Rees thought that in the summer, this room must be bright all afternoon. Although the table was set for four, it was long enough to seat eight. Rees spotted some dried cereal, glued to one of the chairs. This was clearly the room in which the family ate, not a formal dining room. When the two girls brought in the food, they set all the dishes on the table instead of serving courses, as was done in the Farrell household. Rees instantly felt at home.

'We usually eat *en famille*,' Sally said, her cheeks pink.

'So do we,' Lydia said with a warm smile.

'And I am glad of it,' Rees said, eyeing the beef hungrily.

He ate his dinner without worrying about his table manners once.

TWENTY-ONE

Neither Mr nor Mrs Farrell came downstairs for breakfast Friday morning. Although Rees and Lydia did not usually meet her father, since he left very early, they usually saw evidence of his meal. Today, when they arrived in the breakfast room, they found the tea untouched and the tablecloth unmarked. Lydia asked the maid, who replied that Mr Farrell was still feeling poorly and was taking his meal in his room. Lydia directed a quick glance at her husband, but they had no opportunity to comment. Jerusha and Cordelia arrived then, bubbling over with excitement. The dressmaker was scheduled to arrive at nine.

Rees planned to leave well before then. He did not want to be in the house when the dressmaker arrived. He could well imagine the sounds of female excitement and Cordy's non-stop chatter. Seeing the gowns after their completion would be more than enough for him.

He ate quickly, to Lydia's disapproval. 'No need to hurry, Will. The merchants transact business all day.' She added with a sigh, 'How I wish I was going with you. But Isabeau will never forgive me if I do not stay home this morning and meet the dressmaker.'

Nodding, Rees drank the last of his coffee and rose to his feet. 'Don't worry. I'll tell you everything. If there is, in fact, anything to discover.'

He grabbed his greatcoat and left, discovering when he stepped through the door that it was snowing. Small flakes sifted slowly down from the sky and the street outside was already dusted with a thin accumulation. He set off, walking very rapidly, east toward the wharves. The damp cold air bit through his greatcoat but he had not wanted to take any of the carriages. The coachman and the tiger would have learned of his destination, at the very least, and he supposed they shared everything they knew with Marcus Farrell. It was proving difficult to keep the investigation as private as Rees wished.

Despite the early hour, the wharves were already bustling. Sailors from all around the world crowded the docks and were easily distinguishable from the fashionably dressed merchants. Rees stopped one gentleman in a dove-gray coat and fine beaver top hat to ask about the first name on the list. He pointed to a gentleman a distance away down the docks and hurried on, too busy to acknowledge Rees any further.

Rees approached the gentleman, who was engaged in a shouting match with another man. Rees expected it to become physical, but the other man, with a gesture of disgust, stalked away.

'Mr Bartlett?' Rees asked. The other fellow, a solidly built man, turned to eye Rees suspiciously.

'Yes. Who are you?' Portly with success, he was almost completely bald under his fine hat.

'You may have heard about the death of a young man outside the Painted Pig?'

'Ah yes. Relative, are you? You should be speaking to Marcus Farrell.'

'I understand the accusation against him never went anywhere,' Rees said.

'Some influential connection quashed the investigation. Farrell bribed someone, I am certain of it.'

'You are?' Rees said. The belief Marcus bribed his way out of a murder charge seemed to be widespread.

'Absolutely convinced. He murdered that boy as sure as I'm standing here.'

'But why—'

'Why? Who knows why? If that young man wanted something and Farrell didn't want to give it, well . . .' He offered Rees a meaningful wink. 'Farrell is the proudest and greediest man I have ever met. You must know he stole my first company from me. I vow, if I was a murdering kind of man, it would be Farrell who is dead.'

'Is that why you've forbidden your son to court Cordelia Farrell?' Rees asked, guessing Mr Bartlett and Edward were father and son.

'Forbidden? Who told you that?' Bartlett pushed his hat back from his forehead. 'He is a grown man, with his own income, and makes his own decisions. I have nothing to say about them.'

'You didn't threaten to stop his allowance?'

'I couldn't if I wanted. He reached his majority a few years ago.' He tipped his hat and hastened away, shouting after someone. Rees was left standing stock-still on the dock.

The Farrells had lied to Cordelia. But why? To further Mr Hutchinson's suit? After a few seconds of fruitless speculation, Rees shook himself and went in search of the second gentleman. This man was not in quite as much of a hurry but he too had nothing good to say about Marcus Farrell. And another man, overhearing the conversation, interjected a final comment.

'We all trade with him. Well, we have to. But that does not mean we aren't careful. He would sell his own grandmother to purchase a ship. And believe you me, just because slavery has been outlawed in Massachusetts doesn't mean he isn't still doing it. If he told me the sky was blue, I would look up and check.' Rees blinked. What could one say to this? The second gentleman added a parting shot. 'I am only surprised that it is not Farrell who was murdered. There are many of us who have thought of it, of that I am certain.'

Stunned by the outright loathing for Marcus Farrell, Rees began walking home. Surely everyone in Boston did not detest him so. But then, Rees reflected, Lydia, Farrell's own daughter, distrusted her father. That was a sobering thought.

A whiff of molasses-scented air reminded Rees of the distillery and his intention to question Julian Farrell. It was still so early he knew the dressmaker would have just arrived. He hesitated a moment, knowing that Lydia wished to visit her uncle again. But there would be other opportunities and Rees was already nearby. He turned his steps in that direction, arriving at the distillery in just under twenty minutes. He smelled it long before he saw it. When he went inside, he realized he'd forgotten how thick and pungent the aroma of fermenting molasses was. It was so strong he felt dizzy. How could these men work with this smell? But then he thought of the men who worked in the tanneries; at least molasses was sweet.

He waved at the foreman, who waved in response, and bounded up the steps to Julian's office. He knocked on the door but there was no answer. He knocked again. When no one answered the second time, he tried the door handle. It turned smoothly and the door opened. When he peered inside, the office seemed empty. Rees shut the door and went back down the stairs.

'Hey, you,' he called to the foreman. 'Did Mr Farrell leave?'

'No. He's here. Another man came to see him just a bit ago.'

'Another man,' Rees repeated. 'What did he look like?'

The foreman shrugged. 'I couldn't really see at that distance.'

'Was he short or tall?' Rees asked impatiently. 'A tradesman or a gentleman? What color was his hair?'

'Couldn't see his hair; he wore a hat pulled low over his forehead.' The foreman paused, ruminating. 'He was short. Ragged cloak . . .' His words trailed to a stop.

Rees sighed. That description was so vague as to be almost useless. 'Shall we go upstairs to the office now.'

The foreman climbed the steps ahead of Rees and tapped on the door. Since there was no answer, he too tried the handle and pushed the door open. 'That's funny,' he said as he looked inside. 'I swear, he was here less 'n an hour ago.'

He took a few steps inside, Rees almost treading on his heels. They both looked around. To Rees, it appeared even more untidy than usual. Papers were strewn from one end to the other and the desk was buried under a veritable snowstorm of white slips.

'My God,' said the foreman, his voice rising to a shriek.

'What?' Rees took two steps forward to join the man. He followed the foreman's trembling finger. Julian had not left. He was lying crumpled on the floor behind the desk where he'd fallen. A large pool of blood had soaked the carpet beneath him.

'Dear God, what happened?' the foreman moaned.

'Call a doctor,' Rees shouted at the foreman. 'Call the constable.'

While the foreman hurried from the room, Rees knelt next to the dying man and put his arms around Julian's shoulders. He opened his eyes. 'Ja—' he said.

'What's that?' Rees asked. 'Tell me again.'

Julian slumped backwards, dead.

Rees lowered the body to the carpet. Julian had been shot and Rees wondered if the weapon used had been the same muff pistol that had murdered Roark. But Julian had been more prepared and had tried to turn away. The ball had struck him between shoulder and neck so, although he'd dropped to the floor, he'd survived for a little while.

As Rees moved away from Julian's body, the office was suddenly full of people. The workers from downstairs, men who'd drifted in from the docks to gawk, and the foreman. As they crowded around the body, Rees squeezed around the back of the crowd and left the office. He had no doubt that the man who had shot Roark had also murdered Julian Farrell. Why? What did he know? And what did 'Ja' mean?

TWENTY-TWO

Rees stepped outside into the snow. It was falling harder now, a moving curtain of white. He walked a few steps and had to stop. He was shaking so hard he thought his legs would give way beneath him. No matter how many violent deaths he saw, he never found it any easier. If he had seen anywhere to sit down, he would have done so, but there was nowhere around here, and the snow was quickly blanketing everything. He had to continue on.

Turning, he trudged slowly west. Why, oh why hadn't he realized Julian was in danger? Up to now, Roark's murder had seemed to be an isolated crime. It was now apparent that one murder had led to two. What danger had Roark posed to Marcus Farrell – or to the man who had killed him? And what had Julian known? Whatever it was, he could not share it with Rees now.

Half-blinded by the falling snow, Rees plodded forward on his trembling legs. Without realizing it, he made his way to the Painted Pig. Although he had no further questions to ask the proprietor, Rees felt he could walk no farther right now. He went inside.

The proprietor turned and recognized Rees. Seeing something in Rees's face, he said, 'Got bad news, did you? Can I get you something?'

'Coffee?'

'I can make you some. Are you sure you don't want something stronger?'

'Coffee is fine,' Rees said, making his way to the fire. A small blaze, and only recently stirred up, it wasn't putting out much warmth. Rees did not remove his coat but sat huddled as close to the flames as he could. A few minutes later, the tavern-keeper's wife brought a battered coffee pot to the fire and positioned it near the flames.

'I saw you here yesterday. You came with your wife. Red hair, yes?' Rees nodded. 'You're the one been asking questions about the murder.'

'Yes,' Rees said, stirring himself. His visit to this tavern yesterday already felt as though it had happened years ago.

'Why?'

'My wife's father was accused of the murder. So, Lydia's sister asked us to look into it.'

The woman hesitated, clearly debating with herself. In other circumstances, Rees would have pressed her, but he was still too shattered by Julian's death. He waited in silence while she debated with herself. Finally, she spoke. 'The man who was murdered, I believe he came here a few times. Spanish appearing, yes?'

'Yes. You did?' Rees unfolded himself. This was corroboration for her daughter's account. 'Often? Since when?'

'The last few months.'

'Did he ever talk about himself? Explain what he was doing in Boston?'

'A little. He sailed to Boston from the West Indies.' When Rees nodded, she added, 'You knew that?'

'Yes. It is practically the only thing I do know about him. Did he ever mention what he was doing here?'

'He said he'd come to Boston to right a wrong, whatever that means.'

'He never explained what the wrong was?'

'No. I never asked.' She looked at Rees sympathetically when he sighed in frustration. 'It never seemed important.'

'Thank you,' he said.

The woman looked at the coffeepot, now merrily perking away. 'That should be about done now,' she murmured, wrapping her apron around her hand to pull it away from the fire. 'I'll fetch you a cup.'

She disappeared for a bit, returning with a heavy stoneware mug, chunks of sugar in a bowl and a pitcher of milk. Once they were placed on the table in front of Rees, she poured the coffee slowly, so as not to include the grounds, into the mug. He added milk and sugar and took a sip. It was so strong he could feel the skin on his head prickling. It was exactly what he needed right now.

'I thought of something else,' she said once Rees had taken several mouthfuls. 'You asked about a man with blue eyes. That puzzled me since this man had brown. But he did not travel alone. He once said something about a friend. I do not remember the friend ever visiting the tavern. He might have, but I don't remember it.'

Rees recalled the disordered garret and nodded. 'Yes, Roark Bustamonte sailed here with another man. I am looking for him now.'

'Roark Bustamonte? Who is that?' The woman shook her head. 'The fellow I am talking about called himself Benicio.'

Rees almost dropped the mug. 'Benicio? Are you sure that was his name?' He stared at her.

She nodded. 'Absolutely certain.'

'What did he look like?'

'Spanish. Black hair, brown eyes. Not blue.'

Not blue? The young man he had been searching for appeared at least partly Spanish but his eyes were a striking pale blue. Could Roark and this Benicio be brothers? And did this mean Roark Bustamonte was still alive?

As Rees put another chunk of sugar into his coffee, the tavern-keeper's wife stirred up the fire and added another log. 'One more question,' he said to her back. Recalling the yellow jacket his pursuer had worn, he asked, 'What was Benicio wearing?' Perhaps this woman had gotten it wrong and it was Benicio wearing the yellow jacket. Perhaps it was Benicio who was alive. She turned and looked at him.

'Wearing?'

'What color was his jacket?' Rees asked. Of fine linen, that bright yellow coat had been well cut and expensive.

'Brown. Shabby looking. He was not warmly dressed, not warmly enough for this climate anyway. But not everyone who frequents this tavern can afford a coat like the one you wear.'

Rees thought of the warm cloak hanging by the window. One of those young men could afford an expensive jacket and warm clothing. They weren't brothers then. 'Might Benicio have been a servant?'

She pondered the question for a few seconds and nodded. 'Yes, he might have been. Probably was, I would say.'

So if the man who had pursued Rees was not Benicio, perhaps it was Roark Bustamonte. And that would mean he was still alive.

By the time Rees left the Painted Pig, he had finished the pot of coffee and was thinking again. Although the shock of Julian's death had not completely worn off, Rees's mind was clearer.

The falling snow had thinned to a few sparse flakes. Rees thought he remembered how to reach the building in which Roark and Benicio had taken a room. He set off and although he got turned around a few times he soon found it. The landlady said no one had returned and promised she had touched nothing. The young men were paid up until the end of the month. After that . . . But when Rees borrowed the key and climbed the stairs once again, he found some of the clothing and the warm cloak gone. Rees swore under his breath. He had no doubt the young man who was still alive had found other lodging and would not return here again.

With the end of January in a few days, the landlady would clean out the room and rent it to some other poor soul.

Rees would lose the slender lead to the young man that he had. He had hoped to have a bit of good news to temper the devastating discovery of Julian's murder. In a foul mood, Rees stamped back to the street and started home.

TWENTY-THREE

I t was just about midday when Rees returned to the Farrell household. He could hear female voices and Cordelia's shrill giggles emanating from Lydia's bedchamber. He climbed the stairs and entered, stepping into chaos. Lengths of fabric lay on the chairs, the writing table, and over the bed. A large basket with scissors and a measuring tape had been pushed to one side. But only Lydia and the two girls were inside.

'Where is the dressmaker?' Rees asked.

'The dressmaker and her apprentice went downstairs to the kitchen to eat their meal,' Lydia said. Lowering her voice, she asked, 'What happened to you? I expected you home hours ago.'

'I'll tell you later,' Rees replied.

'I do not understand why you allowed them to leave now,' Cordelia complained. 'They aren't finished.' Lydia turned and, clasping her hands together, stared at her sister until she squirmed. 'We want the gowns completed as soon as possible,' Cordelia whined. As Lydia continued to stare at her, she added weakly, 'It's their job.'

'They are still people,' Rees said sharply.

'The apprentice is barely old enough to put up her hair,' Lydia put in reproachfully. 'Really, Cordy, I am surprised at you. They need to eat and to rest just as much as we do. Besides, we will be lunching soon ourselves.'

Sulking, Cordy flounced to the chair and pushed the fabrics to the floor. She collapsed into the seat and scowled at her sister.

'Where have you been?' Lydia repeated to her husband, lowering her voice even further. 'You look disturbed.'

'It is not good news,' Rees whispered.

She looked at him in alarm but did not press him. The only thing she said as she looked at his shirt cuffs was, 'I would change my shirt if I were you. Your cuffs are dirty.'

Rees looked down. When he had held Julian's body, some of the blood had seeped under the cuffs of his greatcoat and smudged his shirt. Just a little. He shuddered. He knew what those brownish marks were. Julian's blood. He hurried into his small room to change.

Mrs Farrell did not join them in the dining room. When asked why she was absent, the maid replied that Mrs Farrell was attending to her husband. He was still feeling poorly, although trying to work with Mr Hutchinson. Lydia rolled her eyes at that. 'I doubt she is doing anything of the kind,' she said to Rees. 'I would guess she arose late and is now taking the opportunity for private fittings.'

Cordelia, who had recovered from her ill temper, chattered the entirety of the meal. For once, Rees was glad of her talkativeness. It spared him from speaking. He did not want to announce his sad news before these young women, at least not until Mr and Mrs Farrell knew.

Cordelia and Jerusha finished eating in record time and asked to be excused. Lydia nodded, and the girls fled. 'I don't know why they are rushing,' she said with a shake of her head. 'The dressmaker may not even be ready.' She glanced around the empty room. 'Tell me now. What happened?'

'Julian is . . . Something happened to Julian,' Rees said in a low voice.

'What?' Lydia's loud shocked question echoed through the room. She turned to stare at her husband. 'You can't be serious.'

'After I spoke with those two businessmen – I'll describe their responses after – I went to the distillery.'

'Oh, Will,' Lydia said in disappointment. 'I would have liked to join you.'

'No, you would not. I went directly up the stairs to his office. In the company of the foreman.' Rees stopped and took a breath. 'At first, we saw nothing. But then the foreman saw Julian, lying behind the desk. He was—' Rees stopped. He did not want to tell Lydia about seeing Julian's blood seeping out on the floor.

Lydia put her hand over her mouth and her eyes welled with tears. 'Is he severely injured?'

Rees reached across the table and took her hand.

'He's dead. Shot, probably by the same gun used on Roark.'

'So, Julian must have known something,' Lydia murmured, fat tears rolling down her cheeks. 'Oh, why didn't he tell us what he knew?' She wiped her eyes with her handkerchief. 'I know I haven't seen him for some time but . . .'

Rees nodded, debating whether he should mention Julian's attempt to speak. Opting not to share even more disturbing information, he cast around for a different subject. 'There's something more. Roark Bustamonte may not have been the victim.'

'What?' Lydia stared at him. 'What do you mean?'

'I stopped at the Painted Pig on my way home. The tavern-keeper's wife said she thinks the young man who was shot might be named Benicio. Not Roark. And Benicio is probably Roark's servant.'

'Not Roark.' Lydia inhaled. 'But that means—'

'Are you coming upstairs?' Cordelia peered around the door. 'We are all waiting.'

'I will be up directly,' Lydia said. Cordelia disappeared. Lydia wiped her eyes and took several deep calming breaths. 'We'll talk again, later,' she said to Rees. 'Say nothing to the girls. Not yet. I want to inform my father first.'

The dressmaker and her apprentice had returned and Jerusha was standing with her arms outstretched as she waited to be measured. Isabeau and her lady's maid, a beautiful young woman with thick dark hair and warm brown eyes, had joined them. Isabeau's cheeks were scarlet and her eyes glittered with excitement. Playing the Grande Dame to the hilt, she was giving instructions to her maid in French. It was not quite the French Rees knew and contained besides a number of unfamiliar words but he understood enough to know the young woman was being sent on an errand. The maid hurried from the room.

'Isabeau,' Lydia interrupted. 'May I have a word?'

'Not now, Lydia,' Isabeau said, turning to the seamstress.

The dressmaker was older, older than Rees anyway, with thin angular features and graying hair, and he instantly felt sorry for her. It could not be easy to work for Mrs Farrell.

'This is important,' Lydia persisted.

'Not now.' Isabeau glanced at Rees. 'You should not be here.'

Rees glanced at Lydia. She nodded at him; she could handle this. As Rees started for the door, he looked at the young apprentice sitting on the floor. He thought she was probably about twelve, with light brown hair and brown eyes. She was too thin and the circles under her eyes spoke of long days and insufficient sleep. Although Rees could do nothing about the child's sleep, he resolved to ask Cook to send up a pot of hot tea and sandwiches and cakes. He suspected that whatever had been offered to her for her meal had been scanty. At least he could make sure the child was fed.

He went downstairs to speak to Cook.

When he returned upstairs before going to his small room, he paused outside of Lydia's chamber. Outside of Cordelia's excited squeals, he heard nothing. Lydia had not succeeded in capturing Isabeau's attention.

Finally, he went into the small room that had been allotted to him. When he had changed his shirt before luncheon, he'd put the sleeves of the previously worn garment into the ewer to soak. He did not want to involve any of the servants. Although he'd done nothing wrong, he did not want to inspire any awkward questions, either from Mr and Mrs Farrell or from the local constabulary.

The water in the ewer was faintly tinted. Rees picked up the sodden cuffs and examined them. The brownish stains were paler, so some of the blood had rinsed out, but the smudges were still visible. Rees scrubbed the two cuffs together, his mind wandering.

What had Julian known? Rees recalled their conversations. Perhaps he'd told the truth about Marcus Farrell and a mistress. With no information about her identity, finding her would be difficult. Rees considered questioning Marcus Farrell but would he even tell the truth?

What connection did Roark – or Benicio, as Rees now suspected was the victim's identity – have with Julian? He had claimed he had met Roark only once, but he'd surrendered Roark's address immediately when asked. So Roark and Julian knew one another well enough to share addresses. It was likely, Rees decided, that Julian knew Roark far better than he claimed. What had Julian said? Roark had approached Julian first, before applying to Marcus Farrell.

Rees nodded. Yes. But that still did not reveal the why behind either murder. At this point, with none of the three talking, Rees could not even guess at the motives behind the murders.

And finally, what had Julian tried to say? Could it have been James, the name of Lydia's brother? Rees hoped that the meeting with James tomorrow would reveal the answer.

TWENTY-FOUR

When Rees left his room, he paused in front of Lydia's door. But, outside of the murmur of voices, he heard nothing. He guessed Lydia had still failed to gain Mrs Farrell's attention. While he stood there irresolute, Mr Hutchinson came up the stairs and turned right, toward the door at the end of the hall. Rees hesitated for a few seconds and then, deciding he would have to take matters into his own hands, hurried after the other man.

Mr Hutchinson tapped on the door to Mr Farrell's room and disappeared inside. Rees paused in front of the closed door. He did not believe Mr Farrell would want to hear this sad news from him, but wouldn't that be far better than hearing it from a workman who suddenly remembered Julian had a brother?

Rees knocked on the door. After a few seconds, Mr Hutchinson opened it. 'What do you want?'

'I need to speak with Mr Farrell.'

'If you are planning to badger me with more questions,' Mr Farrell shouted from inside the room, 'I do not want to speak with you. Anyway, we are too busy.'

'It is not that,' Rees said, moving forward. Mr Hutchinson put out his arm to prevent him from stepping inside.

'What is it, then?' Mr Hutchinson asked, raising his voice so that it echoed down the hall. Rees heard Lydia's door opening behind him and a few seconds later she came up behind him.

'There is something we must tell my father,' she said, glaring at Hutchinson. 'Something important.'

'Let them in, then,' Mr Farrell said wearily. Mr Hutchinson stepped away from the door.

Marcus Farrell was ensconced in a chair in front of a blazing fire. Despite the warmth, and it was so hot perspiration popped out on Rees's forehead, the ailing gentleman had a rug wrapped around his shoulders. He was pale and his eyes were smudged with shadows but he clearly felt well enough to work. Papers were scattered all around him.

'What is it?' he asked impatiently. Rees felt Lydia tense beside him.

'You will prefer to hear this news from us first,' she said, trying to mollify him. Her father widened his eyes in disbelief.

'This had better be important.'

'I am very sorry to inform you that Julian is dead,' Rees said loudly, annoyed on Lydia's behalf. 'He was murdered early this morning.' He watched Marcus Farrell's face freeze and would have sworn he was genuinely shocked.

'No, that can't be. Are you sure? How did you find out?' Marcus struggled to his feet. 'I spoke to him just a week ago.' He turned and glared at Lydia and Rees. 'Are you sure?'

'I found the body,' Rees said. 'In fact, I expect someone from the distillery will soon bring the news to you. I . . .' He glanced at Lydia. '*We* thought you would want to hear it from us first.'

'I've got to find out what happened.' Farrell shrugged off the heavy rug and hurried to the door.

'But sir,' Mr Hutchinson said to Mr Farrell's back, 'you are ill.'

'I've got to go. Now.'

He rushed past Mr Hutchinson and stumbled down the stairs.

Mr Hutchinson ran after him, calling his name. 'Mr Farrell. Mr Farrell. I will accompany you.'

'What did you tell him?' Mrs Farrell asked, stepping through Lydia's bedroom door.

'We told him Julian is dead,' Rees said. 'Murdered.'

Mrs Farrell gasped. 'Are you sure?'

'We thought he would want to know,' Lydia said, adding snidely, 'since Julian is his brother.'

'Why did you blurt it out in such a manner?' Mrs Farrell demanded angrily. 'He is ill. You should have told me first and I would have tried to soften the blow. I certainly would have chosen a more appropriate time.'

'I tried,' Lydia said, eyeing her stepmother with displeasure. 'I did not want to announce it in front of the girls, and you would not permit me to speak to you privately.'

'How long has Mr Hutchinson been here?' Rees asked, wondering if Mr Farrell had visited his brother early this morning. The foreman had mentioned a gentleman visitor before Rees.

'He arrived early,' Mrs Farrell said peevishly. 'He was here when I arose.' Glaring at Rees, she added, 'You cannot suspect my husband of his brother's death. Marcus has been far too ill to leave the house.'

She brushed past Lydia and hurried down the hall. When she opened the door, Rees heard her say to the dressmaker, 'We must have mourning gowns immediately.'

'Not for myself or for Jerusha,' Lydia said, following her step-mother into the bedchamber. Rees, just a few steps behind his wife, glanced through the open door in time to see Lydia shake her head at Mrs Farrell. 'Both of us have dark blue. That will do, I think.'

'But why?' Cordelia wailed. She held up an armful of sheer pink. 'I hate black. I want this.'

Mrs Farrell turned to the dressmaker and her apprentice. 'Can you begin constructing new gowns in black?'

'There will be an extra charge,' the dressmaker said. She spoke softly but Rees spotted a malicious gleam in her eyes.

'Fine,' Mrs Farrell said. 'Whatever you have in your shop, to start. Cordy and I will go out tomorrow and purchase additional fabric.'

The dressmaker turned and nodded at her apprentice, who was already bundling up their supplies. From the speed with which they gathered their things and departed, Rees guessed this was not the first time they had been asked to leave in a hurry.

The bolts of bright fabric were forgotten and left strewn about the room.

'But why?' Cordelia repeated, more quietly this time as she guessed something serious had happened.

'I am very sorry,' Mrs Farrell said, turning a gentle look upon her daughter. 'But Uncle Julian has died.'

'What? No.'

'Your father has gone to the distillery. I daresay we will have more news when he returns.' She held out her arms and drew Cordelia to her bosom.

Jerusha had never met Julian Farrell but, seeing Cordelia's tears, her own eyes moistened.

Mrs Farrell drew her daughter from the room.

As they left, Lydia stepped inside and began picking up the cloth. 'Are you sad, Mother?' Jerusha asked.

'Yes, a little,' Lydia said. 'When I was small, Julian was more of a father to me than my own. But I have not seen him for a very long time . . .' She paused. Rees noticed that she did not tell her daughter Julian had been murdered.

Jerusha sighed and wiped her eyes. As she moved toward the door, Rees said, 'What will you do now?'

'Read. I am halfway through *Strictures on the Modern System of Female Education* by Hannah More.'

'That sounds dry,' Rees said.

'Maddening, more like. I disagree with almost everything she says.' With a smile, Jerusha left, crossing the hall to enter the room she shared with Cordelia.

Lydia shut the door. As Rees sat in one of the chairs before the fire, Lydia stacked the fabric in a corner of the room. Then she joined Rees.

'How nice it is to enjoy some privacy in this house,' Lydia said. 'We've had so little.'

'I know,' Rees said. He felt he could say more but, since this was Lydia's family, he chose not to. She smiled knowingly and patted his hand.

'Thank you for your restraint,' she said. Rees returned her smile. As usual, his wife knew how he felt. When Lydia spoke again, it was on an entirely different subject.

'I suppose you believe my father murdered his brother,' she said. Rees heard a slight tremble in her voice.

'It is possible,' he replied cautiously, adding, 'the same person almost certainly shot both the victims.'

Lydia nodded. 'Yes, that makes sense. But why? He has no reason.'

'I don't know that yet,' Rees admitted. 'But I am beginning to think this has something to do with the West Indies. With Jamaica probably.'

'But what?' she asked, mystified.

'Something else I don't know,' Rees said. 'But Mr Bustamonte, Mr Hutchinson and your father all have a connection with Jamaica. Even your stepmother—'

'Isabeau is not from Jamaica,' Lydia interrupted. 'She was born in Saint-Domingue; the Pearl of the Antilles, as she never fails to remind me.'

'But she met your father in Jamaica,' Rees pointed out.

'Yes. She was sent to Jamaica as a girl for her safety. Saint-Domingue has been wracked with slave revolts for years.'

'That explains the odd French and unfamiliar words,' Rees said. 'Do you think she could be the guilty one?' He paused.

Lydia stared at him for a few seconds and then burst into uncontrollable giggles.

'I am sorry,' she managed to say before another gust swept over her. 'Isabeau? Sneaking around with a pistol?'

Rees tried to imagine the delicate and fashionable Mrs Farrell as an assassin and also chuckled. 'I know it seems improbable,' he said at last. 'But isn't it possible? We have identified other unlikely murderers.'

Lydia wiped her eyes. 'I must be overwrought. It has been an emotional few days. Yes, by all means, let us consider her. I suppose she could have stolen a firearm from my father.'

'Which she would not know how to fire,' Rees said.

'And why? My father gives her everything she could possibly desire.' She sounded almost bitter.

Rees pondered her question in silence. Mrs Farrell seemed devoted to her husband.

'Let's leave Isabeau for the moment,' Lydia said at last. Rees nodded. 'We've got to find Mr Bustamonte. Or Benicio – whatever his name is,' she continued. 'We should return to his lodgings . . .' Her voice trailed away as Rees began shaking his head.

'He's gone from there. The cloak was taken, and the landlady told me no one had returned.'

'Huh!' Lydia said inelegantly. 'She probably never leaves her room if she can help it.'

'Tomorrow . . .' Rees hesitated. 'Do you still want to meet your brother? Especially now after Julian's death?'

'Of course. Speaking with him is more important than ever. Now it is not just Roark who has been murdered but my uncle as well. We have to find the murderer, Will.'

Rees nodded in agreement but added, 'That means we will have to talk to your father again; something none of us will enjoy. Even if he is not the murderer—'

'I know,' Lydia agreed with a nod. 'He knows something.'

TWENTY-FIVE

Rees and Lydia left very early the following morning for their meeting with James at the Green Dragon. Yesterday's snow had ended during the night, leaving a thin coating on all surfaces. The sky was clear and sunny, but the air was very cold.

Rees and Lydia walked briskly to the tavern. It was crowded and busy. They paused by the door and she looked around. She did not immediately see her brother until a man at the back lifted an arm in greeting. Shooing away an approaching servant, Rees took Lydia's arm and guided her around the knots of people.

The figure in the shabby brown coat resolved into a youngish man. The blue eyes were the same as Lydia's but otherwise he bore only a passing resemblance to her. Unshaven and ragged, he had more in common with the poor men who thronged the wharves looking for work. Rees felt his wife jerk to a stop. When he looked at her face, he saw surprise and horror.

'James?' she said, her voice lifting in disbelief.

'Lydia.' He stumbled to his feet, the stink of old alcohol rolling from him in waves. 'And this must be your husband.' He stretched out his grubby hand. Rees shook it as he inspected the man standing before him.

Although Lydia had told Rees her brother was only five years older than she was, James seemed far older than his early thirties. Gray streaked his brown hair and hard living had dug grooves into his cheeks and forehead. He looked like the desperate men who robbed and murdered for something as small as another man's boots. Rees thought again of Julian's garbled last utterance. Had Julian been trying to say James? And was it an accusation?

James waved them to chairs and dropped heavily into his seat. Rees pulled out Lydia's chair and sat down beside her.

'You look well, Lydia,' James said to his sister. 'Happy.'

Rees glanced at his wife and her anguished expression. Since she seemed stunned into silence by her brother's appearance, Rees began the conversation. 'Lydia has been looking forward to seeing you again,' he said, not altogether truthfully.

James, who was summoning the waiter, glanced at Rees. 'She must be disappointed, then.'

'What's happened to you?' Lydia asked in a hushed voice.

'I suppose Father told you I betrayed him,' James said with a bitter smile.

Lydia did not reply and James nodded as though that was exactly what he'd expected.

'Mrs Farrell told us you were estranged,' Rees added.

'Of course she did. But she did not tell you why.' It was not a question.

'Will you tell us?' Lydia asked.

'I couldn't work for him anymore,' James said. 'It's as simple as that.' As the waiter brought over three cups of coffee, James lapsed into silence. They all waited until the server withdrew.

'What happened?' Lydia asked.

'It is very simple. I refused to work on my father's slavers anymore.' The skin around his eyes tightened. 'Lydia, those ships are from Hell. The people are packed in like stacks of cordwood. No room to stand or move around. And the stench! I was told one became used to the reek eventually, but I never did. To do that kind of work a man can have no heart in his body and no soul.'

'But Father said you were sailing to the West Indies,' Lydia said, her cheeks losing color.

'Yes.' James nodded. 'He put me there, thinking it would soothe my "womanly" sensibilities. But that was little better.' He nodded at the sugar on the table, several chunks of which Rees had just put in his coffee. 'Do you know where that comes from? The West Indies. The cane is harvested by slaves, the juice boiled out of it by slave children. The juice has to be cooked . . . some of those kids are scarred for life by burns.' He blew out a breath as he shook his head. 'I brought dried cod from New England to Jamaica and Barbados to feed the slaves. There I picked up the sugar and the molasses, that's what makes rum, and brought them here to Boston. Just because another captain took the rum to Africa to trade for more slaves does not make my part in that filthy trade any less reprehensible. So, I quit.'

'You chose the right path,' Lydia said, her face white with shock. 'I knew Father . . . But this.' She couldn't continue.

'You think I chose well? Father accused me of rank betrayal. He threatened to throw me out of the house and told me he would disown me.'

'Do you have a place to stay?' Lydia asked anxiously.

'So far.' He smiled at her. 'Don't worry about me, Lyds.'

'And enough to eat?' she continued.

'I'm fine,' he said impatiently. Rees eyed him. He did not think James was fine. He was gaunt with hunger. Rees called the servant over to order bread.

'When will you be shipping out of Boston again?' Lydia asked.

'I don't know. Maybe never. Our wonderful father has slandered me to all of his business cronies as well. No one will hire me.'

Lydia stared at him, shaking her head in disbelief.

'Perhaps you could sign on a whaler?' Rees suggested. 'Or on a merchant ship sailing from Salem to the Orient?' He remembered from his visit to Salem that seamen were in high demand.

'My father's reach is a long one,' James said glumly. 'But I expect I will have to do something of the sort soon. I have exhausted the patience and generosity of my friends. Uncle Julian offered to employ me at the distillery. Besides my own reluctance to participate in any industry connected to the slave trade, I fear I would be putting my uncle's own livelihood at risk. What if my father found out?'

'I thought the two brothers rarely speak to one another,' Lydia said, stumbling over the words. Rees could see her struggling not to blurt out the terrible news.

'They loathe each other. But the brothers still meet once in a while.' The waiter brought over more coffee and a loaf of bread, fresh from the oven. As James cut off a large slice, buttered it and took a large hungry bite, Rees and Lydia shared a self-conscious glance.

James intercepted it and hastily swallowed. 'What?' he said, looking from one to another. 'If you know something, tell me.'

'I am so very sorry,' Rees said. 'I went to visit your uncle yesterday and found him – uh, um . . .' None of the euphemisms seemed to work in this situation. 'Dead.'

James stared at Rees aghast for several seconds. 'What happened?' he asked as Lydia reached over and put her hand on his. Rees had hoped he would not have to describe the scene.

'He was shot,' he admitted.

'So, Marcus finally got around to murdering his brother,' James said. 'First Roark and now Julian.'

'You're not suggesting . . .' Lydia stopped, too appalled to continue.

James nodded, blinking rapidly several times. Lydia handed him her handkerchief. No one spoke as James wiped his eyes. 'That is my father for you,' he said at last. 'Removing everyone who stands between him and whatever he desires.'

'You can't be serious,' Lydia said, just as if she had not thought the very same thing. 'Why would Father murder his brother? I know they've been estranged but murder?'

James shook his head at her. 'I suppose Marcus didn't tell you? He wants to sell the distillery. Julian objected, of course.'

'Why would your father do that?' Rees asked.

James shrugged. 'I don't know. He needs money, I guess.' He sighed. 'I suppose I will be murdered next.'

'Surely not,' Lydia gasped, stumbling over the words.

'Did he tell you he threatened to disown me?'

'I am certain he will never harm you,' Lydia protested. Even she did not sound convinced.

'You were right to leave Boston,' James told his sister. 'That was the best action you could have taken. Father lost control of you. And you made your own life.'

'Did you know Roark Bustamonte?' Rees asked abruptly.

'Of course,' James replied in surprise. 'Mine was the ship on which he sailed to Boston. We knew each other well.' He paused and added, 'I was saddened to hear of his murder. But of course, not surprised to hear Father was the accused.' He took an angry swig of his coffee.

'Was he accompanied by a servant?' Rees asked. 'Benicio?'

'Yes. Do you know Benicio?' James sounded even more surprised.

'No,' Rees said, wondering if he should tell James that Benicio might be the victim, not Roark.

'Sometimes I wondered if Benicio was half-witted,' James said with an involuntary smile. 'He was always doing crazy things. But he was fiercely loyal to Roark.' James finished his bread and helped himself to another slice.

'Do you know where Benicio is now?' Rees asked.

James shook his head, his eyebrows rising. 'I haven't seen either Roark or Benicio since I introduced them to Uncle Julian.'

'Why did you do that?' Lydia asked, sounding puzzled.

'Roark had to work. Julian could help. And he knows – knew – his brother's schedule better than I do. I've been away too much.'

'Did Roark confide to you his reasons for traveling to Boston?' Rees asked.

When James did not immediately speak, Lydia said, 'We know about the argument between Father and Mr Bustamonte. You are not breaking any confidences.'

James sighed and shook his head. 'No, I don't know. Roark wouldn't tell me. Something about the sugar plantation.' He smiled wistfully. 'I suppose Roark didn't trust me entirely. He probably felt he couldn't since he knew I was Marcus Farrell's son. He had no reason to know how poor the relationship was between my father and me.' He finished his second piece of bread and asked, 'What are the arrangements for Uncle Julian?'

'There aren't any yet,' Lydia said, throwing a quick look at her husband. 'This all happened yesterday. Is there any way for us to reach you?'

James shook his head. 'No. Make sure Father puts a notice in the newspaper. I will look for it.' He stuffed the last of the bread in his pocket.

'But I might want to see you again,' Lydia persisted, reaching out to grab her brother's wrist. Shaking his head, James pulled free.

'That is not a good idea,' he said. He turned to go but glanced back over his shoulder. 'There is some mystery about the sugar plantation owned by Father. And Julian too, I think.' Rees and Lydia exchanged a startled glance. 'Something clandestine about it,' James continued. 'Maybe Father will tell you what it is.'

Within a few seconds, James had disappeared into the crowd.

Rees liked his brother-in-law, he truly did. But although he did not intend to share his thoughts with Lydia, he wondered if James had reason to wish Roark and Benicio dead. They could have confided more than James had confessed; something that might have seriously damaged Marcus Farrell and his business. James claimed his father was threatening to disinherit him; that remained to be confirmed. If his father did not intend to – and James knew it – he would have a powerful motive for making these men from the West Indies disappear. Although James had said he did not want any money from the slave trade, Rees had learned long ago to mistrust everything people said to him. He thought James had told the truth, that he was genuinely horrified by the slave trade, but planned to keep an open mind nonetheless.

TWENTY-SIX

'So, I was right to wonder about Jamaica,' Rees murmured. Lydia nodded and a tear slipped down her cheek. He touched her shoulder gently, not sure what to say to console her, anything that would not sound like a criticism of her father, that is. Even if Mr Farrell was not the murderer, his behavior toward his son demanded condemnation.

The tavern was growing steadily busier as noon approached. After the waiter eyed them pointedly several times, Rees said, 'We'd better go.' He pushed away his half-full cup of coffee. Now that he knew the association between sugar and slavery, he'd decided to take his coffee without the sweetener. He could not finish the sugarless second cup.

Lydia nodded and wiped her eyes. Rees pulled her chair away from the table and she stood. As they went out into the chilly air, Rees said, 'I wonder if your father is home yet.'

'Probably,' Lydia said. 'Ironic, isn't it. He has not visited the distillery for a long time. At least a year. Today he goes because his brother has been murdered and it is far too late to make amends.' She shook her head.

Rees knew, if he were in that position, he would regret the estrangement the rest of his life. He was not sure Mr Farrell felt the same way. It appeared Mr Farrell suffered from a want of feelings. 'Do you think the estrangement between your father and Julian relates to a disagreement over that plantation?'

'Maybe,' Lydia replied in a trembling voice. 'Probably.' Rees glanced at her. She was wiping away tears of anguish.

When they arrived home, the door to the drawing room was wide open. A coffin lay upon a small table with several men working around it.

'Is Julian's body here?' Lydia asked Mrs Farrell, her voice breaking.

'Not yet.' She cast Lydia a sharp look. 'Your father could not carry Julian home over his shoulder. He made arrangements so he – um – the body should arrive shortly.' She sighed. 'The funeral is planned for next week.'

'Where is Cordy?' Lydia asked, looking around.

'Out with Mr Hutchinson,' Mrs Farrell replied.

Rees could not prevent his quick glance at Lydia.

'Unchaperoned?' Lydia sounded horrified.

'I meant to accompany them but with Julian's accident . . .' She shook her head. 'Anyway, Cordy is perfectly safe with Mr Hutchinson. He will not want to upset your father.'

'But she is so young,' Lydia said in dismay, trying to keep her voice level. 'Are you certain this connection is wise? He is so much older than she is.'

'He is already established,' Mrs Farrell said defensively. 'He would be a good match for her.' She hesitated. 'I know she is interested in Edward Bartlett, but he is not really prepared to set up a household. Besides, since your father's troubles, she has barely seen him and only for a few minutes at a time . . .' Her voice trailed away. A slight frown marred her forehead. 'Yes, Mr Hutchinson is a bit older. Cordy will have to decide. And the wedding can be delayed a year or so, until she is older.'

And the scandal had faded in everyone's memory, Rees thought.

'I am well aware of the pressure that will be brought to bear upon Cordy,' Lydia said disapprovingly. 'She may agree to marry – and soon – just to please Father even if she would prefer to choose otherwise.'

'She is a much different young woman than you were,' Mrs Farrell said tartly. 'Neither so defiant nor so intolerant.'

'You may be surprised,' Lydia replied. 'Cordy is every bit as strong-willed as I was.'

'Is Mr Farrell feeling better?' Rees asked, staring across the hall at the open door to the office. 'It appears he is in his office.'

'He is,' Mrs Farrell said. 'And he wishes to see you both.'

'We want to speak with him as well,' Rees said. He looked at his wife. She offered him a slight nod and they walked across the hall.

Through the open door, Rees could see Mr Farrell seated at his desk sorting through papers. Lydia took in a breath, steeling herself for the interview to come. Rees tapped on the wooden frame and Mr Farrell looked up.

'Come in,' he said. 'And shut the door behind you.' He did not look well; his eyes were reddened with weeping. 'I asked you not to pursue Bustamonte's murder,' he said angrily, before Rees could completely close the door behind him. 'Why were you at the distillery?'

'I wanted to visit my uncle,' Lydia said, her shoulders so stiff they almost reached her ears. Rees threw an approving glance at her, pleased that she had stood up to her father. Marcus threw his handful of papers on the desk and stood up.

'I had a question for Julian,' Rees said. Farrell did not intimidate him. 'If I had not gone, Julian would have lain there, unfound, for God knows how long. You would not have wanted that, would you?'

Farrell began pacing. Rees suppressed his gratification. Of course the other man did not want his brother to lie there alone but he did not want to give Rees the satisfaction of saying so.

'Who else have you spoken to, against my express wishes?'

'We met with James,' Lydia said.

'James?'

'He said you are intending to disown him?'

'Outspoken as usual,' Farrell said critically. 'Did he tell you he refused to work for me?'

'He did,' Lydia said.

'How can he expect me to leave him my business if he refuses to take part in it?' Farrell shook his head.

'Have you?' Lydia persisted. 'Disowned him, I mean.'

'I've done nothing so far. I haven't decided. James is my only son. How I wish Cordy had been born a boy.'

'Well, she wasn't,' Lydia said sharply.

'I'm curious about the sugar plantation in the West Indies,' Rees said.

'James talked about that too, did he? I would not be surprised to hear he suggested I stole it. Nothing is further from the truth. There is no secret to my acquisition of the plantation at all. Roark's father owned it. He owed me a significant amount of money and offered the plantation as collateral. When he couldn't pay his debt, I took the plantation.'

'Is that what you were arguing with Roark Bustamonte over?' Lydia asked. 'The plantation?'

Farrell eyed his daughter contemptuously. 'Your uncle was murdered and this is what you are concerning yourself with? My alleged malfeasance? Yes, that is what we were arguing about. Roark was convinced I had cheated his father when I took the property. He would not listen when I assured him that my recovery of the plantation was entirely legal. And no, I did not kill him over this. Why would I? The law was on my side.'

'We understand you wished to sell the distillery as well,' Rees said.

'Once. I changed my mind. Julian talked me out of it.' Marcus glared at Rees. 'I asked you to refrain from pawing through my private matters. In future, please respect my wishes.'

When neither Rees nor Lydia responded, Farrell added curtly, 'I will see you at luncheon.'

Dismissed, Rees and Lydia prepared to leave. From behind them, Marcus said, 'Wait.' They turned. 'How did James look?' The words were wrung reluctantly from him.

'Fine,' Lydia said briefly.

'Don't be petty,' Rees murmured to her. But she angrily shook her head and marched to the office door.

Mr Farrell did not follow them; he slammed the door behind them.

Only Rees, Lydia and Jerusha sat down to the meal. Cordelia was still with Mr Hutchinson, Mr Farrell had decided to take his meal in his office, and Mrs Farrell was far too overwrought to consume anything. Without Cordy's chatter, the room was very quiet. Even the maids who brought in the dishes seemed to be walking on tiptoe.

'What do you think of Boston?' Lydia asked Jerusha, struggling to find a pleasant topic of conversation.

'I like it well enough,' she said. 'It has been fun. I've enjoyed seeing all the shops.'

Hearing some reservation in her tone, Rees said, 'But?'

'But what?'

'Go on,' Rees said. 'What else?'

'It will be very difficult to study here in Boston.'

'Because of Cordy?' Lydia guessed.

'No! Well, maybe a little,' Jerusha admitted. 'She is fun. But she is not interested in studying. Or even reading a book.'

'Of course, you would not be staying in her room,' Lydia pointed out.

'No.' Jerusha took a meditative bite of her fish.

'I can see you are disturbed about something,' Rees said. 'Come on. Out with it.' Jerusha looked around to make sure there were no servants lurking nearby.

'The problem is, well, Cordy doesn't understand why I want to study. She doesn't wish to allow me enough time to do so much as read a page in a book.'

'Can't you reason with her?' Rees asked.

Jerusha peeked at her mother from under her lashes.

'I've tried. Cordy gets cross and out of sorts. The last time when I wouldn't do what she wanted she ripped the page from my book and threw it in the fire.'

'My goodness,' Lydia said involuntarily. Rees wasn't surprised. He had witnessed too many examples of Cordelia's fits.

'I'm afraid, if I am even in the same town, Cordy will find me and drag me away from my studies.'

Lydia nodded in understanding. 'She misses her friends. I'm afraid she sees you as a substitute.'

'Some days I feel as though I am being torn to pieces.'

'Don't worry,' Lydia said reassuringly as the maid came in to clear the dishes. 'There are other schools. We will manage something.'

TWENTY-SEVEN

Cordelia arrived home with Mr Hutchinson shortly after. Although she tried to mask her feelings and thank him civilly for such a pleasant outing, it was plain she was in a foul temper.

'He tried to discuss politics,' Rees overheard Cordelia tell Jerusha as he and Lydia followed the girls up the stairs. 'Politics! Of all the boring topics. Mr Jefferson is an atheist. Mr Jefferson will destroy the country in three months. Mr Jefferson this, Mr Jefferson that. Eddy would never bore me so.'

'What does he talk to you about?' Jerusha asked.

'Oh, he tells me the latest gossip. Who married who; that sort of thing.'

'Perhaps Mr Hutchinson was attempting to ease your grief and take your mind from your uncle's recent passing,' Jerusha suggested.

'Then he should have chosen a more entertaining topic. I was like to doze off from sheer boredom.'

'Why did you accompany him, then?' Jerusha asked. 'You could have claimed you were prostrate from grief.'

'My parents insisted. I did not want to go. I feel terrible about my uncle.'

'Maybe they were trying to protect you?' Jerusha suggested.

'Oh, pish,' Cordelia said. 'People die all the time. No, they are determined I should wed the boring old stick they have chosen.'

Lydia and Rees paused at the door of her bedroom and she turned a grim look upon her husband. 'I was afraid of that,' she muttered as she watched the young women continue down the hall.

'My father would never do that to me,' Jerusha said with such obvious affection Rees felt himself blushing.

'I'm hungry,' Cordelia said. 'I'm going to send to the kitchen for a tray. Do you want anything?' As they stepped inside the room, Cordelia's voice faded. A few seconds later, the door slammed shut.

Within the hour of Marcus Farrell's return home, the house was thronged with people. Rees and Lydia kept out of the way, remaining upstairs unnoticed until Mrs Farrell appeared searching for them. Upon an invitation to enter Lydia's bedchamber, she came in and collapsed into the desk chair. Plunging her hands through her fashionably arranged hair, and leaving it a disordered mess, she exclaimed, 'I am worn to a thread! Besides the dressmaker – we must all have black dresses made – I met with the coffin-maker and the church pastor.'

Rees thought of the young apprentice who had already seemed so tired. He did not doubt Mrs Farrell expected the new clothing immediately. That poor child would be up to all hours trying to finish this new commission.

'I can wear my navy blue,' Lydia said. 'It is quite dark and will be appropriate. Jerusha can wear one of her blue gowns. The dressmaker will have enough to do with you and Cordy.'

Mrs Farrell nodded abstractedly just as though Lydia had not already told her this. 'Very well. How fortunate we have all already been fitted.'

'How is my father faring?' Lydia asked her stepmother.

'He is more distraught than I expected. Quite laid low, in fact. I am finding it surprising. Marcus and his brother scarcely spoke for months, if not years. Yet now . . .' She sighed heavily.

'Did you like your brother-in-law?' Rees asked.

'Like? What do you mean, like?'

'Find him compatible? Enjoy his company?'

'Of course I do.' She directed an insincere smile at Rees. 'But I am angry with Julian. Marcus gave his brother everything. After Julian lost the cargo, the entire cargo, mind, and the *Flying Fish* as well, Marcus still allowed his brother to work in his employ at the distillery. One would think Julian would be grateful but he was not. He implied his brother should do more. In addition, he sided with James when he defied his father. Such disloyalty! So, even if Marcus is disposed to forgive and forget, I will not.'

Despite her words to the contrary, it was clear she did not like her brother-in-law.

'What will Father do about the distillery now?' Lydia asked.

'I don't know. Sell it perhaps. That is another problem I will lay at Julian's door. He has left Marcus in a terrible spot. Although,' she added thoughtfully, 'I daresay the foreman might be able to take over the distillery operations. Once the vats and the stills are set up, screech is not so difficult to make.'

'Screech?' Rees asked.

'Rumbullion. Kill-devil. The lowest grade of rum.'

'Ah,' Rees said, remembering Julian and his offer of the 'good stuff'.

At that moment one of the maids poked her head through the open door. With a soft tap, she said, 'Begging your pardon, Mrs Farrell, but Mr Farrell has been looking for you these past five minutes.'

Mrs Farrell rose to her feet. 'I must go.' She started for the door but turned back. 'I will forget my head next. I came to tell you that dinner tonight will be a cold collation in the breakfast room.'

'Thank you,' Lydia said.

Mrs Farrell hurried out. Lydia closed the door. 'Isabeau truly disliked Julian. If I could imagine my stepmother visiting the distillery, I might suspect her of Julian's death.'

'I suppose that is possible,' Rees said with a chuckle. 'Although her dislike does not seem intense enough to result in murder. Besides, the foreman saw a man.'

'Yes, I know,' Lydia agreed. 'And I can't see her creeping through the streets of Boston in the dark to shoot Roark. Or Benicio. Whoever the other victim is.'

Sunday passed almost wholly occupied in services. The minister, a plump white-haired fellow, was pleasant but some of the congregants were not. Glances ranged from the dubious to the openly hostile, despite the sad news about Julian. Although Farrell himself seemed oblivious, both Mrs Farrell and Cordelia noticed. Mrs Farrell lifted her head even higher, daring these erstwhile friends to say something, while Cordy withdrew into herself.

'We shan't see many of these people at Julian's funeral,' Mrs Farrell predicted in a low voice.

Lydia, Rees observed, appeared unmoved. She greeted the minister politely, introduced her husband, nodded to the few who welcomed her and ignored the rest. 'After all,' she said when Rees commented upon her demeanor, 'I left this life behind a long time ago.' She paused and added, 'An excellent decision, I believe.'

Rees awoke very early Monday morning, so early the sky was just beginning to lighten. Leaving Lydia sleeping, he went into his little room to wash and dress. When he descended the stairs to the breakfast room, he found the servants beginning to lay out the food. Since the fire had just been lit, the room was chilly.

The maids glanced at him but were too well trained to reveal their surprise. 'Would you like coffee, sir?' one of the maids asked timidly.

'No thank you,' Rees said. He expected Quentin Fitzpatrick would soon be working in his shop; not for him the luxury of lying in bed. After speaking with him, Rees would find a tavern and eat his breakfast there.

He went out into the cold clear morning. A few stars still shone on the horizon, but they were fading rapidly as the sun rose. Walking briskly, Rees crossed the street and headed east. He'd been confident in his memory, and sure enough, he soon recognized the Fitzpatricks' house. When he went around the corner, he saw the silversmith's shop, just as Quentin Fitzpatrick had described. As Rees approached the door, Quentin himself opened it.

'Mr Rees,' he said in surprise. 'I am just opening my shop. Do you want to come inside?'

'Thank you,' Rees said, following Fitzpatrick through the door.

The shop was still empty of journeymen and apprentices. Quentin, it appeared, had been eating his breakfast at the back table before tackling the day's projects.

'Are you hungry?' Quentin asked, following the direction of Rees's gaze. He pulled a cord that ran above his head. 'We'll get something for you.'

'That is not necessary,' Rees began but Quentin interrupted.

'Oh, it is no trouble.'

When the young maid Rees recognized from the Wednesday before entered, Quentin asked for another plate of breakfast, bread, and coffee. 'Now, sit down and tell me why you're here.'

'I was wondering if you'd identified the gambling house my father-in-law frequents,' Rees said, adding 'I am ashamed to admit one of my major sins is impatience.'

Quentin smiled. 'I understand. And yes, I did. Forgive me for not sending around a note immediately.'

Rees waved away the apology. 'It is nothing.'

'I mentioned Mr Farrell to a few of my customers. Your father-in-law plays at two or three houses, but his favorite is Mrs Lunn's on North Street. I would try there first.'

'And the second?' Rees asked. He wanted to be prepared in the event Mrs Lunn denied Mr Farrell was in attendance that night.

'It is on Franklin but I don't know the name,' Fitzpatrick said as two young maids brought in Rees's plate and cup and a pot of coffee. Milk and sugar soon followed. Rees poured the milk liberally into his cup but did not add sugar. He could not repress a shudder at the first sip of the dark brew. He couldn't help it; coffee cried out for sugar. He put in half of his normal amount and decided, after a tentative sip, that the beverage was at least drinkable.

He spent a pleasant half hour chatting with Quentin as they both ate their meals. By the time they were finished, the shop was filling

up with a journeyman or two and several apprentices. It had become
so noisy Rees could scarcely think. Rising to his feet, he shook
Quentin's hand and set off for Mrs Lunn's gambling house.

TWENTY-EIGHT

'Psst.' Rees stopped and looked around. After leaving the
silversmith's shop, he'd walked alongside the Fitzpatrick
home and was just preparing to cross the street. 'Psst.' The
whisper sounded again. 'Here.' Rees looked at the wall of the house
and spotted a gate. Cautiously he approached. The high, solid
wooden door swung open a crack and the Fitzpatricks' nursemaid
peered out. 'Mr Rees.'

'Gertrude, is it?'

'May I have a word?'

'All right,' Rees said, taking a few steps closer.

'I want to talk to you a little bit about Miss Cordelia.'

'What about her?' Rees asked. What could Gertrude have to say
about Cordelia?

'I've known her all of her life. She isn't a malicious girl, but she
is spoiled, very spoiled.'

'All right,' Rees said, wondering where this was going.

'I didn't want to say anything to Miss Lydia. She is protective
of her sister. But she should know.'

'What has Cordy done?' Rees asked in resignation.

'There is a young man.' She stopped and started again. 'Since
Mr Farrell's troubles, most of the young people Miss Cordelia
was accustomed to seeing have been forbidden to associate with
her.' She peered into Rees's face to see if he understood. He
nodded.

'I've heard.'

'Cordelia has been seen slipping out of her house at night.'

'She's been what?'

'I know,' Gertrude said with a nod. 'She could get into no end
of trouble.'

'Who has seen her?' Rees asked. And did Jerusha know?

'One of the servants saw her. She passed the information along to me, thinking, I suppose, that Sally would tell Lydia.'

'She didn't,' Rees said.

'I know. Because I haven't told Sally yet.' Gertrude shook her head. 'I wasn't sure what Sally would do. She's a good-hearted girl but flighty, you see. I thought it best to tell you instead. I have no doubt in my mind that Cordelia is sneaking out to meet that young man she was seeing before her father's troubles.'

Of course she is, Rees thought.

Gertrude took a deep breath. 'I see you understand. Well, you know how girls are.'

Rees wasn't sure he did know. Jerusha had never given him any cause for concern, not in that area anyway.

'Cordelia probably fancies herself in love with him,' Gertrude continued. 'And in a few years, under normal circumstances, he would be a decent match. But he is not established yet. And I am quite certain her parents do not want to marry her off in a hurry, if you know what I mean.'

'I do,' Rees said, nodding his head. 'And who is the servant who told you?'

'Bridget. Do you know her?'

'Yes,' Rees said, recalling the shy child who was responsible for minding his baby girl Sharon. 'Thank you for telling me. I will look into it.'

The gate quietly eased shut. Rees stood before it for a moment, thinking. He hoped this was not as serious as Gertrude claimed. But the nurse did not even understand the full import of what she'd confided. Cordelia, it seemed, had more freedom to move around town than Rees had realized. Could she have had something to do with the deaths? Surely not. She was a young and gently bred girl. Still, Rees could not erase the apprehension that shadowed him as he continued to Mrs Lunn's.

He was surprised by the elegance of the establishment. Like the Farrell home, the Lunn house was three stories and boasted a small garden in front. When Rees knocked on the door, it was opened by a butler as proper as Morris and even more forbidding. 'We are closed, sir,' he said.

'Fine,' Rees said. 'I would like to speak to Mrs Lunn, if I may.'

'Is she expecting you?'

'No. But it is urgent. It concerns Mr Marcus Farrell.' Rees kept his gaze upon the butler until he dropped his eyes.

'Very well. Wait here.' He firmly shut the door, leaving Rees staring at the wooden panels. He guessed Mrs Lunn wished to be discreet. Boston was not London and many of the amusements in that more cosmopolitan city were considered suspect in a country founded by the Puritans.

After a minute or more, the butler opened the door once again and invited Rees inside.

He was astonished by the grandeur of the front hall: the elegant carpet, the crystal chandelier, albeit with the candles unlit, and the elegant sideboard positioned on the right wall. A woman of about thirty slowly descended the stairs. She was quite lovely with large brown eyes thickly fringed with dark lashes. Rees wondered if Julian had told the truth about his brother and his brother's mistress.

But she inspected Rees with a gaze as battle hardened as an old soldier. 'You said this is about Mr Farrell,' she said in a husky voice.

Rees nodded. 'You must have heard? He was accused of the murder of a young man a few months ago.' Rees paused. Would it serve him to admit he was trying to prove Farrell's innocence or the reverse? He decided to tell the truth. 'He swears he is innocent. I am trying to track his movements on that date, November 15th, and discover the truth.'

'That was a long time ago. I do not remember every night Mr Farrell has frequented my establishment,' she murmured in her low voice. She regarded him in silence for several seconds and finally decided to trust him. 'The ledger, please,' she said to her servant. Turning to Rees, she said, 'Come into the salon.' She preceded him into a large room, filled with couches and comfortable chairs. Rees wondered if this was where the games took place or whether that activity went on in some other chamber.

Mrs Lunn sat down on a couch and gestured Rees to the chair across from it. When the butler brought in the ledger, she put it on the table between the couch and the chair and opened it. 'November 15th, you say.' She ran her finger down the left side, finally pausing at an entry. 'Yes, here it is. Marcus Farrell. He arrived just after six and played until almost four the next morning. He ate both dinner and breakfast here. I cannot tell you exactly when he left, but he indicated he was on his way to his office.' She pushed the ledger across the smooth wood of the table so that Rees could confirm her information for himself.

He quickly found Farrell's name. It was written in the exact same hand and ink as the names above and below. Although Rees knew Mrs Lunn did not mean for him to do more than corroborate Farrell's whereabouts, he noted that one of those gentlemen, the name right above Mr Farrell's, was listed as a judge. Maybe Farrell had applied to the judge to quash the investigation into the murder at the Painted Pig.

Rees, moreover, could not help reading across the lines. The final figures made him stare. He decided Mrs Lunn could not be Farrell's mistress; he had owed her in excess of nine hundred dollars. And she clearly intended he should pay; so far, she had listed a total of three hundred dollars paid on that account.

'Thank you,' Rees said, returning the ledger. Stunned, he couldn't help wondering if he had misread the sums.

'There are others who can also corroborate his presence here,' she said. 'I would prefer you not ask them.'

'I understand,' Rees said, wondering if all of the players lost as much as Mr Farrell.

'He promised me he had nothing to do with that young man's death,' Mrs Lunn said. 'He also promised me no one would know of his presence here; that I would never be asked. He said he would deal with the accusation a different way.'

'He did,' Rees said. 'He does not know of my visit here and I will not share it with him or with anyone else. I just wanted to assure myself of his innocence.'

Mrs Lunn nodded. 'Thank you. I maintain my house by offering this modest pleasure to a small number of carefully selected gentlemen. You understand, I rely completely on their discretion as they rely upon mine.'

'Of course,' Rees said. 'Does Mr Farrell visit the house often?'

'Occasionally,' she said with a smile. 'Although it is rare that he plays so deep.' She paused. When Rees said nothing further, she asked, 'Do you have any more questions?'

'Not at present,' he said.

Mrs Lunn rose and offered him her hand. He took it, uttering some pleasantries that afterwards he barely remembered. 'Please consider yourself welcome if you ever wish to try your luck at

French hazard or whist,' she invited him with a professional smile. 'Although you do not look as though you could afford the stakes.'

'Thank you.' He followed the butler to the door and found himself on the porch.

He walked home with his mind whirling. Farrell still owed Mrs Lunn six hundred dollars. Why, a man could buy six farms with that, build and outfit a merchant ship, live like a king.

And what would Lydia make of the cost of her father's pastime?

TWENTY-NINE

'How much?' Lydia said, her eyes widening. They had taken refuge in the nursery where they were alone but for Sharon. Even Bridget had disappeared on an errand.

Lydia was seated on the floor playing dolls, or rather trying to play dolls with her daughter. The little girl demonstrated an unfortunate tendency for using the baby dolls like soldiers and staging mock battles with them. Lydia kept suggesting they put the dolls to bed, but Sharon refused to even consider anything so tame.

'Six hundred dollars,' Rees repeated. 'And the amount was once nine hundred. He has paid three hundred on his account so far.' He watched Sharon pick up a baby doll with a broken head and use it to mow down the figures Lydia had arranged on the other side. 'Sharon has learned to play with her brothers,' he said with a grin. 'Your efforts are futile.'

'Appalling,' Lydia said, carefully arranging the scattered toys once again. 'Maybe the dollies should go to school,' she suggested to Sharon.

'No. Soldiers.' She sent the damaged doll against Lydia's forces once again. Rees wondered if Sharon had broken the toy with her roughness.

'I could almost prefer he keep a mistress,' Lydia continued. 'It would cost less. Are you certain this Mrs Lunn does not fill that role?'

'She is a beautiful woman,' Rees said. 'But no, I don't believe so. His entry in the ledger looks the same as the others; exactly like the business transaction it is.'

'The two are not mutually exclusive, you know,' she replied, eyeing him as though he were naïve. 'She might serve as his mistress but still expect him to pay his shot. It is business, her business, after all.'

Rees considered that for a moment and nodded. 'Yes, I suppose that's true.'

He had decided not to mention Gertrude's accusation quite yet. He hoped to speak with Bridget privately at some point and corroborate that part of Gertrude's claim. Not that he didn't trust Gertrude or Bridget, but Cordy could be perfectly innocent of any wrongdoing.

'Anyway,' he said aloud, 'you must be relieved to know your father is innocent of Roark's – or Benicio's – murder, just as he said he was.'

'That may be true,' Lydia said unsmilingly. 'But what about Julian? My father might be guilty of that murder. By his own admission, he had reason.'

'What reason?' Rees asked.

'The distillery.'

'He said Julian talked him out of the sale.'

'We don't know if that is true,' Lydia said mournfully. She turned an anxious gaze on Rees. 'He might still be guilty. And, if not him, who?'

'That remains to be discovered,' Rees said. At the moment his only suspects were other members of his wife's family, a fact he did not wish to say out loud. 'I understand why your father refused to tell the truth,' he continued. 'Why he told us that ridiculous story. I wouldn't want anyone to know how much money I'd lost at cards either.'

'I imagine Isabeau would be furious,' Lydia agreed. She shook her head. 'So, we prove his innocence in the murder by discovering a different, maybe somewhat less serious, sin. Unbelievable.' She did not sound comforted.

'What's unbelievable?' Jerusha asked, following Bridget into the nursery.

'That your sister insists on using these dolls as soldiers,' Lydia said quickly. 'Where's Cordelia?'

'Being fitted for mourning gowns.' She shook her head. 'I don't know why they don't take some of her older gowns and dye them. Cordy already has more clothing than can fit in her press. She doesn't need anything new.'

'Spoken like a true daughter of your frugal mother,' Rees said, grinning.

'The dressmaker has had to pause in the finishing of our new gowns,' Lydia said to Jerusha. 'Do not expect them as soon as they were promised.'

'I asked her that,' Jerusha said. 'She told me we will still receive them in a few days.'

Rees listened with half an ear as he watched Bridget. She bustled around the room, ostensibly tidying. He could see she was listening. He picked up some of the dolls and joined her by the window. As he handed her the toys, he whispered, 'Gertrude told me you saw Cordy sneak out of the house?'

'I saw her sneak back into the house,' Bridget corrected. Rees looked at her interrogatively. 'I don't live in. I was on my way here when I saw her.'

'What time was that?'

'About four in the morning.'

'But how would she get in and out?' Rees asked.

Bridget looked at him in disbelief. 'The servants' stairs, of course.'

'The servants' stairs?' Rees glanced around as though a flight of stairs would magically appear.

'They don't come this far up. They go to the door at the end of the hall next to Miss Cordelia's room. You'll see. Then the stairs go straight down to a hall and a door out to the drive.'

Rees noticed Lydia looking at him. 'Do you want the rest of the dolls?' Rees asked more loudly. 'We'd better pick them up before she breaks them all.'

'Yes, thank you. She will be eating her dinner soon anyway.'

As he turned around and began collecting the scattered toys, he was aware of Lydia's intent gaze. She did not want to question him in front of Jerusha but he knew she would pounce as soon as they were alone.

'I'm going downstairs for a bit,' he said and was out the door before Lydia could say anything. He descended to the second floor. The hall to the right went to Mr and Mrs Farrell's bedchamber. To the left, the corridor passed first Lydia's bedchamber and then Cordelia's. Across the passageway from Rees's small room was another door. It had been distempered white so that it disappeared into the white wall.

Rees opened the door to disclose a set of narrow stairs dropping into the gloom. He stepped down the first few. When the door above closed automatically, the stairwell was suddenly in complete darkness. Rees put his hand on the wall to steady himself and very slowly began to follow the twisting flight down. No attention had been paid to the comfort of the servants. The steps were narrow, and the staircase twisted like a corkscrew all the way to the bottom. Rees was surprised that the maids didn't fall down and break their ankles.

He came to a wall at the bottom, which, as he felt his way forward, resolved into a wooden panel. When he pushed, it opened into a small hall. Four other doors led off this tiny space. To his left was the kitchen; he could hear the clatter of pans and the murmur of voices. To his right, the passageway led to another hall leading toward the front of the house. And behind him was a door that led directly into the formal dining room.

But the door that interested Rees the most was located next to the servants' stairs. As Bridget had promised, when Rees went through, he found himself on the drive outside. He was almost invisible from all sides. The mews to the back were all the way to the rear of the house. Unless someone was coming down the drive and turned the corner, this entrance could not be seen. There were no windows in the wall of the building next door and as for the Farrell home, it was Cordelia's room that looked out upon the drive.

If Bridget had not been coming up the drive to this, the servants' entrance, at the exact moment Cordelia had been slipping through the door, she would have escaped detection. Especially so early, before sunrise, when everything was still dark.

Rees resolved to stay up late the next few days and watch for Cordelia. He wanted to know if this was something she engaged in regularly. Then he would share the information with Lydia.

When he went inside and up the stairs once again, he found Lydia lingering in the doorway of her bedchamber. He tried to escape by hurrying into his small room, but she followed him. 'What did Bridget tell you?' she demanded. 'And where did you go?'

'Um, er.' Rees floundered for a few seconds. He did not have Lydia's quickness of thought. 'I just – um – went outside for a few minutes.'

'The truth,' Lydia said, fixing him with her stern gaze.

Rees sat down on his bed. 'When I went out yesterday, I met Gertrude. She accosted me outside Quentin Fitzpatrick's shop.' The entire tale spilled from his lips. 'I wanted to make sure Cordelia was truly guilty of something before I told you,' he concluded. She shook her head at him.

'You know how your attempts to protect me anger me,' she said in exasperation.

'I understand. But this is Cordelia.'

'I know my sister,' Lydia said with an amused smile. 'I am not surprised to discover she is slipping out to meet Edward Bartlett. Gertrude is right; Cordelia is spoiled. She does not often accept the word no.'

'Did you know of the other stairs?'

'No. I should have realized there would be some. I never thought. Trust Cordelia to use them for her own purposes.' She paused for a few seconds. 'We will set watch tonight. We can see the end of the driveway from my front window.' Lydia's forehead wrinkled. 'If she is meeting that young man, we need to put a stop to it. If it continues, at best her reputation will be in tatters. No one will want to marry her.'

'There is always Mr Hutchinson.'

'No one decent anyway. Mr Hutchinson is a lackey of my father. I cannot believe his feelings are truly engaged and we know hers definitely are not. He will only make Cordy miserable.'

THIRTY

Claiming fatigue, Rees and Lydia retired early. They had agreed that Rees would enter his room and then use the connecting door into Lydia's after the maid came in to turn down the bedding. To give credence to the ruse, Lydia changed into her night rail.

As soon as Rees came through, she jumped out of bed. They pulled the drape away from the window and Rees took up a position by it. The cold air streamed in around the sash and Rees began shivering. After a few minutes, in which his fingers and toes went numb, he drew the drapery once again and tiptoed downstairs to collect his greatcoat and scarf. He could hear voices and since there were burning candles in the sconces, he assumed some of the family was still awake.

When he returned to Lydia's bedchamber, he found she had stirred up the fire so that it blazed merrily on the hearth. It was quite warm near the fireplace but when Rees returned to the window, he found that the heat did not penetrate so far. Despite his warm coat, his gloves and the scarf enveloping his neck, he quickly felt the cold.

Fortunately, he did not have to wait long. In a little more than an hour, a slight form illuminated by a lighted candle appeared on the drive. From Rees's position above, the figure appeared to be that of a young man; a young man with Cordelia's pale blond hair peeking out from underneath the hat. The short cape dropped to just above her knees, but as she hurried toward the street Rees could clearly see white stockings. Light glinted from the silver buttons at the knees. It was a somewhat old-fashioned costume.

Rees hissed at Lydia. Wrapping a heavy quilt around her shoulders, she joined him at the window. Together, they watched Cordelia turn left, and start walking east, toward the wharves. She very quickly disappeared from sight.

'That's it, then,' Lydia said unhappily. Rees allowed the drape to drop over the window.

'We-we will have-have to speak to your sister to-tomorrow,' he said through chattering teeth.

Lydia took off his gloves and felt his fingers. 'My goodness, your hands are like ice,' she said.

'And I'm hungry.'

She hesitated for a moment. 'Everyone is abed. Follow me to the kitchen,' she whispered. She took one of the lighted tapers and together they tiptoed through the dark and silent house. Taking his hand, she led him through the dining room and into the kitchen. The fire was banked but the residual heat from the day's cooking lingered, warming the room so that Rees could remove his coat. The faint enticing aroma left by the roast they'd eaten earlier wafted through the air and Rees became even hungrier.

Lydia lit several candles from hers. Then she pulled bread, fresh that morning, and what was left of the joint from the pantry. Mustard followed. She handed him a plate and knife.

'Did you see?' Rees asked. 'Cordelia went toward the docks. Why would she go there?'

'I cannot imagine.'

'Next time I should follow her,' he said as he slathered mustard on the bread.

'That may be a good idea,' Lydia agreed.

As Rees took a bite of his sandwich, Lydia said, 'She would have no reason to walk to the wharves in the dark. And I can't imagine that young man she is so fond of meeting her at the docks. It is dangerous at the best of times. He would be lucky to lose only his purse.' She bit her lip and stared blindly across the room.

'Perhaps Bartlett's wagon is parked at the corner,' Rees said. Lydia's anxious expression did not ease. 'What's the matter?'

'Could you see what she was wearing under that cape?' Lydia asked.

'Stockings and shoes. Breeches I suppose.'

'Will, did you see those breeches?' Lydia looked at him, her eyes wide with worry and fear. 'They were white.'

Rees's thoughts flew instantly to the young barmaid at the Painted Pig. She had given them only one specific detail, that the young man who had run away after the shooting wore white breeches. 'You don't think . . .?' He met Lydia's anxious gaze.

'Cordelia could not possibly be the murderer,' Lydia said. 'Could she?'

'Of course not,' Rees assured her heartily, pushing away his sandwich. He was no longer hungry. 'But until we know for certain, we can't tell anyone what we saw.'

Lydia nodded unhappily. 'I concur. But her reputation . . . I must still speak to her about her meetings with young Mr Bartlett. They cannot continue.'

She stacked the dirty dishes in the sink. 'Cook will speak to you about those,' Rees said.

'I know she will,' Lydia agreed. 'Let's go upstairs. We can still get a few hours of sleep before morning.' She blew out all the candles she'd brought but one and she used that to light their way up the servants' stairs. Rees did not think it was very useful; the stairs remained narrow, dark and twisty.

Despite this late-night excursion, Rees did not fall asleep immediately. He turned over and over, finally flopping onto his back. As he stared at the ceiling, he pondered this new development. He did not want to believe Cordelia was the murderer. She was so young.

And what possible reason could she have to wish not only Roark but also Julian Farrell, her uncle, dead? It did not make sense.

With a rustle, Lydia rolled over. 'Can't you sleep?'

'No.'

'Me either.' She heaved a sigh. 'It looks like the murderer is a member of my family.'

'It may not be Cordelia,' Rees said consolingly. Lydia snorted rudely.

'No, it may be my father. In any case, we now know she's been dancing all over Boston.'

Rees thumped his pillow in frustration. 'Yes, and we know why; meeting that Edward Bartlett. I cannot conceive of a reason why Cordy would find it necessary to murder, first, a young man from the West Indies, and second, Julian Farrell. I can't force it into any kind of sense. Especially since it was Cordy who invited us here.'

Lydia was silent for so long Rees thought she'd fallen asleep. He closed his eyes and tried to find that elusive unconsciousness. 'Of course, that could be a tactic to mislead us,' she said so suddenly Rees jumped. His eyes popped open. 'It is exactly the sort of thing my sister would find clever. Then there's my brother. I am convinced he knows something more. I was so upset by his appearance on Saturday I wasn't thinking clearly. We have to locate him. Press him to tell us what else he knows.'

'I agree,' Rees said. 'But where is he?'

'I have an idea about that,' Lydia said. 'It's unlikely but . . .'

'And we still have to find Roark Bustamonte,' Rees said. 'I am persuaded this whole scandal relates back to something that happened in the West Indies. Your father won't tell us, and Julian is dead. Only Roark – or Benicio – whoever it is, is left.'

THIRTY-ONE

Heavy-eyed and tired, Rees and Lydia went down to breakfast a little later than usual. Apparently having experienced no ill effects from last night's jaunt to the wharves, Cordelia, bright-eyed and lively and chattering gaily to Jerusha, was already at breakfast. She wore one of her new gowns, a frock of palest yellow.

'Does your mother know you are wearing that?' Lydia asked in dismay.

'No. I thought I'd wear it before I was forced into mourning,' Cordelia said. 'So spring-like, don't you think? And much prettier than black.'

She did look lovely. But Rees, as he eyed the short, puffed sleeves and the gossamer fabric, thought she must be cold. He would be. Almost as if she could hear his thought, Cordelia pulled up the shawl and wrapped it around her shoulders.

'Is the dressmaker coming again today?' Lydia asked as she buttered a piece of toast.

'Yes. I am not quite sure why my mother is so eager to outfit us in black.' Cordelia shook her head. 'She did not even like Uncle Julian.'

'It is expected that one will at least pretend to grieve for a relative,' Lydia said drily.

'It is also considered bad form to toss the body into the ground and walk away,' Rees added. Cordelia giggled.

'I do understand that. I just don't believe we require quite so many black gowns. After all, we will not be in mourning forever.'

'What will you be doing while Cordelia is otherwise engaged?' Rees asked Jerusha.

'I have only a few chapters remaining of *Pamela*,' Jerusha said. 'I hope to finish it today.'

'Why do you want to read that boring old thing?' Cordy asked dismissively.

'I want to find out what happens.'

'I can tell you. She's ruined and has a miserable life. The End.'

'The tale is not quite so simple as all that,' Jerusha protested. 'In fact, she isn't ruined. She successfully defends her virtue.'

'The Lord marries her in the end,' Lydia said.

'Mother!' Jerusha cried. 'You shouldn't have told me.'

'Surely you guessed,' Lydia said, unmoved.

'We have more important matters than books to discuss,' Rees said impatiently. Lydia nodded.

'Cordelia,' she said sternly.

'What did I do now?' her sister asked. 'I hate it when you speak to me like that.'

'We saw you slipping out of the house last night,' Rees said.

'What? I didn't,' Cordelia cried. Rees could almost believe her surprise was genuine.

'We know you've been meeting Mr Edward Bartlett,' Lydia said.

'No, I haven't,' Cordelia said, shooting an angry frown at Jerusha.

'You knew?' Rees stared at his daughter in disappointment.

'Cordy made me promise not to tell.' Jerusha couldn't meet his gaze.

'She didn't break your confidence,' Rees told Cordelia. 'We discovered your reckless behavior another way.'

'What you are doing is very dangerous,' Lydia scolded her sister.

'No, it's not. Eddy would never hurt me.'

'Your reputation—' Lydia began.

'My reputation? My reputation? What about my father's reputation? He's made it impossible for me to see the man I love.'

'Please, Cordy,' Lydia said coolly, 'don't be so melodramatic.'

'But it is true.'

Lydia sighed. 'Cordelia, you must cease these late-night rendezvous with that young man. Immediately. Your behavior is rash and dangerous.'

Cordelia smiled at her sister innocently.

'Edward might not harm you,' Rees said, trying to drag the conversation back to the matter at hand. 'But you are abroad, at night, without protection—'

'My father gave me a muff pistol for protection,' Cordy said. 'He wanted his family to be secure. And he taught us how to use it. I am perfectly safe.'

Rees glanced at Lydia as all the blood drained from her cheeks. 'You own a muff pistol,' she said in a strangled voice. Cordelia nodded.

'And I always carry it, so you don't need to worry about me.' Cordy sat back with air of certitude.

'Where is your mother?' Rees asked. At some point, she would have to be informed about her daughter's escapades.

'She has another of her sick headaches,' Cordelia said. 'She won't appear until later, probably not until noon. But Mr Hutchinson is already with my father so I must hurry away, before he comes downstairs.' She rose from the table and left the room. After a moment, Jerusha followed.

Lydia turned a frightened look upon her husband. 'She owns a pistol.'

'I know,' he said. He too was worried.

Lydia stood up. 'It is even more important we identify the murderer now. We must speak to my brother and to Mr Bustamonte as soon as possible.' She led the way to the hall.

'Where are we going?' Rees asked as he put on his greatcoat.

'You'll see.' Lydia tied her bonnet under her chin and donned her gloves. 'Come with me. I hope this succeeds.'

They walked toward the docks. Rees was quite surprised when they paused in front of the distillery.

'Why here?'

'I happened to think that, when we asked for Roark's address, my uncle Julian went straight to a pile of papers on his desk. I think we might find my brother's direction in there.'

Rees was not so optimistic. And would the foreman even allow them entry?

But Lydia marched into the distillery without hesitation. When the foreman hastened toward them to head them off, Lydia asked, 'Do you recognize us?'

'Yes. He' – he pointed at Rees – 'was here Friday.'

And today was Tuesday. With a shock, Rees realized they had arrived in Boston just a week ago. He felt as though he'd been in Boston for a year.

'Has my father, Mr Marcus Farrell, been in to examine his brother's papers?'

'No one's been in.'

'He sent us,' Lydia said, lying without compunction. The foreman stared at her for several seconds and then his gaze moved to Rees.

'You was here when I found the body.'

'Yes. I came to meet with Mr Farrell. I brought the sad news of his death home.'

'Go on up then,' the foreman said, waving his hand at the upper floor. 'Nobody's been in there since the death. Mr Farrell gave me permission to use it.' He shuddered. 'I'd rather not.'

'Naturally, my father is much shocked,' Lydia said. 'And there are arrangements to be made. But eventually someone will come down and clean it out.' The foreman nodded and withdrew. Lydia looked at Rees. Now that they were here, she hesitated to climb these stairs to the office.

'I'll go first,' Rees said.

He ascended the stairs and pushed open the unlocked door. The first rush of air stank of old blood and rum. 'Wait here,' Rees said. He put one arm over his nose and mouth and crossed to the window on the other side. He pushed it up a crack to allow a draft of cold, brine-soaked air to flow inside.

Then he turned. The office was even messier than it had been on his previous visit; someone had been here and had searched the office. All the piles of paper on Julian's desk had been tossed in every direction and now the floor was covered in white sheets.

Lydia took a few tentative steps into the office. 'My goodness, what a mess,' she said as she looked around.

'It was not quite so untidy when I was here last,' Rees said. 'The foreman said he hasn't been inside so I suspect it was the murderer who went through Julian's papers.'

'What was he looking for?' Lydia stepped further inside.

'I don't know.'

Lydia stopped with a gasp and when she turned to look at Rees her eyes were filled with tears. She gestured to the floor at the end of the desk.

The spot where Julian had drawn his final breath was stained with blood, the carpet stiff and dyed dark brown. Lydia inhaled a deep sobbing breath as Rees pulled her into his arms.

Her shoulders shook for a few seconds, but she quickly took herself in hand. Stepping back, she wiped her eyes. 'Let's begin,' she said. 'The sooner we finish, the sooner we can leave.' She righted the small table and put the globe on it. The bottle of rum had spilled and left a glossy brown pool dried over several papers. 'Do you think the murderer found what he was looking for?'

'I doubt it,' Rees said.

'Hmm, perhaps he thought no one could sort this mess,' Lydia said, picking up a handful of papers. With just a few pauses to wipe her tear-filled eyes, she began organizing them into batches.

Rees sat in the chair so recently vacated by Julian and began examining the papers that had fallen to the floor. Almost every piece of paper he picked up was an invoice, an unpaid invoice. When he looked at the stacks Lydia had begun sorting into, he saw the unpaid accounts was the biggest pile by far.

'Why haven't these been paid?' Lydia asked. 'Some of these bills go back months. And yet,' she went on, holding up a fistful of paper, 'the distillery is making money. Lots of money. It is well able to pay its accounts and still show a tidy profit.'

'I don't know,' Rees said absently. 'We know your father lost a lot of money at Mrs Lunn's. Maybe that's why he wanted to sell.' He had decided to abandon the papers on the desk and move to the stacks on the periphery. 'Don't get too involved in the invoices. We could be here for days sorting them.'

Lydia looked at him and nodded. She put down her handful of papers and moved to the other side of the office. 'This is disgraceful,' she muttered as she began sifting through the ledgers stacked on a chair.

Rees had found a small pile of miscellaneous notes that he thought might prove useful. No invoices or other bills were included; from what he could see at first inspection, these were more personal papers.

'Will. Look at this,' Lydia said.

'What is it?' Rees turned around. She held up a framed drawing of a property; it was something of a cross between a map and a drawing.

'La Belle LeClerc,' she read. 'I think this is the plantation my father owns.' She handed it to Rees over the messy desk. He examined it.

Under the words La Belle LeClerc was the legend 'Jamaica. 1782'. A structure occupied the center and areas around it were marked with words: sucre, indigo, and cacao.

'Yes, I think you are right,' Rees said, peering at the drawing. '1782?'

'I was eight that year,' Lydia said. 'My father disappeared for several months, leaving me with his parents. He returned and then, a year later he left again. He returned with Isabeau. And, of course, two years later, Cordy was born.'

'Julian must have been involved somehow,' Rees said. 'Otherwise, why would he have that picture?'

Lydia nodded. 'They owned the plantation together, at one point. I'd forgotten that.' She looked at her husband. 'Roark is from Jamaica.'

'I'll wager he knows something,' Rees said. He handed the picture back to her and, after another careful inspection, she put it back in the pile. He returned to the stack of miscellaneous documents he'd been working through. After another few minutes of searching, he found something close to the bottom. It looked like the draft of a letter, the lines blotted with cross-outs and ink spots.

'*I know you are in want of funds,*' the letter read, '*particularly as you feel you must support your* vice,' written very large and underlined twice. '*But I will not and cannot agree to the sale of the distillery which brings in, as you know, a handsome profit. If you insist in pursuing this course I will be forced to corroborate Mr Bustamonte's account of the happenings in the West Indies.*

'*I warn you, brother, do not pursue this course.*'

'I guess Julian warned your father not to sell the distillery,' Rees said, handing Lydia the paper. She read the letter and looked up, her mouth pinched.

'Not just warned him. Threatened him. This note certainly gives my father reason to murder his brother.'

'Reason, perhaps, but that alone does not make him the murderer,' Rees said. 'James's address is on the back side.' Lydia flipped the paper.

'I know this address,' she said. 'He had a school friend who lived here. I should have thought of this young man. What was his name?' She stared over Rees's head as she tried to bring it to mind. 'Franklin something.'

'James may not even be staying there anymore,' Rees said.

'But perhaps they'll know where he went,' Lydia said hopefully.

'At least we have a place to begin,' Rees agreed.

THIRTY-TWO

When they left the distillery, they walked north. Rees could see this section of Boston was in transition. Many mansions remained but some were beginning to display an air of neglect, like a ball gown trimmed with fraying lace. He supposed all of the wealthy would soon live on Beacon in the new estates designed by Charles Bullfinch.

The address they had found brought them to a house designed in the neo-classical style with large white pillars and statuary in the front garden. The butler put them in an elegant drawing room to wait while he fetched the master of the house. Lydia's memory of the name had proven correct; it was Franklin; Franklin Chiltern. When he descended the stairs and entered the room, he rushed across the floor with hands outstretched. He was a small round man with bright eyes and almost no hair. 'Lydia. My goodness, I haven't seen you for many years. But it isn't Miss Farrell anymore, is it?' he asked, turning to inspect Rees with an expression of frank curiosity.

'No. This is my husband, Will Rees.'

'Delighted,' said Mr Chiltern, pumping Rees's hand enthusiastically. 'Come, sit down, and take some refreshment.'

Rees and Lydia followed Mr Chiltern to a couch and matching chairs. Although the furniture looked expensive, Rees noticed some careful darns on the seat upholstery.

'I am surprised to find you still in residence here,' Lydia said.

'I never married,' Mr Chiltern said. 'When my parents found this house difficult to manage in their declining years, I returned home to care for them.' He rang for tea and then gave Lydia and Rees his full attention.

'We found your address in Uncle Julian's papers,' Lydia said. 'We thought you might know where James is living now. Is he here?'

Mr Chiltern's expression became very grave. 'He was for a time. But he . . .' He paused and cleared his throat. 'I'm not sure where he went when he left here.' He paused as a maid brought in a tray with tea and a few small cakes. When Rees picked one up, it was hard. Stale. Yesterday's baking at the most recent. But the tea was hot.

'What happened?' Lydia asked.

'I believe James quarreled with your father. Not too surprising since James's youth was punctuated with arguments, but this one was especially bad. He told me his father threatened to disinherit him. James threw the threat back in his father's face. He said he didn't care. He did not want to take one penny of that blood money.'

'That must have infuriated my father,' Lydia said.

Mr Chiltern nodded. 'I'm sure. But when James came to stay here, I must admit I felt a certain amount of sympathy with your father. James spent all his time drinking in his bedchamber. I finally asked him to leave.'

'Do you know where he went?' Rees asked.

Mr Chiltern shook his head without looking at them.

'He said something about going to one of those boarding houses that caters to seamen. I believe the one he had in mind was located near Long Wharf.'

'Oh dear,' Lydia said. 'There are so many boarding houses. And we were just near there.' Rees nodded. Not only had they just been in that neighborhood, but Long Wharf was within a ten- or fifteen-minute walk of the distillery. James could easily have gone to the business, murdered his uncle, and returned to his boarding house, almost unnoticed. The entire visit, murder and all, would have taken less than an hour. Although, at this point, Rees thought James had more reason to murder his father than his Uncle Julian.

Rees glanced at his wife. Would she prefer suspecting her brother to suspecting her sister?

'I am quite comfortable here,' Mr Chiltern was saying in answer to Lydia's question. 'Several of my neighbors have decided to move to Beacon Hill as soon as their new residences are completed. But I was born in this house. I expect I will die in this house. It suits me.'

After exchanging a few more pleasantries, Lydia thanked Mr Chiltern and rose to her feet. He followed his guests to the door. Rees suspected Mr Chiltern had few guests. As they stepped out into the portico, Mr Chiltern invited them to return. 'If only to share any news about James,' he said, his forehead furrowing with concern. 'I did give him some money . . .'

'Of course,' Lydia promised, taking Rees's arm.

In silence, they walked to the street. 'I don't think he is doing well,' Lydia said.

'What does he do for a living?' Rees asked.

'I don't know.' She smiled at her husband. 'You would not believe it to look at him now but as a boy he had a mop of curly hair. I envied him those ringlets.'

Rees laughed. 'I liked him, curls or no.' He paused. He wanted to initiate a conversation about James but he couldn't think of a good way to begin. They walked for a few minutes in silence.

'But he lied to us,' Lydia said. 'I think he knows exactly where my brother is living.'

Rees nodded. 'And James lives close to the distillery.'

'It would have been easy for him to murder my uncle,' Lydia said bleakly.

Rees blew out a breath of relief.

'Yes, I thought of that,' he said. 'But why would he do it?'

'I can think of a reason,' Lydia said. 'But it would mean James lied to us. My father said he had not disowned my brother, that he was still considering it. Right now, his will leaves everything to James, including the responsibility for my stepmother and for Cordy. If James is disinherited, or if he dies first, everything would go to Julian. James might have decided to remove the other male heir.' Her voice trembled and ended in a suppressed sob. Rees drew her arm through his, understanding she needed comfort. She did not want to think so terrible of her brother.

'I wondered if James lied,' Rees admitted. 'Where is your stepmother in all of this? Your father does not plan to leave her anything?'

'My father has no confidence in the female brain,' Lydia said sourly, after a few seconds composing herself. 'I would guess she is mentioned third, if at all, and will inherit only once all the male heirs are dead or unavailable.'

Rees's thoughts were running ahead. 'Are your stepmother and Cordy in danger from the killer?'

Lydia considered the question for several seconds. 'No, I don't think so. Cordy has her dowry of course. Isabeau may have money of her own. I do not know. But they will inherit nothing from my father. Not unless there is no male heir.'

'We know your father and his brother were fighting over the future of the distillery,' Rees said. 'But I am having a hard time believing your father would kill Julian over it?'

'Not over the distillery, perhaps,' Lydia said. 'But if Julian knew something—'

'And threatened Marcus with it,' Rees agreed with a nod.

'But why now?' Lydia wondered. 'Julian must have known my father's secret for some time. I can scarcely believe Julian cared so much about the distillery that he would ruin my father over it.'

'He must have,' Rees said. 'Your father believed him. When Julian threatened Marcus over the proposed sale, your father gave in.'

'True. This certainly does not look good for my father,' Lydia murmured.

Rees nodded.

'No. But we haven't completed our investigation yet. Is there anyone else who might benefit from Julian's death?'

Lydia shook her head. 'I don't know. I doubt it, though. He owned nothing. My father took everything from him.'

The majority of the boarding houses frequented by the sailors could scarcely be dignified by the name. Most were so ramshackle Rees found it hard to understand how they remained standing. Some were dirty, a few scrubbed to a sparkling cleanliness. But no matter who they asked, no one had heard of James Farrell.

Finally, as the sun climbed to the zenith, Rees and Lydia set off for home. Footsore and weary, they began the long walk to State Street. As they trudged west, through the narrow lanes where the brick walls loomed over the crowded streets, Rees saw a familiar yellow jacket emerging from a doorway ahead. A black cloak had been thrown over the canary-colored shoulders, but it served only to make the bright jacket more visible.

Grasping Lydia's arm, Rees pointed. They began hurrying after the man and for a few streets Rees was able to keep the yellow collar, bright over the dark cloak, in sight. Roark – or Benicio – never turned around or gave any sign that he knew they were following him. Gradually, they narrowed the distance. But when their quarry turned onto a wider main street, he disappeared.

Almost ready to swear with frustration, Rees looked from side to side. But the man was gone, swallowed up by the mass of people.

THIRTY-THREE

'At least we now have a place to look for Mr Bustamonte,' Lydia consoled Rees as they walked home.

'I suppose,' he said glumly. 'I expect I'll have to set up camp outside and wait for him. And I know, if he sees me there, he will run. Again.'

'He's afraid,' Lydia said. 'And I don't blame him. Benicio has already been shot. Or will it be Benicio you are waiting for? In any case, the man we are pursuing knows someone is after him with intent to do him harm. I think if we can convince him we do not intend to hurt him, we will have a better chance of persuading him to speak with us.'

'And how are we supposed to do that?' Rees asked in frustration.

'I'm not sure yet,' Lydia said. 'I'm still thinking.'

They arrived at the house just before the midday meal. Lydia barely had time to smooth her hair before they were called into the dining room. Both Mr and Mrs Farrell took their places at the table. Lydia's father still did not look healthy, but Rees was not sure whether he was ill or pale from grief. Probably the latter since the funeral was scheduled for the following afternoon.

'Where have you been going every day?' Mrs Farrell asked as soon as everyone was settled.

'I hope you are not meddling,' Mr Farrell warned them.

'I've been showing him Boston,' Lydia said, darting a quick glance at her husband.

Well, that was true, Rees thought, although not in the manner either Mr or Mrs Farrell expected.

'Boston has much to recommend it,' Isabeau agreed.

For a moment, there was silence. No one wanted to mention the approaching funeral. Then Jerusha burst into speech.

'I'd like to visit the school again,' she said brightly.

'Why?' Cordy asked. 'Why do you want to visit that dreary place?'

'It is not all that interesting watching as you are fitted for one gown after another,' Jerusha retorted. 'And I have seen almost nothing of Boston.'

Rees and Lydia exchanged guilty glances. 'I am so sorry,' Rees began.

'I will gladly offer you my seat in Mr Hutchinson's carriage this afternoon,' Cordelia offered with an impish smile. 'Your last chance to accompany him.'

Jerusha rolled her eyes. 'No thank you. Anyway, he wishes to see you. Not me.'

'He does not find me all that interesting,' Cordelia said indifferently. 'He prefers talking to my mother. He told me the last time we went out that I was terribly young. And it was not a compliment.' Her mother smiled. Before she could respond, Mr Farrell spoke.

'He will always be able to support you, Cordy. Perhaps if you made more of an attempt to please him?' He did not reprove her with his usual zeal. Startled by his lackluster tone, Lydia turned to look at him. He managed a faint smile. 'Don't worry, daughter. I am not ready to turn up my toes quite yet. But I confess to feeling a certain melancholy. Now that Julian is gone, I am the last of my generation left alive. I am the only one who remembers my childhood.' He heaved a sigh.

Lydia gaped at her father in astonishment.

'You have never spoken of it,' she said. 'You always preferred to keep it in the past. The past is the past, isn't that what you said?'

'That is so,' he admitted. 'But now, with Julian's death, I realize I am mortal too. And once I am gone, no one will know what it was like, growing up in my family. That hardscrabble life . . .'

Rees, surprised, eyed Mr Farrell with sympathy.

'Why don't we arrange a drive through Boston?' Mrs Farrell said. 'After the funeral, of course. We can take the carriage and show everyone the sights.'

Silence greeted her proposal. Rees thought it inappropriate. Lydia stared at her stepmother in shock.

'Really, Isabeau,' she murmured.

As the servants brought in the plates, Mr Farrell said, 'I don't feel well enough to participate. Especially not now, not so close to my brother's funeral. But I think it is a grand idea. Jerusha should see something of Boston, particularly if she plans to attend school here.' He glanced at his wife. 'Julian certainly wouldn't mind.'

'Well, I would like to do that,' Cordy said candidly. 'I haven't attended a party for months and now that we will be in mourning it will be longer still until I see my friends. By the time everything is back to normal, no one will want to marry me. I will be too old.'

That was so patently ridiculous that everyone, including her father, burst out laughing. Cordy pushed her plate away and sat back, her lips pressed together in an affronted line.

'Well, if you're going to mock me.'

'Really, Cordy,' Lydia said with fond exasperation, 'don't be silly. It won't matter if you are ten years older. You are such a beauty you will always receive offers. Besides, if you wait a little longer, that young man you are so interested in will be much closer to earning enough to support a wife.'

Cordelia tried to remain petulant, but she could not help smiling.

'Oh, all right. But it is hard to always stay home and never have any fun,' she added wistfully.

Rees and Lydia exchanged a glance. Cordelia was out, somewhere, almost every day, openly or in secret.

'Don't worry,' Lydia said. 'People's memories are short, and mourning doesn't last forever. I promise you, you'll be attending parties soon.'

For a minute or two, there was no sound but the scrape of cutlery on plates. Then Mrs Farrell turned to Lydia. 'Have you spoken with your brother again?'

'No. Why?' Lydia asked, looking at her stepmother.

'I just wondered. You were once so close,' Mrs Farrell said. 'I haven't seen my brothers since I was nineteen.' She heaved a sigh.

'In Jamaica?' Rees asked.

Isabeau shook her head. 'Saint-Domingue. My parents sent all of us away, for our own safety. Slave revolts. I could kill that Touissant L'Ouverture.'

'You've never been back?' Lydia asked. Isabeau shook her head.

'No. Someday, I hope. My brothers went to France for their schooling, but they at least returned home. I've never been and—'

'Do you have James's direction?' Mr Farrell asked Lydia, interrupting his wife. She turned a look of annoyance upon him.

'He didn't leave it with me,' Lydia said truthfully.

'When James left, he did not tell me where he was going,' Mr Farrell said. 'I didn't ask, foolishly, I suppose. Now I have no idea where he is.' He sighed heavily, startling another surprised expression from Lydia.

'He told me you threw him out of the house,' Lydia said.

'I was extremely angry,' he said to her. 'I told him I never wanted to see him again.'

'Did you put a notice in the newspaper about the funeral?' Lydia asked. Her father nodded. 'James will see it and I know he'll wish to attend.'

'But surely,' Mrs Farrell said, glancing from her husband to her stepdaughter, 'it is too late for any kind of a rapprochement? You've already disinherited him.'

Marcus Farrell looked down at the table and did not reply. Rees and Lydia exchanged a glance. Marcus had told them he had not disinherited James, not yet anyway.

'I doubt James will care about that,' Lydia said into the awkward silence.

Mrs Farrell shook her head. 'He would be a fool not to,' she said.

'Well, I would like to see him,' Cordy announced. 'He is the only brother I have.'

When Rees and Lydia retired to her bedchamber, and were finally alone, Rees asked curiously, 'Why didn't you tell them about James' friend, Franklin Chiltern?'

'For the same reason I did not betray my father to his wife. He told us he did not disinherit my brother.'

'I noticed that. But your stepmother believes he did. Your father lied to us.'

'Or to her. Until we know which it is, I will say nothing to either one. After all,' she pointed out reluctantly, 'although it now appears unlikely my father is Roark's murderer, he is involved. Somehow.'

'We have not learned enough yet about Julian's death to say . . .' Rees began. He stopped when Lydia turned an anguished glance upon him.

'Yes, I know. And what if my father threatens Mr Chiltern?'

Breathing a silent sigh of relief, Rees nodded in agreement. 'Or Roark Bustamonte. We still don't know how he fits into all of this.'

'Yes. That young man is still in danger. I don't want anything to happen to him.'

'Especially before we speak to him,' Rees said drily.

A soft scratching on the door broke into the conversation. 'Come in,' Lydia said. Rees thought it might be one of the maids but instead it was Jerusha.

'Is Cordy still with the dressmaker?' Rees asked. Now the poor woman was hurrying to complete the mourning gowns.

'No, she is with Mr Hutchinson,' Jerusha said. 'I don't know why she agrees to join him on these drives. I doubt either one enjoys it; she certainly doesn't.'

'It is an excursion of a sort,' Lydia replied. 'She does not want to remain home all the time.'

'Are you bored?' Rees asked his daughter. She shook her head.

'I wanted to tell you – I don't need to drive around Boston. Or visit the school once again. I just wanted to . . .' She paused and stared at her parents beseechingly.

'I understand,' Lydia said. 'Cordelia is strong-willed and deter-mined. She tends to drag people along with her, doing what she wishes.'

'Yes,' Jerusha said gratefully. 'That's it exactly. It is surprising. I have brothers and sisters but all together they do not absorb as much of my time as Cordy.' She glanced at Lydia and, afraid she had given offense, said quickly, 'I do like your sister. It has been mostly fun staying with her. But I never seem to have any time to think my own thoughts.' The last words rose almost into a wail. 'I know you are looking into the murders and may not want me with you. But I am content to wait at a coffeehouse or something. I'll bring my book.'

'I hope it won't be necessary to abandon you in a coffeehouse,' Rees said with a chuckle.

'I'm glad you told us,' Lydia said.

'She is already cross with me for, as she put it, betraying her confidences,' Jerusha said.

'But you didn't,' Rees said.

'She doesn't believe that,' Jerusha said. She looked from one parent to another. 'I did try to stop her from sneaking out of the house, but she is determined to spend time with her Eddy.'

'I hope that is all she has been doing,' Rees muttered under his breath.

'I hope you are not joining her,' Lydia said in sudden concern. Jerusha shook her head.

'No. But Cordy talks about him all the time. Truly, I already almost dislike him.'

Laughing, Lydia said, 'Go on. Enjoy your time without Cordelia.' Jerusha nodded and fled.

'You don't really believe Cordelia is the murderer, do you?' Lydia asked Rees anxiously. 'I know she is spoiled but she is so young . . .' She and Rees had seen other young murderers.

'N-no,' Rees said without conviction. 'You must admit, though, that Cordelia had as much opportunity to shoot both Benicio and Julian as your father or James did. I just don't know why she would. Both your father and your brother could have a financial incentive. But Cordy?'

'Cordy will not inherit,' Lydia agreed, her expression lightening. 'Not unless everyone else is gone and even then . . .'

Rees, who wondered if money was at the root of the murders,

given it so often was, nodded. 'Even then she would be a ward of a relative,' he said.

'Probably us,' Lydia agreed. Rees sighed. 'Still, I would like to meet Mr Bartlett. Isabeau did not even introduce me before.'

'Just to be sure he's a good man?' Rees asked. Lydia nodded unhappily.

'Just to be sure.'

THIRTY-FOUR

When Rees and Lydia went down to breakfast the following morning, only Jerusha and Cordelia were present. They had their heads together and were giggling so Rees guessed Jerusha was once more in charity with her cousin.

'Were you close to your uncle?' Rees asked. Such hilarity seemed inappropriate on the day of her uncle's funeral. But then, he had not gotten the impression Cordelia knew Julian well. She shook her head with a moue of regret.

'Not really. My father and his brother rarely spoke to one another and my mother did not favor Uncle Julian.'

'That does not mean the rest of us are not grieving,' Lydia said. Rees touched her wrist comfortingly. He knew she had been awake most of the night. She looked it now; her eyes were heavy lidded and smudged with shadows. She poured herself a cup of tea and held it to her lips with trembling hands.

Rees looked at the coffeepot. He was finding it difficult to surrender taking sugar in his coffee. Finally, he poured out half a cup. He added almost as much cream and one tiny fragment of sugar. When he took a sip he shuddered a little but decided he could choke it down. He helped himself to breakfast: bacon, eggs, and fried potatoes. Lydia ate only a small piece of toast.

Rees could not bear staying inside, not for the morning anyway. The family would be busy with last-minute arrangements for the funeral. Few had come to view the body the last few days; probably everyone who intended to support the family would come today. Many would arrive early and expect refreshments and conversation.

Rees shivered at the prospect of making polite conversation with strangers and drank the last drops of his coffee. He would much rather stand in the cold and wait for Roark to appear.

'I'll return in time for the service,' he promised Lydia.

'I wish I were going with you,' she said, rising to her feet. She walked him to the door and watched as he donned his disguise: a jacket instead of his greatcoat and a scarf wrapped around his neck for warmth. Instead of his hat, he wore a flat-brimmed cap. In these, he hoped to fit in a little bit better.

The funeral carriage, draped in black, was already drawn up in front of the house. Marcus Farrell had spared no expense for his brother. Made of mahogany, the hearse sported gold leaf trim around the windows and the doors. Six matched ebony horses with black plumes snorted in the cold, curls of mist spiraling from their nostrils.

'Julian would hate this,' Lydia murmured, examining the vehicle.

'I guess your father feels guilty for the estrangement between him and his brother,' Rees said. 'It is a pity he did not reach out to Julian while he was alive.'

Lydia threw her husband a dark glance. 'This is Isabeau's handiwork; a grand show of grief to conceal the lack of family affection.'

Silenced by that grim assessment, Rees kissed Lydia and left.

Rees spent the morning leaning against a wall near Long Wharf. His attempt at camouflage was only somewhat successful; he was the object of many curious glances. Although he lingered there, across from the building in which his quarry had disappeared, the man in the yellow jacket never appeared. Rees could not be sure if Roark did not live in the ramshackle building, if he had spotted Rees waiting for him, or if today he had just not left his rooms. It was disappointing but Rees felt he would still rather be here than at the Farrells' house.

Finally, as noon approached, he left his post to return home and change.

When he entered the house, the parlor was already filling with mourners. Most appeared to be men released from the distillery, still wearing their rough workmen's clothes and smelling powerfully of molasses and spirits. Isabeau had been expecting a crowd and a lavish cold lunch had been laid out in the dining room. Rees thought there was far more food than people to eat it. He did not see James Farrell anywhere.

The minister from the church was already present, in the dining room helping himself to a plate. He glanced at Rees but did not speak. At first startled by the pastor's rudeness, Rees realized that, as the minister had only met him once, he was unrecognizable in his disguise, and hurried upstairs to change.

When he returned downstairs, he joined Lydia in the parlor. Unlike her stepmother, who was conversing solely with Edward Bartlett, Lydia was making an effort to thank the distillery workers for coming. Most did not stay more than a few minutes. Awkward and clearly feeling out of place, they remained only long enough to pay their respects, and eat something, before leaving again. And young Mr Bartlett departed, probably with a flea in his ear, before Cordy made an appearance.

When Lydia was called away by her father, Rees took up a position by the wall and watched the people come in and out of the room. It seemed to him that there were far fewer than there should be, and almost all men, and guessed that the social shunning affected funerals as well as all other occasions.

'Mr Rees. Lost in a brown study, I see,' Sally Fitzpatrick said. Rees looked up to see Sally and her husband standing before him. She was wearing a dark blue dress under a shawl. Rees spotted a yellowish (it looked like cornmeal mush to him) stain on her skirt as though a child had grabbed at her to prevent her from leaving.

'Lydia will be so glad to see you,' Rees said as Quentin extended his hand.

'How is she doing?' Mr Fitzpatrick asked.

'Well enough,' Rees replied. He was tempted to admit that only Lydia and her father were genuinely grieving. Cordelia and her mother seemed too concerned about their own affairs to spend any energy on Julian.

'We'll see her later, then,' Sally promised as she and her husband turned to the chairs.

Just after one o'clock, the minister began the service. All the family were seated together but for Rees, who had elected to remain by the wall. He'd liked Julian well enough and thought they might have become friends. On such short acquaintance, however, he felt he could not claim the grief of a close connection.

Marcus and Isabeau Farrell must have agreed. Rees had not been asked to serve as pallbearer, although Mr Hutchinson had been, no doubt in the expectation he would marry Cordelia.

An outsider would never guess Rees was connected to the Farrells in any way. Although the exclusion was hurtful, Rees was glad of it. He was able to observe the proceedings, and everyone in the room, without attracting any attention whatsoever.

James Farrell did not arrive until the funeral was almost over. He joined the few distillery workers still present and lingering at the back. In his shabby cape and battered hat, he looked like one of them. None of his family seemed to recognize him or paid him any attention. He did not follow the coffin out of the parlor, on its journey to the vault to wait until spring. Rees pushed his way through the crowd to cross James' path. 'A word,' Rees said in a low voice as he grasped the other man's arm. James turned in alarm but relaxed when he saw who it was.

'Join me in the dining room, then,' he said. 'I am wicked hungry.'

Rees followed James through the rapidly clearing drawing room to the chamber at the back. It was almost entirely empty and the lone fellow inside quickly stuffed his pockets with food and departed.

James chose a plate and began circling the table. 'I suppose you want to ask more questions about the murders,' he said as he picked up a roll and began gnawing on it.

'Yes,' Rees said. 'I have several.' He hesitated, not sure where to start.

Flinging off his cape, James sat down in the nearest chair and began eating hungrily. 'I did not kill Julian,' he said with a full mouth. He swallowed and replied to Rees's surprised expression. 'Well, that is one question you were going to ask, isn't it?'

'I was hoping to work up to it,' Rees said, a trifle wryly.

James waved his fork at Rees. 'Continue, then.'

'On the night of Benicio's murder—'

'Benicio?' James interrupted.

Damn, Rees thought. He had meant to maintain the fiction Roark was the victim. 'We are not entirely sure who the victim was,' he admitted. 'But it is likely Benicio.'

'So, Roark is still alive,' James murmured thoughtfully. 'Good. Although I am sorry about Benicio. Roark and Benicio were brothers, you know.'

'I know,' Rees said, staring very hard at James.

'You can't believe I murdered him. I know the difference between the two men, for all that they resemble one another.'

'Of course I don't believe that,' Rees lied. He had to admit to himself that James had a good point. 'On the night Benicio was shot, your father was seen at a gambling house.'

'Mrs Lunn's,' James said with a nod.

'You knew?'

'That he was gambling away every penny of his income? And my patrimony? Yes.' James hesitated.

'Yes?' Rees said encouragingly.

'That is one of the topics we argued about,' James admitted. 'He would not be so desperate for money, and so involved in that filthy slave trade, if he were not a gambler.'

'That is true,' Rees agreed. 'But he could not have shot Benicio. Your father was on the other side of Boston.'

James did not speak for several seconds. Finally he said, 'That is a mercy, I suppose. Does that also clear him of his brother's murder?'

'No,' Rees admitted. 'But I am not certain he is guilty of that either. He may have been in conference with Mr Hutchinson.'

'Or it may have been a conspiracy between the two of them,' James said, putting his finger on Rees's very thought.

'You don't care for Mr Hutchinson?' Rees asked in a soft voice.

James hesitated for several seconds. 'No, I do not,' he said at last. 'Mr Hutchinson has never done an honest day's work in his life. And he is far too comfortable with the slave trade for my liking.'

'But do you believe he would commit murder at your father's command?' Rees asked, peering into James's face. Once again, the young man paused.

'I don't know,' he admitted when the silence grew too uncomfortable. 'I think he might but that is a serious accusation to make about any man.'

Rees nodded. 'Indeed,' he agreed. 'But you did not refute the suggestion immediately so, on some level, you believe it might be possible.'

James, who had a bite of chicken halfway to his lips, put down his fork. 'I suppose so,' he said. 'And damn you for saying so.'

'One final question. Do you know if your father has made good on his threat to disinherit you?'

'I don't know,' James said. 'He swore he would, but I have seen nothing in writing. No legal notices. Not even a letter.'

'Hmmm,' Rees said. Although James had claimed he did not want the money, he might have lied. And if he knew his father had not disinherited him and knew moreover that his father was gambling away every penny he owned, why, that was a powerful motive. A motive to murder Marcus Farrell, who was still alive. Rees exhaled in frustration.

'I did wonder if he might have changed his mind when he calmed down and reflected upon my arguments.'

'If you suspect he calmed down, why have you stayed away?' Rees asked with genuine curiosity. He could see James was living the life of a poor man; he was ragged and hungry. Yet, his privation might not even be necessary.

'You mean other than the fact my father threw me out?' After a few seconds of silence, James said, 'Promise me you won't tell Lydia.'

'I would like to make that promise,' Rees said. 'But . . .' His voice trailed away. After his infatuation with a rope dancer the previous summer, and all the drama and pain that had stemmed from it, he had sworn to himself that he would never keep secrets from his wife again. 'I don't know if I can,' he admitted. 'If you tell me, I will decide then.'

James regarded Rees. 'Many men would have lied to me to hear the secret,' he said. 'You told the truth.'

'I am not a very good liar,' Rees said with a smile. James nodded slowly.

'Very well. I will trust you to do what you think is best. I left because someone, and I suspect that Mr Hutchinson who is in this house way too often, tried to poison me.'

THIRTY-FIVE

'Are you certain?' Rees asked, only realizing after he'd asked it what a stupid question that was.

James stared at him incredulously.

'I mean, what happened to make you think so?'

'I always keep – kept – a bottle of wine in my room. One night I came home late and finished off the bottle. It was bitter but I drank it anyway. Oh, was I sick! Nausea and diarrhea. All right, maybe the wine was bad. Then, another night, I found a plate waiting for me. Again, after eating some of it, I fell ill. By then, I was becoming suspicious. I tested it and, every time I did not dine with the family, the food and drink left for me made me ill. That was when I left.'

Rees nodded. Although he understood why James might be worried, Rees did not find the story entirely convincing. 'Why Mr Hutchinson?' he asked. 'The poisoner could be Mrs Farrell? Or even Cordelia?'

'Not my sister,' James said. 'We love each other dearly. My stepmother? I admit, I considered her. But why? Neither she nor Cordy inherit from my father. If I die, it all goes to Julian . . .' His voice trailed away.

'Exactly,' Rees said. James lapsed into silence for a few seconds.

'I have seen father's will. Nothing goes to Isabeau,' he said at last. 'Cordy inherits if all the male heirs are dead. And she is not of age yet, so a guardian would be appointed.'

'Unless she marries,' Rees guessed. James nodded.

'Unless she marries. Then her husband takes it all. And right now, it looks as though Mr Hutchinson plans to be in that position.'

Surely Mr Farrell must have thought of this? Rees stored that bit of information away for further analysis and discussion with Lydia. 'And then you went to your friend,' he said.

'Yes.'

'He told me he asked you to leave,' Rees said. James smiled.

'Frankie is a good friend. I suggested he say that if anyone came asking. You see, I saw someone lurking outside, more than once. No one came to the door but still I was afraid for him. So, I left.'

Rees stared at his brother-in-law for a long moment. He'd wondered how James could survive and now he thought he knew. 'He's been helping you. And he lied to me when he said he did not know your address. He's known all along.'

James ducked his head in acknowledgment. 'I owe him more than I can ever repay. And now . . .' He rose to his feet and began stuffing bread and fruit in his pockets. 'I should leave.'

'But you haven't seen Lydia,' Rees objected. 'I know she wants to see you.'

'I dare not stay,' James said.

The back door opened with a soft hiss and Cook entered with a package in her hands. 'Now, Master James,' she said with affection, 'you know that won't keep you fed. Here is something to take with you.'

'You know Herself,' James said, 'Queen Isabeau will threaten to turn you off if she finds out you fed me.'

'Well, she won't. Will she?' Cook said, shooting a look at Rees.

'Not from me,' he promised. 'Lydia would skin me alive.'

'Well then, thank you.' James took the package with trembling hands.

'You take care,' Cook said with a warm smile at James. 'And if you need something more . . .' With a wink, she withdrew.

Rees followed James from the dining room. 'Are you going to eat that?' he asked, James's story still fresh in his mind.

'Of course. I know Cook isn't trying to poison me,' he said.

'Was Mr Hutchinson here every time?' Rees asked. He had not considered Mr Hutchinson seriously and now he wondered why he hadn't. It was true Marcus Farrell's assistant spent a great deal of time here, at the house.

'I don't know,' James replied honestly. 'I don't remember. But once I began paying attention, he was. Every time. One could almost believe he lived here. Of course, at that point, he was just my father's assistant. We didn't know he was being pushed forward as Cordy's suitor.' He started up the stairs.

'Where are you going?' Rees asked in surprise.

'I still have some things here. Not much. I've sold almost everything. But there are still a few old clothes here; used clothes can always be sold,' he added throwing a glance at Rees. 'And I still have some possessions I can pawn. I don't want Frankie to entirely support me.'

Rees watched James until he made the turn on the landing and disappeared from sight.

Rees waited eagerly for Lydia and her family to come back so he could discuss James's revelation with her. But, by the time they did, it was well after dark and had begun to snow. Rees had been waiting in the breakfast room with a pot of coffee, courtesy of the cook, for some time. As soon as he heard the door open and voices in the hall, he rushed out to greet them. In the candlelight, her face above the dark neckline of her gown looked white and gaunt. Red rimmed her eyes and the lids were puffy from crying. She managed a feeble smile.

Rees reconsidered his urge to tell her about James. He did not want to confide this concern in front of the others, but more importantly Lydia looked too tired. Instead he asked if she were hungry.

'I am far too drained to eat,' Mrs Farrell said, clutching at her throat. 'I must retire.' Calling for her maid, she started for the stairs.

Lydia, who appeared far more grief-stricken than her stepmother, examined her father and her sister. Mr Farrell's eyes bore no sign of weeping, but his hands were shaking. Rees thought his father-in-law looked as though he were keeping himself together by sheer will. And Cordy, tearstained and pale, was swaying as though she might collapse. Since she had not displayed much sorrow previously, Rees concluded that the weight of the grief expressed by the others had finally brought the seriousness of this situation to her.

Lydia looked at her sister and mustered a smile. 'I think we can all do with a hot cup of tea and something to eat,' she said. Taking Cordelia's arm, Lydia propelled her sister into the breakfast room.

Rees felt himself swell with pride. That was Lydia, always thinking of others before herself. His heart almost bursting with love, he said, 'I'll ask Cook to send out a pot of tea and some sandwiches.'

As Rees followed Lydia into her bedchamber that night, he realized he was tired. It didn't seem possible. Few of his activities here in Boston had been physically difficult. But the experience of staying in this household was proving exhausting in other ways. He was so afraid he would put a foot wrong. He could not enjoy his meals because of Mrs Farrell's gimlet eye fixed upon him. Maybe he was imagining things but he thought she wanted him to make a mistake so she could laugh at him later. There was some kind of tension between her and her husband; Rees could not guess at the cause, although his treatment of other merchants probably had something to do with it. As for Marcus Farrell, Rees found him arrogant, self-satisfied and rude. He did not blame Lydia for fleeing her family.

As Lydia went to her writing desk, Rees settled himself in a chair before the fire and continued his cogitations.

Cordelia seemed oblivious to the undercurrents. She was lively and appealing, but Rees judged her spoiled. He wondered how much of Cordelia's attachment to her young man sprang from defiance, on both her and the young man's sides. He was glad Jerusha was a steadier, more reliable girl. He would rather a bluestocking for a daughter than a frivolous one.

Of all of Lydia's family, Rees preferred James. And James himself was keeping secrets. Were they the secrets of a murderer? For the life of him, Rees couldn't see why James would wish Uncle Julian and Roark dead. Now, if Marcus Farrell had been found shot, James would be Rees's number one suspect.

'What's the matter?' Lydia asked, hearing him sigh. She looked up from her letter. She had already written home several times and was now engaged on another communication. She missed her children, despite having Jerusha and Sharon with her.

'Oh, just thinking of the murders,' Rees replied.

Lydia put down her pen. 'And what are your conclusions?'

'That although your father has the best motive, he is not the only one,' he said. 'And others are keeping secrets as well. I am even beginning to entertain the notion Cordelia murdered both your uncle and Benicio and then concocted a scheme to throw suspicion on her father, all so she can wed her young beau.'

'I doubt Cordelia has the intelligence to fashion such a plan,' Lydia said with a smile.

'She has proven remarkably adept at slipping out of the house to meet her suitor,' Rees pointed out.

'That is true,' Lydia agreed. 'I wish James had come to the cemetery. I know he's angry—'

'He says he left home because someone tried to poison him,' Rees said bluntly.

'What? Surely not my father?' Lydia gasped, putting her hand to her throat. She was so pale Rees wished he had not told her.

'No.'

'Isabeau then? I know they dislike each other . . .'

'James suspects Mr Hutchinson.'

'Mr Hutchinson,' she repeated slowly.

'James has no evidence,' Rees said. 'And he dislikes Mr Hutchinson, even more than he does your stepmother.' He sighed. 'Of course, James could be lying. But why? I swear, the murders would make more sense if your father had been the victim. We know he and Mr Bustamonte argued.'

'And my father was estranged from both Julian and James. Either one of them might have been moved to murder by their anger,' Lydia said dispassionately. 'Is that what you think?'

'Well, it is a possibility.'

'Except my father is not the victim.'

'And Mrs Lunn was definite that he was playing cards at her house the night of the murder,' Rees said. 'Moreover, she has a ledger with his name in it to back up her story.' He exhaled noisily in angry frustration.

'Yes, I know. But listen. Maybe my father went to the gambling house on purpose, so he would have proof he could not have shot that young man. Mrs Lunn, oh so reluctantly, would admit he had been at the house all night. But meanwhile, my father instructed Mr Hutchinson to remove Roark Bustamonte. That would explain why the victim was Benicio. My father knew Roark, knew what he looked like, but Mr Hutchinson did not. And who would suspect Mr Hutchinson? He has no reason to murder that young man. Mr Hutchinson has been involved all along, exactly as my brother said.'

'James also suggested Mr Hutchinson is plotting to wed Cordy to eventually inherit, through her, the entirety of your father's fortune,' Rees said.

'Yes. And since my father wishes Mr Hutchinson to marry Cordy, that implies a conspiracy between them,' Lydia said.

'As you proposed,' Rees said. Lydia nodded. 'Is it possible Hutchinson murdered Julian for your father? Or, do you believe your father did that deed himself?'

'My father was home sick when Julian was murdered,' Lydia argued.

'We were told he was. We did not see him until noon. In fact, Mr Hutchinson was supposed to be in your father's company and we did not see him until then either. One or both of them could have left the house without our knowing it,' Rees said.

Biting her lip, Lydia nodded. With Cordelia slipping out, seemingly at will, Lydia could not argue that her father could not do so as well.

'That is true. But it is as likely Mr Hutchinson went on that errand. My father was genuinely ill.'

She was trying so hard to defend her father, Rees thought. Still, she had made several good points. 'It is true we know nothing about Mr Hutchinson,' Rees said thoughtfully. 'He is the only member of this little group whose movements we have not tracked at all.'

'Exactly,' Lydia said, trembling with relief.

'I think we need to learn more about Mr Hutchinson,' Rees said.

'Yes, we do. And we need to speak to Mr Bustamonte,' Lydia agreed with a determined nod. 'We must discover the connection between this young man and my father. And that plantation in Jamaica.'

THIRTY-SIX

When Rees went downstairs for his scarf next morning – he had donned his shabbiest jacket and the cap in his small room – he found Lydia waiting for him. 'What are you doing here?' he asked her.

'I'm going with you,' she said as she put on her gloves. 'I think this will need both of us. And anyway, it will be less threatening for him if he sees a woman.' She put a basket over her arm as her disguise and stared at him defiantly. Rees took one look at her expression and knew better than to protest.

'Very well,' he said and gestured her through the door.

It was still very early but the streets were already crowded with people on their way to their jobs. This was one of those crystal-clear days one sees in winter; very cold, with a deep blue cloudless sky. Rees could feel the chill even through his coat. But as they began walking, he began to warm up.

He took up his position on the wall with his gaze fixed firmly on the door across the street. Basket over her arm, Lydia wandered from shop to shop, always remaining within a few feet of her husband.

'There he is,' she said at last.

'Where?' He frantically searched the crowd.

'Coming through the door. In the black cloak.'

Rees, who had been searching for something bright yellow, said, 'Are you sure?'

'Yes.' Lydia was already starting across the street. Rees quickly followed.

The fellow in the black cloak, with the cuffs and collar of a shabby black jacket just barely visible, did have tanned skin, now that Rees looked at him more closely. Of course, many of the sailors were also tanned brown from their sojourns to southern climes. And Rees, fixated on the yellow jacket, had not looked at faces.

At first sauntering casually along, the man soon realized Rees was heading for him and speeded up. Rees broke into a sprint. His quarry took several running steps, and almost collided with Lydia, who had stepped directly into his path. His effort to avoid her slowed him down sufficiently for Rees to catch up and grab him by the arm.

'Roark,' Rees said.

'Let me go,' he cried, trying desperately to pull away. His face ashy with terror, he stared at Rees. 'Why have you been following me? I don't know any Roark.'

'Too late for that,' Rees said. 'We know who you are.'

'You are Mr Bustamonte, are you not?' Lydia asked. He stared at them both before finally nodding his head.

'Yes.'

'So, it was Benicio who was shot,' Rees said.

'We won't hurt you,' Lydia assured him. 'We just want to ask you some questions.'

Rees looked around. The people nearby had begun to stare. 'We just need to talk to you. Can we go somewhere?'

'Were you on your way to breakfast?' Lydia asked, keeping her voice low and even. 'We'll join you.' When he did not respond, she added, 'You must know we will not hurt you, especially not in public.'

After a few more seconds, Roark reluctantly nodded. 'Very well.' He started forward. Rees kept a tight grip on his arm.

'What happened to your yellow jacket?' he asked. Roark threw him an angry look.

'I traded it. It was too noticeable. I loved that coat too,' he added accusingly.

'You were right,' Rees said. 'It was too noticeable.' He nodded at the young man. 'So. Do you know why someone is trying to kill you?'

This neighborhood did not support coffeehouses, but the tavern Roark brought them to served coffee, tea and breakfast. Lydia quickly glanced around when they entered and, seeing other women at some of the tables, stepped inside more confidently. Roark headed for a table at the back; his regular table, Rees assumed. Rees and Lydia joined him, seating themselves on either side so he could not flee.

The waiter brought a plate of bacon, eggs, fried cod and potatoes, glancing at Roark's companions in surprise.

'Coffee for me,' Rees said. 'And tea for the lady.' He glanced at her and added, 'Maybe some toast as well.'

'And could you wipe down the table,' Lydia added, pointing to the food solidified in lumps on the wood.

The waiter, frowning, whipped out a grubby rag and dragged it over the table. Lydia stared at the still dirty table.

'Who are you?' Roark asked. 'And why have you been following me?'

'Will Rees. This is my wife, Lydia.'

'Why have you been following me?' Roark demanded.

'We have some questions,' Rees said.

Roark took a large bite of his cod and then wiped his mouth daintily on his napkin. 'Why?' he asked.

'There has been another murder,' Rees replied. He was not sure whether he should admit to Lydia's connection with the man accused.

'Julian Farrell,' Lydia added.

Roark paused with the fork raised to his mouth. 'I am shocked,' he said, dropping the fork to the table. 'Julian was kind to me. He helped me when Benicio and I first arrived in Boston.' He grimaced. 'The only man I can think of who would wish to see both me and Julian dead is Marcus Farrell.' He paused, going silent as the waiter deposited a battered teapot on the table and added a mug of coffee, slapping it down so the beverage slopped over. Sugar and cream followed. Rees poured in a generous amount of cream but, although he eyed the sugar longingly, he did not take any. It was difficult to wean himself from the sweetener but he was trying.

When the waiter departed, Roark continued. 'Does this mean Marcus Farrell murdered his brother?'

'That is what we are trying to discover,' Rees said. 'So, I repeat, why would someone want to murder you? And why was Benicio at the Painted Pig in your place?'

Roark's face crumpled and for a moment he could not speak.

'He wanted to go. To make sure it was safe, he said. I heard the gunshot.'

'Did you see anyone running away?' Rees asked. Roark shook his head.

'As soon as I heard the shot, I hid. When I came out, I went directly to the tavern. But, by then, someone else was there. So I left. I was afraid . . .'

'But why?' Lydia asked. 'Why does someone want to kill you, Mr Bustamonte?'

He picked up his fork and moved the food around on his plate.

'We know it has something to do with the plantation,' Rees said.

Roark eyed Rees for a long moment and then, finally, spoke.

'It was my father's plantation,' he said. 'We grew coffee, indigo, and sugar. Mr Farrell was starting up a shipping business, traveling between the plantation and Boston. At first, he and his brother were content with the products my father sold. But somewhere along the line, they began to pressure him to grow more sugar.'

'Surely you don't remember this?' Lydia said. 'You would have been no more than a baby.'

'I was a child then,' Roark said, with a nod. 'But my mother has told me the story many times. And I was old enough to remember the ending.'

He put down his fork once again and stared unseeingly at the grease congealing on his plate. The bread came, along with a lump of butter and a crock of jam. Lydia cut a slice and began buttering it.

'What I don't understand,' she said as she added a layer of jam, 'is why my— Mr Farrell wanted to grow sugar instead of coffee.'

'Sugar makes a man rich,' Roark said drily. 'And Mr Farrell desperately craved wealth. Still does, I think.'

'But he must already have been quite well off,' Lydia said, her voice shaky. Despite all she and Rees had discovered, she held on to a flimsy hope her father was innocent.

'He was planning to marry,' Roark said. 'And this woman had many suitors and desired many things. Mr Julian told me his brother wished to support her as she wished.'

Lydia looked at Rees, her eyes wide.

'That must be Isabeau,' she said.

'For several years, the partnership went well. Then Mr Farrell,'

Roark spat out the name, 'began pressuring my father to increase the number of sugar fields.'

'He objected to that?' Rees asked.

Roark shook his head. 'No, he was agreeable. And he did. But once there was more sugarcane growing, we needed more slaves. Many more slaves. They are costly and my father went into debt. To Mr Farrell, who had begun importing them from Africa. The following year, most of the sugar crop was lost in a hurricane and my father couldn't pay. Mr Farrell lent him more money to replant the following year, with the plantation as the collateral.'

Lydia nodded. 'Your father couldn't pay.'

'That is not what happened,' Roark said, his voice rising angrily. 'That year was a good one for sugar. But when my father brought Mr Farrell the money he owed him, Farrell threw it in his face. Farrell wanted the plantation.'

'That is what your father told you?' Rees asked. He wondered what Marcus Farrell would say to this.

'My father did not tell me this,' Roark said. He examined Rees's expression. 'You doubt me. I have proof; a signed affidavit from my father's lawyer attesting to what transpired in his office. My father brought the sum he owed. Mr Farrell refused it, claiming it was not enough to cover interest. My father promised to gather some more money and pay him but Mr Farrell refused. He wanted the plantation. He offered to allow my father to serve as an overseer. An overseer! My father!' Roark moved suddenly and his plate jumped on the table. 'Mr Farrell was greedy and selfish.'

'Did you bring the affidavits with you, Mr Bustamonte?' Rees asked. 'To Boston, I mean?'

'Yes. That is why I agreed to meet Mr Farrell. He promised to surrender the deed to the plantation if I showed him the affidavits and paid him the sum my father owed. It was all in the note he sent me.'

Lydia's eyebrows rose. 'That does not sound like him,' she said. 'He would argue and probably fight this through the courts.'

Roark nodded in agreement. 'I know. I see that now. And by agreeing to meet Mr Farrell, I cost my friend Benicio, my brother, his life.' His face contorted as he fought tears.

'This does not prove Mr Farrell shot Benicio,' Rees said although he thought, at best, Lydia's father was guilty of defrauding Roark's father. 'Anyone could have sent the note.'

'Why did you come to Boston?' Lydia asked. 'Why didn't your father come instead? He could have faced Mr Farrell in a court of law.'

Roark stared at her. 'He couldn't come. Didn't you know? Mr Farrell shot my father to death not two days after they argued over the plantation.'

Both Rees and Lydia stared at the other man in shock.

'Are you sure?' Lydia stopped, the words sticking in her throat. 'Are you saying he murdered your father?' Her face was white.

Rees reached over and put his hand over Lydia's.

'Did your mother tell you this?' Rees asked.

'Yes, she did. And she told me the truth,' Roark said, leaning forward and speaking emphatically. 'I know you think she was making up stories. But Julian Farrell, Marcus Farrell's own brother, said he would testify that he saw Marcus shoot my father to death so that he might keep the sugar plantation. And that is probably why that monster, Marcus Farrell, murdered his brother.'

THIRTY-SEVEN

I n the shocked silence that followed, Roark Bustamonte took up his fork and continued eating.

'N-n-not my father,' Lydia said. Rees looked at her. Although she had told him she thought her father could commit murder, this credible accusation horrified her. She did not want to believe it.

'Your father?' Mr Bustamonte said. 'Now I know why you are so interested in the murders.' He shook his head. 'First my father, then Benicio, and now Julian Farrell. And your father has so far escaped punishment.'

'Do you have the affidavits with you?' Rees asked the other man.

He nodded but turned a suspicious look on Rees.

'I do. I carry them with me. Why?'

'I would like to see them.' When Roark made no move to remove them from his jacket pocket, Rees added, 'I will examine them here. You can show them to me one at a time, if you wish.'

Roark stared at Rees for several seconds before reaching into his

jacket and pulling out a wad of thick paper. He examined them
carefully and finally pulled the top few from the bundle. Rees
skimmed the first, the paper indicating the debt owed by Michael
Bustamonte, and handed it back.

'It says nothing about interest,' Rees commented.

Roark nodded. 'I know. How he got away with claiming
interest . . .' He peeled another sheaf of papers from the bundle and
handed it over. This one was a deed in Michael Bustamonte's name.
The stamps and wax seals all looked authentic to Rees. Of course,
he reminded himself, it could be an excellent forgery.

Finally, he read the affidavit from the lawyer attesting to the
scene in his office. Marcus Farrell refused payment of the debt and
threw the money in Michael Bustamonte's face. Rees read this
document over twice. It was damning. He no longer wondered why
Marcus Farrell wanted to recover this; it clearly demonstrated his
theft of the plantation and gave him a strong motive for the murder
of this young man's father.

When Rees handed it back, he asked, 'What happened to you
and your mother?'

'We moved in with relatives. Benicio and his family.'

'Tell me about Benicio,' Rees said. 'I know he accompanied you
north to Boston.'

'He was my brother, my half-brother. His mother was a slave.
Fortunately for my mother and her children, my father freed
Benicio's mother before he was murdered. So, we all lived in poverty
together.' Roark added bitterly, 'We lost my father, our livelihood,
and our home.'

'One thing puzzles me,' Rees said. 'You'd met Marcus Farrell.
Several people have told us about the argument.'

'Yes,' agreed Roark. 'I approached him, told him who I was, and
demanded my property. He refused. In fact, he threatened to set the
sheriff on me if I didn't leave him alone.'

'But you have the deed,' Rees said. 'That is a legal document.'

'He said he would claim it was a forgery. Who would everyone
believe? A successful and wealthy merchant in Boston or a boy
from the West Indies.' Roark's voice was thick with rage.

Rees glanced at Lydia. 'I certainly understand why he would
want these documents,' she said.

Roark nodded. 'He offered me money because, he said, he felt sorry for me. I refused. The next day, I received a note suggesting a meeting at the Painted Pig and promising to void my father's debt and return the plantation to me.'

'Wait,' Rees said. 'How did he know where you were staying?'

'He didn't. I don't know how he knew I'd been to the Painted Pig; I'd only been there two or three times, always with Benicio. Mr Farrell sent the note there and Lily, the young girl who works there, gave it to me.' He smiled slightly. 'I sent a reply agreeing to the meeting.'

'Didn't you wonder about the location?' Lydia asked sharply.

'And the time,' Rees added.

'That is why Benicio went in my place,' Roark said. 'If it was legitimate, he was to signal me.' His face crumpled and tears filled his eyes. 'You know what happened then.'

'But he didn't have the documents,' Rees said. Now he knew what the murderer had been searching for. Roark nodded.

'I had them. I knew then Farrell meant to murder me as he had my father. When I saw you at my lodgings, I thought he'd found me. I've been running ever since. And now you've found me,' he added simply.

'Yes,' agreed Rees. 'But this is the important fact. If Marcus Farrell had met you and knew what you looked like, why would he have shot Benicio?'

Lydia looked at Rees. 'Because it wasn't my father who shot Benicio.' He knew what she was thinking; it had to be Mr Hutchinson.

Rees knew that when they left Roark, he would immediately collect his possessions and flee his lodging again, despite the assurances both Rees and Lydia offered him. As they started back to the Farrell household, Lydia said, 'We now know why my father would have wanted Mr Bustamonte dead.'

'Yes,' Rees said. 'But we have proof your father was elsewhere.'

'He involved Mr Hutchinson,' Lydia said. 'Has to be. My brother was right to fear him.'

'We have no evidence so far that Mr Hutchinson is the murderer,' Rees cautioned. 'We could still be searching for someone else.'

'Then we need to find it,' Lydia said.

'Determining Mr Hutchinson's whereabouts will be difficult,' Rees said. 'Benicio's murder was months ago.'

'If Mr Hutchinson lives in lodgings, someone will know if he was at home.'

'Perhaps,' Rees agreed. 'But how are we to find his address?'

'I'll ask my father where Mr Hutchinson lives,' Lydia said.

'Will he tell you?'

'Oh, I'll make up some story,' Lydia said grimly.

'Are you sure you want to do that?' Rees asked, knowing how reluctant Lydia was to engage with her father.

'We must if we are to learn the truth.' She sounded determined.

'I wonder.' Rees paused, thinking. 'Does Mr Hutchinson frequent the Painted Pig? It would be more his sort of place than your father's.'

'We will have to ask the tavern-keeper,' she replied. 'But that would explain why the meeting with Mr Bustamonte was arranged for there.'

'Then there is your Uncle Julian's death,' Rees said. 'We know a gentleman called upon Julian before my arrival at the distillery. If that man was Hutchinson, he would have arrived at your father's house late. Somehow, we must discover when he arrived.'

'My father will not tell us directly,' Lydia said.

'No. We must find another way,' Rees agreed. Lydia looked at him, her forehead furrowed with worry.

'What?' Rees asked. 'What's the matter?'

'I've been thinking . . .' Her voice trailed off. Rees waited. 'If my father contrived Benicio's murder, thinking he was ridding himself of a threat, then he has a strong motive to murder Julian. Far stronger than an argument over the distillery.' Lydia's voice broke. She shook her head fiercely. 'Julian knew about the murder of Roark's father. And he was willing to testify to it. Even my father could not have survived that scandal.'

Rees nodded to show he understood. It was not only a plausible motive but a likely one as well. 'That doesn't mean your father conspired to commit the murders,' he said, although he thought she was probably right. Lydia looked at him, her eyes blurred with tears.

'No,' she said. 'But I think we can agree that my father is still the most likely murderer, despite his seemingly iron-clad alibi.'

THIRTY-EIGHT

Neither Rees nor Lydia wished to return to the Farrell home. Like the sword of Damocles, the threat of questioning Marcus Farrell hung over their heads. But they were reprieved – and their rescue came from an unlikely source.

'Today,' Mrs Farrell announced at luncheon, 'we will tour Boston.'

'What if one of your Society friends sees you?' Farrell asked.

'No one from Society attended the funeral,' Mrs Farrell pointed out. 'Besides, Cordelia is quite laid low by her uncle's death.'

Everyone looked at Cordy. She endeavored to appear prostrate with grief. The emotions from yesterday's funeral had dissipated, apparently leaving no lasting mark. Rees and Lydia exchanged a doubtful glance.

'This would not be just for me,' Cordy said, clasping her hands together. 'Jerusha has seen nothing of the town.'

Since this was true, Mr Farrell nodded. 'I have far too much work to do to plan on joining you. Besides, I would not be good company.' His eyes moistened and he looked away from the others. Rees could not help a surge of sympathy. Marcus at least was genuinely grieving.

'I must beg off as well,' Rees began. He did not want to drive around Boston admiring elegant buildings. He was not surprised when Mrs Farrell refused to accept his excuse.

'We must have a male escort,' she said firmly. 'Besides,' she added archly, 'don't you want to see this wonderful town?'

Lydia stared at her husband with a 'Please don't abandon me' expression.

'Very well,' Rees said, submitting with bad grace.

Mrs Farrell proved to be both proud and knowledgeable about Boston. She spoke at length on every grand structure; what had come before and what it was currently. As Rees had seen several of these buildings during his walks, he quickly lost interest and his mind began to wander. Mrs Farrell's monologue became a steady background buzz that he could ignore.

Could Cordelia be the murderer, he wondered, staring across the carriage at her. She looked particularly fetching today despite her black gown and pelisse, her pale blond hair arranged in artful curls. The scent of roses clung to her in a choking cloud. She chattered gaily to Jerusha as though she had not a thought in her head but her gowns. She looked beautiful and vain and silly, and far too delicate to kill a fly, let alone two men. And Rees could not conceive of any reason she would wish either the young man from the West Indies or her Uncle Julian dead. Although, with her uncle dead, she was one step closer to inheriting a fortune.

Rees's gaze moved to Mrs Farrell. She was flushed with excitement; the outing agreed with her. Was she aware of her husband's dealings or had he kept everything from her?

As the carriage headed east, toward the wharves, Rees's thoughts moved to James. Perhaps he knew his father had not disinherited him? Perhaps he had lied and, knowing Roark's purpose in Boston, had tried to remove a threat to his patrimony? That would be a strong motive.

But James, in his shabby clothes, did not appear willing to surrender his principles for money. Far from it.

Lydia suddenly jabbed him in the ribs with her elbow and Rees roused himself. The carriage had drawn to a stop outside of Faneuil Hall. Mrs Farrell wanted to know if everyone wished to go inside. Rees, who had already visited the Hall in his pursuit of Roark, shook his head. But Cordy was so eager her companions were carried along on her enthusiasm. 'You will see such marvelous things,' she said to Jerusha.

Mrs Farrell was as excited as her daughter.

They had barely gotten through the door when a young man detached himself from his friends and hurried to Cordy's side. He greeted everyone very politely, bowed over Mrs Farrell's hand, and expressed his condolences for their recent loss. Blushing and smiling, Cordelia accepted his attention as her due.

'This is my friend, Eddy,' Cordy said.

Although short – he did not even reach Jerusha's height – Edward Bartlett was an uncommonly good-looking young man with thick chestnut hair and dark brown eyes. The cut of his clothing revealed him as the scion of a wealthy family.

'I wonder how Cordy got word to him that she would be here,' Lydia murmured.

'Do you think one of the servants brought a note?' Rees asked, contemplating the smiling couple.

'No doubt,' Lydia said. 'Cordy probably fancies herself Juliet to his Romeo.'

'Why isn't Mrs Farrell more alarmed?' Rees asked, watching Isabeau smile graciously at the young man.

'How nice to see you again, Eddy,' she said warmly. He met her gaze and returned her smile.

'I thought she and your father were both eager to see Cordy wed to Mr Hutchinson,' Rees continued.

'Yes, why isn't she?' Lydia wondered, eyeing her stepmother. 'Of course, this is a public venue. She will not wish to become the subject of malicious gossip. Any more than my family is already,' she added in a dry voice.

'How old do you think he is?' Rees asked. Cordy's beau looked young.

'Twenty-five or so. His father still controls the purse strings. If they do not favor my sister, I fear Cordelia is doomed to heartbreak.'

Rees turned to stare at his wife. That was not what the elder Mr Bartlett had told him. Before Rees could say anything, Isabeau called them over to be introduced. 'Since my daughter seems to have forgotten her manners,' she said.

'Of course, I remember Mrs Rees,' the gentleman said as he bowed.

'My husband,' Lydia said, gesturing to Rees.

'Edward Bartlett,' the young man said, shaking Rees's hand with a firm grip.

'I believe I have met your father,' Rees said.

Both Lydia and Mrs Farrell looked surprised; Edward looked alarmed. 'I hope he was polite,' he said.

After a few minutes of further conversation, young Mr Bartlett made his excuses and took his leave. But Rees saw, when Cordelia offered her hand, the exchange of a small slip of paper. With a sigh, he realized Cordelia had never intended to obey Lydia's prohibition on meeting her young man. Rees and Lydia would have to keep watch. Again. Only this time they would have to intervene.

When Rees claimed he was too fatigued to continue on the sightseeing tour, Cordelia, who had gotten what she'd wanted from the beginning, made no further demur.

'I daresay we have seen enough,' Mrs Farrell agreed, directing them to the waiting carriage. They would not have been able to continue for too much longer anyway. It would soon be dark. Snow was beginning to fall from a steel-colored sky. Rees suspected that this time they would see several inches, more than the dusting Boston had welcomed earlier.

'Cordy,' Mrs Farrell said, settling herself more comfortably in the cushions, 'Mr Bartlett is from a good family. In another few years, when you both are older and he is prepared to support a family, he would have been a perfect match. But not now. Please hand me the note Eddy gave you.'

Cordy clutched it even more tightly. 'You know his father would not have looked kindly on the match even before the scandal,' she said, the blush of happiness fading from her cheeks. 'He and Father were always at loggerheads and after Father ruined him—'

'I do not think we should be discussing this now,' Mrs Farrell said, darting a quick glance at Rees and Lydia. 'It is not appropriate. Edward Bartlett's note, please.'

'I am comfortable enough with my sister and her husband to share the entire sorry tale,' Cordy said. 'The truth is, Mr Bartlett and my father have always loathed each other—'

'Please do not regard my Cordelia,' Mrs Farrell said quickly, turning to Lydia. 'They quarreled over a business deal. I don't understand all of it but there were hard feelings. It has nothing whatsoever to do with the events that occurred afterwards.'

'Oh, I wish I was an orphan,' Cordelia cried. 'Then Eddy and I could marry. I do not want to wed Mr Hutchinson.'

'Do not be so dramatic, Cordelia,' Isabeau said. 'It is unbecoming. Hand me the note. Now.'

'I've barely had a chance to read it,' Cordy complained as she handed the missive to her mother. Isabeau dropped the paper into her reticule. 'The world hates me,' Cordy continued.

Rees grinned, amused. He glanced at Lydia and saw her answering smile. But, as she leaned forward and put her hand over her sister's, Lydia's smile faded, and her lips thinned into a frown of determination. 'Don't worry, Cordy,' she murmured. It sounded like a promise.

As they deposited their outer clothing with Morris, Lydia asked if he knew when her father planned to return home.

'He is in his office now,' Morris said.

'So early?' Lydia said, exchanging a glance with her husband.

'He suffered an attack of the ague,' Morris said with a frown.

'I feared he returned to the office too soon,' Mrs Farrell said, shaking her head. 'He didn't rest.'

Turning toward Rees, Lydia murmured, 'I don't suppose there is any point in putting this off.'

Rees nodded glumly and followed his wife to Mr Farrell's office door.

He was sitting at his desk, head resting in one hand while the other held a rug tightly about his shoulders. He looked up before Lydia knocked and barked, 'Come in, then. Did you enjoy the drive?'

'Very much,' Lydia said politely.

'What do you want?'

'Where is Mr Hutchinson?' Rees asked.

'At my office. Why?'

'I wished to discuss his financial situation with you,' Lydia said.

'What? Why?' Mr Farrell looked up in astonishment. He was no more surprised than Rees, who turned to stare at his wife.

'I feel it prudent to confirm he is able to support Cordy, should this courtship go forward,' Lydia said smoothly.

Mr Farrell chuckled. 'Of course he is well able to support her. I would not countenance the connection if I thought he could not.'

'Where is he living now?' Lydia asked. 'Does he own a house?'

'He is living in lodgings,' Mr Farrell said. 'At 34 Hanover Street. But he is building a fine house on Beacon. By the time Cordelia is old enough to marry, it should be finished and entirely furnished. Neither she, nor you, will have anything to complain of.'

Lydia nodded, smiling slightly, while Rees stared at her in frank admiration. He would not have thought of couching his question so indirectly. Instead, he would have blurted it out and probably been told to mind his own business for his pains.

'And will he treat her well?' Lydia asked, the words almost wrung out of her.

Raising his head, Farrell stared at his daughter.

'Of course he will,' he replied, bristling. 'I will watch him and make certain he does.'

Lydia nodded and turned to go.

'I thought . . . I expected Micah to make a good husband for you,' Mr Farrell said to his daughter's back. 'I did not expect . . . I did not realize . . .' He hemmed and hawed a second longer and finally forced out the words, 'I'm sorry.'

Although Lydia hesitated, she did not turn around. After a few seconds, she continued on through the door.

Darkness was falling. It was too late to begin searching for Mr Hutchinson's lodgings, although still several hours before dinner. Rees and Lydia climbed the stairs to her bedchamber. Dropping into the chair by the fire, he kicked off his shoes and stretched his stockinged feet toward the fire.

'Cordy and Mr Bartlett were planning another meeting.' Lydia sat down across from him, knotting her hands together.

'Yes,' Rees agreed. 'But your stepmother took the note.'

'Cordy still read it. She knows what it says. We'll have to keep a watch on her, that foolish child.'

A tentative knock sounded on the door. Lydia hurried to open it, startling the maid who was carrying a tray. Coffee, tea and sandwiches. 'I asked for sandwiches instead of cake,' Lydia said as she watched the maid place the tray on the table. 'After eating cake, I am hungry again an hour later.'

Rees ran a thumb around his waistband; it was growing snug. But he helped himself to several sandwiches anyway. He didn't want Lydia to eat alone and anyway eating helped make his sugarless coffee palatable.

THIRTY-NINE

Rees arose early the following morning, a struggle since he had waited by the window until well after midnight. He had expected to see Cordy sneaking out but, to his relief, she had not made an appearance.

Both he and Lydia had agreed they would begin their inquiry into Mr Hutchinson with Cordelia since, outside of Marcus Farrell, she had spent the most time in Hutchinson's company. They hurried down to the breakfast room early to make sure they were already there when Cordelia came downstairs.

To their disappointment, she quickly disavowed all knowledge of Mr Hutchinson's inclinations or interests.

'I have seen him only a few times,' she said. 'Almost always in my mother's company. Or in my father's.' She grimaced. 'When he was still just my father's employee.'

'Huh,' Rees grunted in dissatisfaction.

'We are trying to determine his movements,' Lydia said.

Cordelia's expression brightened with interest. 'Do you think he might be the murderer? Why, nothing could serve us better. My father would be declared innocent and I . . .' Her voice trailed away but her intent was clear. If he were the guilty man, she would not have to marry him.

'What do you know of him?' Rees asked.

Cordelia's lips drooped. 'Nothing. Except he displays an inordinate interest in politics. What do I care who is President? That has nothing to do with me.'

Rees eyed her with disfavor. 'Politics affects everyone's life,' he said.

'We are hoping if we can track Mr Hutchinson's movements, we will know if it is even possible he could be the murderer,' Lydia said.

'I wish I could help you,' Cordelia said, shrugging. 'Truly, I do.'

'Help with what?' asked Mrs Farrell as she entered the breakfast room. She picked up the teapot. 'This is cold.'

'With Mr Hutchinson's movements,' Cordy said.

'Mr Hutchinson? Why?' Mrs Farrell looked from Lydia to Rees and back again. Rees, who had hoped to keep this investigation secret, said nothing. It was left to Lydia to explain.

'We wondered if he might be guilty of the murders,' she said.

'You aren't still meddling in that, are you?' Mrs Farrell said disapprovingly.

'Uncle Julian's dead,' Lydia said. 'Surely you don't wish his murder to go unsolved.' She met her stepmother's gaze and for a few seconds they stared at one another. Finally, Mrs Farrell replied.

'No, of course not. But Mr Hutchinson did not murder your uncle. He was here that morning, meeting with your father. As I told you previously, when you were accusing Marcus of the murder. So, Mr Hutchinson could not have done it.' She smiled.

'And what time did Mr Hutchinson arrive?' Lydia asked, unprepared to surrender.

'I don't know,' Mrs Farrell said. 'He was here when I arose at nine. So, quite early I imagine.'

'That is early for you,' Lydia said, shooting a significant glance at her husband. He nodded; message received. Mrs Farrell did not know exactly when Mr Hutchinson had arrived. It could have been early – or later, after the murder of Julian Farrell.

'I was worried about Marcus. Why are you looking at Mr Hutchinson anyway?' Mrs Farrell asked. 'He would have no motive; he is devoted to Marcus.'

'We just wondered,' Lydia said airily.

'I, for one, wish he is guilty,' Cordelia said. 'He would be the perfect murderer.'

That was such a callous statement everyone turned to stare at her in shock. 'Really, Cordy,' her mother said. 'How can you say such a thing?'

Cordelia, snorting in an unladylike manner, rose from her seat and flounced from the room. Mrs Farrell glanced at Rees and Lydia and followed.

'Isabeau did not persuade me Mr Hutchinson is innocent,' Lydia said as soon as the ladies were gone.

'I agree,' Rees said. 'We know Benicio's murderer was a young man.'

'Yes. He was seen running away by that young woman. Since my father could hardly be described as a young man, Mr Hutchinson is a distinct possibility.'

Rees sipped his coffee and grimaced at the bitterness. 'But why? Because he is working with your father?'

'Or to protect him?' Lydia stirred the eggs on her plate.

'Pardon,' Mrs Farrell said as she hurried into the breakfast room. 'I forgot my wrap.'

'Do you think she overheard us?' Rees whispered when the other woman was gone. Lydia shook her head but she looked worried.

Rees and Lydia left as soon as they'd eaten; Lydia was eager to pursue the possibility of Mr Hutchinson as the murderer. Rees suspected she wanted to believe he had acted alone, without the involvement of her father at all. While it was possible, Rees thought Lydia's hope sprang more from wish than from reality.

'We have only Isabeau's word that my father was meeting with Mr Hutchinson,' Lydia said now, as they crossed the street. 'What if she saw Mr Hutchinson after he murdered Uncle Julian? He might have committed the crime before meeting with my father.'

'That's true,' Rees said. He tried to imagine anyone being so coldblooded they could go to their office and transact business immediately after murdering someone and failed. 'We have to ask your father when Mr Hutchinson arrived.'

'I'll have to think of another excuse,' Lydia said glumly.

Rees glanced at her. 'I know. Let's talk to the young maid at the Painted Pig again. This afternoon. She was the only person who saw the murderer running away. I will quiz her and hope to elicit a better description. After all, Mr Hutchinson is tall and dark-haired. Surely the girl would see the difference between him and your father, a shorter, older man with reddish hair.'

Lydia nodded, brightening.

'We must not forget to ask her if Mr Hutchinson is a patron of the Painted Pig as well,' she added.

FORTY

M r Hutchinson's address brought them to a house away from the center of town, and from the wharves. It had probably once been a farm on the outskirts of Boston but as the town had grown, the fields had been taken over by buildings. A few apple trees still grew in the yard. Rees looked at the frozen brown branches edging the path to the door and thought this must be a pretty spot in the summer.

An older woman, clad all in black, opened the door to Rees's knocking. 'Are you the landlady?' Lydia asked.

'Oh my no. I help out, that's all.' She smiled, her face falling into familiar creases. 'My husband was a sailor, so this position helped me keep body and soul together. Now that he's died, well . . .' Her voice trailed away. 'But you don't want to listen to me. I'm sorry to tell you that the Missus is out.'

Realizing that they were more likely to hear something useful from the talkative woman than from the landlady, Rees said, 'Please, don't trouble yourself. We just had a few questions. I am certain you can answer them as well.'

'Do you live in?' Lydia asked, guessing her husband's intent.

'Yes, I do.'

'Mr Hutchinson is employed by my father,' Lydia said, smiling warmly at the old woman. 'And he is courting my younger sister. We are attempting to hear something of his character.'

The woman's smile faded. 'Come in, then, out of the cold.' She stood away so they could enter. Rees did not feel much difference in the temperature of the hall to the front step outside. 'Mr Hutchinson pays his rent on time,' the woman said.

'Do you think he is a suitable husband for my sister?' Lydia asked her.

'I think Miss Florence would be the one to answer that,' said the woman primly.

'Very well,' Lydia said, leaving that question for the moment. 'We are curious about one night in particular, a night he claims to have been home all night. November 15th. Might you remember if he was here or not?'

'He was not,' she said firmly.

'Why do you recall that so clearly?' Rees asked, surprised by the woman's certainty.

She hesitated and then said, 'Perhaps you should come into the kitchen.'

They followed her to the back of the house. A large fire was burning on the hearth. Rees gratefully shed his coat and held his hands, very cold despite his gloves, to the flames.

Lydia put out a hand and laid it over the old woman's gnarled fingers. 'I sense a certain reservation on your part about Mr Hutchinson. If there is anything you can tell me, I will be grateful. My sister is just seventeen, you see.'

The woman nodded and busied herself for a few minutes pouring hot water into a teapot. She cut wedges of cake and passed them around. Then she sat down while the tea steeped. 'Miss Florence believes – hopes – Mr Hutchinson will marry her despite the fact he is many years her junior. She is a widow, as I am, although,' she added with a smile, 'she is at least fifteen years younger. He had promised to escort her to a fete on November fifteenth. But he did not come home until the early hours of the following morning. I think he was spending the night with another woman.'

Rees darted a glance at his wife before continuing the questioning. 'And you are sure that is the date?' he asked.

She nodded. 'I am not likely to forget it.' She rose and poured tea into cups.

Rees accepted one although he did not care for tea. He thought this woman was lonely, despite her billet here in this house.

'Miss Florence cried for hours.'

'I believe you have answered my initial question,' Lydia said. 'Mr Hutchinson is not a suitable husband for my sister.'

'I don't want to say,' the woman said quickly. 'He is a young man, well set up, and, as he tells it, growing wealthy. He is still unmarried, so I suppose it is not surprising he looks for female companionship.'

'But that isn't all, is it?' Rees asked, eyeing the woman carefully. She met his gaze.

'Miss Florence will tell you how charming he is,' she said. 'But I don't care for his manner.'

'I believe I understand,' Lydia said. 'To him, you are nothing and he does not trouble himself to treat you politely.'

'That is it exactly,' the woman said, looking at Lydia gratefully. 'As he sees it, I am only a servant and not deserving of even a glance.'

'Definitely not an appropriate husband for a young and impressionable girl,' Lydia said emphatically. She looked at Rees before taking an angry sip of tea.

'This is good cake,' Rees said. The woman smiled.

'Thank you. I do pride myself on my baking.'

Lydia took a bite and nodded. 'Truly excellent,' she agreed, cutting off another mouthful.

Rees smiled. He knew she would finish the piece.

The woman sat back with a satisfied smile. 'Thank you, my dear. And I do hope you save your sister.'

Windblown and cold, they arrived home just before luncheon. 'I must freshen up – or at least comb my hair – before we eat,' Lydia said as she started up the stairs. Rees followed, turning to look as he heard the front door open and close. Mrs Farrell and Cordelia, with Mr Hutchinson behind them, entered on a gust of cold air.

Cordelia hurled her coat to the floor and ran across the hall, brushing past Rees and Lydia as though she were being pursued.

'Thank you for a most delightful outing,' Mrs Farrell said, offering her hand to Mr Hutchinson. 'I do hope Cordelia offers you a more cheerful countenance next time.' Mrs Farrell was garbed in black, and the dark color suited her fair hair and skin.

'Well, Cordy is still a child,' Mr Hutchinson said, raising the gloved hand to his lips. 'We cannot expect her to possess the poise and maturity of her mother.'

'You are generous, Mr Hutchinson,' she said. 'More generous than Cordy deserves. Do you wish to join us for luncheon?'

Mr Hutchinson hesitated but, seeing Mr Farrell walk into the hall, he shook his head.

'I fear I have far too much work waiting for me at the office,' he said. Directing a polite nod all around, Mr Hutchinson withdrew into the cold.

Smiling, Mrs Farrell removed her bonnet, gloves and pelisse.

'What did Cordelia do?' Mr Farrell asked wearily.

'She was quite rude. I am ashamed for her,' Isabeau replied to her husband. 'After her initial greeting, Cordy barely spoke to him. I vow, I conversed with him more than she did. It was embarrassing.'

'I am still hopeful she will look with favor on his suit,' Marcus said as he extended an elbow to his wife. 'His marriage to Cordelia would bring him into the family.'

'Mr Hutchinson does seem to work hard,' Lydia said now, in the tone of someone conceding a point. 'Why, Isabeau told me he came to receive instructions from you quite early the day Julian was murdered.'

'He did,' Marcus said. 'He has been a great help to me these last few months. I don't know what I would have done without him. Eventually, I'd like to take him on as a partner. Wed to Cordy, he could take over the business when I'm gone.'

'That would be a perfect solution,' Mrs Farrell agreed, smiling.

Lydia took her husband's arm and urged him up the stairs. Rees went willingly, wondering how it was possible the Farrells could avoid seeing their daughter's resistance to the match. Mrs Farrell especially. She knew her daughter had her heart set on Edward Bartlett. Marriage to Mr Hutchinson would make Cordy miserable.

He said as much to Lydia when they reached the privacy of her bedroom. 'I know,' she said, her brow furrowed with worry. 'I understand why Cordy feels she must meet young Mr Bartlett on the sly. Without in any way approving of such reckless behavior, of course.'

Not for the first time, Rees thanked Heaven for his sensible and level-headed Jerusha.

When they left the room for lunch, they met Jerusha in the hall. 'Come on, Cordy,' she called over her shoulder. With a patter of running feet, Cordelia hurried out of her room. She had straightened her black gown and combed her hair, but she was not smiling. She linked arms with Jerusha and they fell into step with the adults.

No one spoke until after grace was said and the first course had been put before them. Then Mrs Farrell, placing her napkin in her lap with an annoyed snap of her wrist, said to Cordelia, 'You were quite rude to Mr Hutchinson today.'

'What do you mean?' Cordelia asked with a sulky curl to her lips. 'I thought I was polite to him, considering the circumstances.'

'What circumstances? He wishes to spend time in your company.'

'He has no interest in my company,' Cordelia said. 'He forces himself to speak to me.'

'Nonsense,' Mrs Farrell said firmly. 'He tries and tries hard to engage you in conversation, but you rebuff every attempt.'

'That is because he asks questions about politics,' Cordelia said angrily. 'He must know by now I have no interest in politics. Or he speaks about the business, as though I should understand what he is saying. He would rather talk to you.'

'That is because I respond to his questions,' Mrs Farrell said, her own eyes glittering. 'If I do not understand, I ask him to explain. Really, Cordelia, I do wish you would not make your disinterest so obvious. At best, you are unnecessarily rude.'

Cordelia flung herself backwards into her chair and crossed her arms.

'And please,' her father said sternly, 'behave like a young lady instead of a hoydenish child. It is unbecoming.'

Rees and Lydia said nothing and kept their eyes on their plates. But Rees knew from the curve of Lydia's lips that she was glad Cordelia was disinterested in the older business colleague of their father.

FORTY-ONE

The awkward meal continued. Cordy ate little and said nothing. In an attempt at polite conversation, Mrs Farrell asked Lydia how she and Rees had spent the morning.

'We visited an old friend,' Lydia lied.

'How nice,' Mrs Farrell said politely.

Conversation languished as the diners searched for a neutral topic of conversation. Finally, Jerusha jumped into the silence.

'I finished my book,' she said.

'I always thought *Pamela* was a little too ready to wed Mr B. I would never trust him,' Lydia said, seizing on the topic with relief.

'I thought exactly the same,' Jerusha agreed enthusiastically.

'Reading such tripe is a waste of time,' Mr Farrell said.

No one spoke after that. Everyone ate quickly and escaped from the dining room as quickly as they could.

Rees and Lydia left promptly after the meal, more than glad to escape the house. They walked quickly and arrived at the Painted Pig by three o'clock. To their astonishment, the door was closed and locked. Rees stared at it in chagrin. The tavern was always open at this time. A sudden fear stole over him. 'Something's happened,' he said. Remembering that there was a door from the kitchen to the back yard, Rees walked around to the rear.

The tavern-keeper was standing in the yard, his hands held helplessly before him. He stared at the body of his wife, lying prostrate on the ground before him, as though he didn't know what to do. His daughter knelt beside her mother, weeping convulsively.

'What happened?' Rees asked, pulling the young girl to her feet. The tavern-keeper looked at Rees as though he were speaking a foreign language. As Lydia took charge of the weeping girl, Rees added, 'Has anyone notified the constable?' When there was once again no response, Rees followed the alley around to the street. He grabbed a man, a bricklayer by the looks of him, and told him to fetch someone as there had been a death. When the workman shot off, Rees returned to the yard. 'What time did this happen?' The tavern-keeper did not respond. Rees grabbed him by the arm and shook it. 'When did this happen?' The man turned his shocked gaze on Rees.

'I don't know. Sometime this morning. I don't know. Oh, what will I do without her?' He began to weep. Seeing the man was too distraught to respond intelligently, Rees released his arm and knelt by the side of the body. Gently, he turned it over. As he'd suspected, it was the tavern-keeper's wife. She'd been shot, close range, and Rees would wager everything he owned that she'd been murdered by the very same gun that had been used against Benicio and Julian Farrell.

But why shoot *her*? Rees muttered to himself. What did she have to do with the murders?

He rose to his feet and joined Lydia and the victim's daughter. She was still weeping, but her sobs had lessened. Without a cloak, she was shivering with cold and her lips were blue. As men began surging into the yard, Rees gestured to the back door. 'Let's go inside,' he said.

Lydia wrapped a fold of her cloak over the girl and urged her through the back door, to a seat by the fire. Rees took one last glance at the body on the ground before he followed his wife inside.

'What happened?' Lydia asked the tear-stained girl.

'I don't know,' she replied. 'It was quiet. My father was shouting at me to wash the dishes.' She paused. 'When I went through the common room, I saw my mother talking to someone. Then she went outside . . .' She broke down.

Lydia began stroking the girl's back. 'What time was this?'

'I don't know exactly. Early. Eight thirty maybe. Nine? We got busy then and it wasn't until a little while ago we noticed she'd never come back inside. My father went out to find her.'

'I am so sorry,' Rees said. 'So, so sorry.' Sniffling, the young girl nodded. 'May I ask some questions? We need to find this man.' He wished he had realized the murderer might go after the tavern-keeper's family.

'I suppose.'

'Did you hear anything?' Rees asked. 'Like a pop?'

'Not that I remember. But it is noisy here. Why would anyone shoot my mother?' She raised streaming eyes to Rees. 'Why?'

'I don't know. But we will find out.' Rees felt moisture flood his own eyes. If he had found Benicio's murderer last week, this would not have happened.

'This isn't your fault,' Lydia said, directing a stern look at her husband.

Rees nodded although he didn't agree. He wiped the back of his hand over his eyes. 'Can you tell me anything else about the man you saw running away from the first shooting?' he asked. She shook her head. 'You said you thought he was young.'

'He was running,' she choked out. 'Running fast. No old person runs like that.'

Rees, who at forty was probably one of the old people to whom she referred, shook his head. He could still run and, from a distance, might pass for a young man.

'Are you sure it was a man?' Lydia asked. Rees knew she was thinking of her sister who, they already knew, slipped out at night.

'He was wearing white breeches. Silver buttons at the knees. I could see them sparkle in the light of his lantern.'

'What color was his hair?' Lydia asked. 'Could you see it?'

'I think it was dark,' she said. She raised her head and turned to look at Lydia. 'But that could have been a hat.' She stifled a sob. 'I wasn't paying attention.'

'Was he tall or short?' Rees asked.

'Short, I think. And thin. But he was not that close by.' Bowing her head, she began sobbing once again.

'Don't worry,' Rees said. 'We will catch this man. I promise you that.'

The girl nodded but she did not raise her head.

'One final question,' Lydia said softly. 'There is a man by the name of Hutchinson—'

'Mr Hutchinson?' the young woman said.

'Dark hair?' Lydia continued.

'Wavy hair? Yes, that's him. He comes by once in a while.'

Rees and Lydia stared at one another. Although they had discussed the possibility Hutchinson was a customer here, Rees had not considered it very seriously. Now he was too stunned to speak.

'Listen,' Lydia said to the girl. 'Tell no one what you have told us. No one. Do you understand?'

She nodded.

'We will find the man who murdered your mother, I promise you that,' Rees repeated, bending down so he could look into the young woman's eyes. She nodded. Rees wasn't sure if she even understood what he'd said; she was trembling with shock and her eyes were unfocused.

Rees and Lydia withdrew, leaving the tavern-keeper and his daughter in the care of their neighbors.

'So, Mr Hutchinson is a regular patron of the Painted Pig,' Lydia said grimly as they returned to the street outside. Snow had begun to fall; a few small flakes.

'That does not mean he is the murderer,' Rees cautioned. 'She did not see the man running away clearly enough to identify him.'

'She couldn't even tell the color of the fellow's hair,' Lydia agreed.

'Or whether he wore a hat.'

'So we don't know if the man she saw was the murderer,' Lydia said.

Rees cast her a skeptical glance.

'I think we can be pretty sure he was,' he said. 'Unless you believe someone unconnected to the murders just happened to be in the neighborhood at the same time Benicio was shot.'

Lydia nodded absently, as though she were not really listening to him.

'I think we can both agree the same person murdered all three of our victims.'

'But that is important.' Lydia looked at her husband. 'Why was *she* shot? Do you believe she, or her husband, had any connection at all with my father? Or with Roark Bustamonte?'

'No,' Rees said. 'No, I don't. That is why I am so puzzled.' He paused. 'Unless the murderer thought the wife was the witness and that she could see him clearly enough to identify him.'

'Exactly. And there was a witness, but it was not the wife. It was the daughter. So, why did the murderer think it was the wife who saw him? And perhaps more important, how did he find out there was a witness?'

FORTY-TWO

As they walked home, Rees and Lydia discussed the ways that the murderer could have learned of the witness. 'We didn't tell anyone, did we?' Rees asked his wife.

'I don't think so.' She sighed. 'But everyone in my house listens at doors.'

'There is no knowing if the tavern-keeper and his family said something to someone either,' Rees said, smiling at her comfortingly. 'And now that we know Mr Hutchinson is a regular patron here, it seems possible, maybe even likely, he heard about it.'

'And acted upon it?' Lydia asked, turning to look at her husband.

Rees nodded. Lydia remained silent for several seconds.

'I must admit,' she said at last, 'that I would rather the murderer be Mr Hutchinson than my father.'

Rees was not surprised.

'I just can't see my father murdering Julian. The others, maybe . . .' Her voice trailed away.

The snow fell more and more thickly as they walked home. By the time they reached the Farrell household, the snow was falling so rapidly it was impossible to see more than a few feet ahead. The world was shrouded in white and it had become very quiet. The cart traffic on State Street had thinned as everyone hurried home. In the candlelight from the windows, the snow resembled a lace curtain moving in a breeze.

'I wouldn't be surprised if we saw a foot or more by tomorrow morning,' Morris said as he took their outer clothing. 'Everyone is in the drawing room, around the fire,' he added.

Rees and Lydia joined the others by the roaring blaze. Every now and then, as a drift of snow would fall down the chimney, sparks would rise up with a hiss.

'I'll ring for more tea,' Mrs Farrell said, adding with a smile, 'and coffee of course.'

'And cake?' Lydia asked hopefully.

'Of course, cake.'

A burst of giggles from Cordy and Jerusha drew Rees's gaze. Cordelia seemed in fine spirits tonight, her cheeks flushed and her eyes sparkling with excitement.

'I received an invitation to a tea party today,' Mrs Farrell announced.

'I daresay there is a new outrage for people to gossip about,' Lydia said.

Her father nodded.

'There is always another scandal. I hope this means we have been forgotten. Society is important to Isabeau.'

Conversation languished as the wind picked up and began to growl around the house. Dinner was a hurried affair, and everyone decided to make an early night of it. Although Rees was not sleepy, he followed Lydia upstairs. Long after her breathing evened out, he lay awake, thinking. Although he found the town of Boston captivating, he was ready to go home. He missed his children. And, although he would not tell Lydia, he was not fond of his in-laws. He was still reserving judgment about Lydia's siblings. Cordy was spoiled. Whether she would develop a better character as she grew remained to be seen. And James was an enigma. Rees could not decide if James's tale of poisoning was to be believed or not.

Rees fell asleep mid-thought and dreamed he was home. His children were all sick, sick with the smallpox, and in danger of death. He needed to go home to protect them.

He awoke suddenly, tears on his cheeks. Shadowed by his dream, he believed for a moment they were sick. But then he remembered he'd inoculated them and they'd all survived the epidemic.

A faint creak outside the room brought Rees to a sitting position. For a moment, when he heard nothing further, he wondered if he was imagining things. Then he heard the soft click of a closing door. He jumped out of bed and ran to the bedchamber's door. The hall outside was so dark he could see nothing. Wait. There was a faint gleam of light, quickly extinguished, seeping from under the door to the servant's stairs.

Cordelia was sneaking out of the house. And Rees was in his nightshirt and could not pursue her. Closing the door, he hurried to the front window that overlooked the drive. In the dark, he banged into Lydia's writing desk and bruised his hip against it. With a muttered epithet, he limped to the window and pulled aside the drape.

Hoarfrost incised lacy patterns across the glass. Rees used a corner of the drape to scrub a small circle clear. The snow outside was falling in an opaque curtain, pattering against the glass as the wind whirled it around. Rees could see nothing beyond the falling white.

Then a faint circle of light appeared on the drive. A small figure holding a lantern, high enough for Rees to identify Cordelia, made her way toward the street. Although she wore a dark cloak, she did not have the hood up. Instead, she wore a charming and entirely useless bonnet of some lighter color. Rees thought it was pink but could not be certain; the falling snow bleached all color from the world outside. He saw a flounce of the same color as the hat beneath the hem of the cloak. Despite the risk her fashionable bonnet and gown would be ruined, Cordelia wore them to impress her beau.

She did not turn at the end of the drive and walk out of sight, as she had done before. Instead, she paused by the street and waited. And waited. Rees, who was shivering with cold, thought she stood there for almost an hour. He had just decided to dress and go downstairs to meet her, when she turned and made her way back up the drive and into the house. A few minutes later, he heard her footsteps whispering up the servants' stairs and the slide of the door across the carpet. She was weeping. Her sobs faded when she went into her bedchamber and closed the door.

When Rees awoke the following morning, the room was shrouded in a grayish gloom. Lydia, a blanket wrapped around her, was standing by the window. The snow was still falling and all Rees could see outside was whirling white.

Despite the fire burning in the hearth, the room was bitterly cold. When Rees rose from the warmth of the bed, he felt as though he had stepped outside into the snowstorm. He too pulled a cover from the bed and wrapped it around himself. As he padded to his wife, she turned and smiled. She had unplaited her nighttime braid and her dark auburn hair fell almost to her waist in a shiny wave.

'How long have you been awake?' he asked, putting his arms around her shoulders.

'Not long.' She gestured to the fire. 'The maid woke me.' She returned her attention to the white world outside. When Rees followed her gaze, he thought Morris's prediction was probably correct; they would see a foot of snow. Maybe more. 'When I was a girl, I could not imagine myself living anywhere but Boston. Leaving was the hardest thing I had ever done. If I had not been so distraught with rage and humiliation, I probably would not have had the strength to do it. But now I realize I don't belong here anymore.'

'Because of the murders?'

'Partly. But . . . my life has taken several different turns. I never had much interest in Society. Now all I want to do is go home and spend time with my children and my friends.' She heaved a sigh. 'One of my few remaining connections to Boston is gone. I still have Cordy and Sally but with Uncle Julian dead . . .'

'I know you were close once,' Rees said.

She smiled bitterly. 'My father never had time for his children. Not until they were useful to him anyway. It was Uncle Julian who taught me to ride and to drive a trap. He gave me my favorite doll. She must have been fearfully expensive; she came all the way from Paris and had a porcelain head.'

Rees thought of the doll Sharon had been using as a soldier, and that now had a crack on the side, but he said nothing.

'Cordy will soon marry and who knows where she and her husband will settle?'

'We will always return to visit Jerusha,' Rees said consolingly.

'I believe she had decided to attend a school elsewhere,' Lydia said. 'Jerusha fears she will not be offered the leisure to pursue her studies. And Jerusha is very serious about her education.' Rees nodded in agreement. 'I hope my brother is all right,' she murmured.

Rees did not think James was doing very well. He was gaunt and shabby and when he'd left, he'd filled his pockets with food. 'Do you think he told the truth? About being poisoned, I mean?'

'Once I would have sworn my brother was one of the most honest people I knew,' Lydia said regretfully. 'Now? I don't know. What do you think?'

Rees hesitated 'Your brother is still keeping secrets,' he said at last. 'If your father was the victim . . .'

'I know. James would inherit everything.'

'Only if he hasn't been disinherited,' Rees said. He paused a moment, thinking. 'James said if he died, Cordy would inherit everything. I wonder how he knows that. Is there a will? If he died now, Cordy, unmarried and not of age, would be assigned a guardian.

And of course, if she is married, her husband will take it all. Hutchinson would become a very wealthy man.'

'Only if my father hasn't gambled away his entire estate,' Lydia pointed out drily.

'Mmm. That is true. I suppose it would be important to remove Marcus before he loses everything. By now, Mr Hutchinson must have met all of your father's business contacts. How difficult would it be for him to step into your father's shoes?'

Lydia stared at her husband for a few seconds and then nodded. 'Not difficult at all,' she said. Dropping the drape over the window and the storm outside, she crossed the floor to a chair in front of the fire and sat down. As she stretched out her hands to the flames, she said, 'We know he wasn't home the night Benicio was shot so it is possible he did that. But he *was* here the morning my Uncle Julian was murdered.'

'Isn't it possible Mr Hutchinson murdered Julian before he arrived here,' Rees said. 'It would be tight. But, if your father is involved, then he could have pretended they were meeting early.'

'And meanwhile, Mr Hutchinson was at the distillery, murdering my uncle?'

Rees nodded. 'No one would know what time Hutchinson arrived, as long as he made an appearance during the morning.' Rees shuffled to the chair opposite and sat down. As James had said, Hutchinson was always here. Almost as though he were already one of the family; something that was worrisome considering the light shone on Hutchinson's character by the housekeeper at his lodgings. Moreover, besides Hutchinson's connection to the Farrells, he was a patron of the Painted Pig so he knew of the tavern. He could have easily arranged the meeting.

Hutchinson would certainly present a tidy solution to the murder. If he were guilty. Would he have murdered three people at Marcus Farrell's instigation? Or had Hutchinson conceived of the murders and followed through alone? Did he assume that, once he wed Cordelia, he would take control of the company? And become rich.

'How deeply involved in the murders do you suspect your father might be? Do you think Hutchinson is acting at his command?' Rees asked aloud.

'I don't know,' Lydia admitted. 'But I would hope my father has some reservations about murdering his only brother. Although they have been estranged these last few years, they were close once. And they were the only two left of that family.'

'Yes,' Rees said, nodding at his wife. 'He seems genuinely broken up.'

'And James is his only son. Of course, James did not die, only made ill.'

'Your father could not even bring himself to disinherit James,' Rees said slowly. 'Would he harm his only son?'

'Probably not,' Lydia agreed, looking more cheerful.

'But would Hutchinson commit several murders in the hope Cordy will accept his suit?' Rees asked. 'She fancies herself in love with another man. I think she might refuse Hutchinson.'

'Perhaps. Remember, she is under pressure from both parents,' Lydia said.

'Still, she has not accepted him yet. And if the marriage was to go forward, is Hutchinson planning to murder your father the day after the wedding?'

'You mean, now that he knows how easy it is to take a human life, he might continue?' Lydia asked, horrified. 'That means Cordy would be in danger too. She might meet an unfortunate accident after her marriage. Hutchinson would walk away with everything.'

'What would happen if Cordelia elopes with Edward Bartlett?' Rees looked at Lydia.

She bit her lip. 'I guess that would depend on whether my father is alive, for one thing, and forgives her for ruining his plans, for another. I don't believe he would disown her . . .'

'I saw her last night,' Rees said. 'She slipped out to meet her young man. But he did not arrive, and she returned to the house.'

'Poor Cordy,' Lydia said. 'So disappointing for her. Still, I suppose it is a mercy the snow prevented another of her thoughtless escapades.'

'This will not be the last one, I am sure of it,' Rees said. He lapsed into silence as, with a soft scratching at the door, the maid brought in a tray with a teapot, one cup, and a plate of biscuits.

'Shall I bring up coffee?' she asked.

'No need,' Rees said. 'I'll walk down to the breakfast room as soon as I'm dressed.' It was not a great sacrifice. He did not enjoy sugarless coffee at all.

FORTY-THREE

The room Rees had been assigned was even colder than Lydia's bedchamber. He had no fireplace for one thing, and the wind whipped through the small window overlooking the drive, for another. White powdery snow dusted the sill.

He dressed hurriedly and left the freezing box. Even the landing outside was warmer. When he descended to the lower floor and entered the breakfast room, it felt positively balmy by comparison.

Rees was astonished to see Marcus Farrell sitting at the table. He was drinking coffee and had already eaten halfway through a full plate of food.

Rees helped himself to coffee, adding so much cream the black brew turned white. 'Are you going to your office today?' he asked with a quick glance at the white world outside.

'Of course,' Farrell replied. 'Business does not stop for poor weather. I am later than usual, I know. I had to wait until the servants cleared a path to the street. But I shall be leaving shortly.'

'Are you sure that's wise?' Lydia said as she entered the room. 'You've been ill.'

'That has nothing to do with the weather,' Mr Farrell said. 'The ague comes and goes. I feel better now.'

'What if you take a chill?' Lydia asked in genuine concern. 'This is not the West Indies, you know.'

'Have you ever been to the West Indies, Rees?' Farrell asked. He shook his head no. 'It is beautiful country. Very lush and green. Anything can grow in that soil. But disease flourishes there as well. And the bark helps only somewhat. That is why the plantations require slaves. They tolerate the heat, the disease, and they work far better than a white man.'

Rees almost burst into an argument. He remembered his friend Tobias suffering in the Great Dismal Swamp as much as Rees himself. Lydia put her hand on his arm.

Unaware of Rees's anger, Farrell rose to his feet.

'Couldn't Mr Hutchinson come here?' Lydia asked. 'He came before, when you were ill.'

'He would, if I was still feeling poorly. But I prefer he join me in the office. He is already behind in his work.'

'Was he late arriving at the office yesterday?' Lydia asked. Rees stared at her. He could feel her tension from across the table.

'Yes. You may remember he took Cordy for a drive.'

'So, when did you see him yesterday for the first time?' she asked, her voice taut with strain.

'I saw him when you did,' Marcus said. 'When he delivered my wife and daughter home.'

'I remember,' Rees said.

'Yes, Cordy had not behaved well,' Lydia said almost at random. 'It could not have been a pleasant drive. It was cold yesterday.' She glanced at her husband, her eyebrows rising meaningfully.

'Why are you asking these questions?' Mr Farrell asked, bending a suddenly suspicious glance on his daughter. She forced a smile.

'You cannot blame me for my curiosity about Mr Hutchinson when I know you wish my sister to marry him,' she said.

'You worry needlessly,' he said as he rose from the table. 'I have it well in hand.'

He disappeared into the hall and a few minutes later the front door slammed.

'What's the matter?' Rees asked.

'Don't you see? We know Mr Hutchinson could have murdered Benicio and my uncle Julian—'

'Possibly,' Rees interjected. 'I am not at all sure—'

'Yes, perhaps,' Lydia said with an impatient nod. Her hands were shaking. 'But it's possible he did. Yes?' Rees nodded. 'So, I suddenly realized we had not investigated anyone's whereabouts yesterday morning when the tavern-keeper's wife was shot.'

'You're right,' Rees said, staring at her. 'But we don't know exactly when the murder occurred—'

'We know it was early morning. Mr Hutchinson did not arrive to collect my sister until after ten. In fact, it was after eleven, if Cordy is to be believed.'

'We know he was not at the office,' Rees said. Lydia nodded.

'There's more. My father did not see Mr Hutchinson, that is true. But no one saw my father either. He could have slipped out and shot that poor woman, with no one . . .' She couldn't finish the sentence. Shaking her head angrily, she wiped her eyes. With a sympathetic smile, Rees reached over and put his arms around her.

'Look,' he said, 'your sister asked us here to prove your father's innocence.'

'I know,' Lydia said. 'But I doubt he is innocent. I am convinced that somehow he murdered those three people.'

'Perhaps,' Rees agreed. 'But let's return to that point, that your father is innocent. Now, let's look for proof.' Lydia flashed a skeptical glance at him. 'Maybe someone, say, Mr Hutchinson, is trying to frame him. Maybe the murderer did not know your father would be out gambling that night. Maybe the murderer shot the tavern-keeper's wife because he thought she could identify him as someone else; not Marcus Farrell.'

She hesitated, staring at him.

'Really, Lydia,' he said in a gentle voice, 'do you believe your father would kill his brother and poison his own son?'

'I don't know,' she admitted. 'I just don't know. I don't want to believe it. But we know my father probably murdered Roark Bustamonte's father.' She stared at her husband. He nodded.

'That's true. But your father seemed genuinely shocked and grieving for his brother,' Rees said.

'A murderer might still weep over his victim,' Lydia said. 'My father needed money; we know he was taking it from the distillery. And Julian knew my father murdered Roark Bustamonte's father. If my uncle threatened to reveal what he knew . . .' Her voice trailed off and she stared at Rees in anguish.

'We have to start over,' Rees said. 'Go right back to the beginning.' Then, hearing the voices of Cordelia and Jerusha outside, he stopped talking.

'Why did it have to snow?' Cordelia complained as they entered. Her eyelids were heavy and reddened from crying.

'Don't bother trying to keep your midnight excursion secret,' Rees said. 'I saw you.'

He picked up his coffee cup and took a sip. 'Who were you waiting for? Edward Bartlett?'

'I don't know what you are talking about,' Cordelia said, tossing her head.

'I saw you,' Rees repeated.

'Really, Cordy,' Lydia said reprovingly. 'After I scolded you too.'

Rees watched with interest as the emotions streamed across Cordy's face. Although trained from birth to conduct herself with good manners, she was so annoyed she could barely overcome her pique to respond.

'Well, he did not come, did he, so it didn't matter,' she said.

'It was snowing,' Rees pointed out. 'It still is.' He glanced over his shoulder at the white world outside. 'He probably could not get out.'

'Are you finished?' Cordelia asked Jerusha.

'Not quite,' Jerusha replied cheerfully, piling food on her plate.

'Excuse me,' Cordelia said and flounced out. After a few seconds, Lydia rose to her feet and followed her sister.

Rees looked at his daughter. Leaning forward, she whispered conspiratorially, 'She wore one of her new gowns, not a mourning gown either, to meet him. When she returned to the room, her gown was soaked and quite ruined.' She buttered a piece of bread and added jam. 'She is still very upset.'

Rees cut his sausages into pieces. 'What do you think of Cordy's young man?'

Jerusha took a bite and chewed meditatively. 'I have met him only once and seen him maybe twice more. He is very good-looking. And I do not like Mr Hutchinson at all. He always seems artificial to me.' She looked at her father. 'He doesn't know what I am; someone deserving of politeness as simply a servant. He is just short of brusque with me. But Eddy was as nice to me the time I met him as he was to her.'

'But . . .?' Rees prompted. Jerusha sighed.

'It is a small thing, I know. But, from Cordy's own reports, he seems to treat her like a child. No serious conversation at all. I simply cannot prattle about inconsequential topics the way Cordy can. So maybe it is me,' she added honestly.

'He sounds a fine match for your cousin,' Rees said drily. He ate his last sausage and stood up.

'Where are you going?' Jerusha asked.

'Out for a walk. I am already tired of being inside.'

'You should read more books,' Jerusha said critically. 'Then you wouldn't find staying inside so boring.'

Shaking his head, Rees went to fetch his greatcoat. He didn't care to stay indoors all the time, that was true, but boredom was only a small part of his reasons. He needed to think. He couldn't string two ideas together in the hothouse of the Farrell household. There were too many people talking and too many disturbing undercurrents; it all kept him on edge and too distracted. And Lydia, who usually provided a calm perspective, was herself buffeted by the emotions generated by her family.

It was bitterly cold outside, and the wind was blowing a gale. The snow fell so thickly Rees could barely see two feet in front of him. His skin began to sting and the hairs inside his nostrils stiffened. He wrapped the scarf around his neck and the lower part of his face and walked to the drive. Several of the stable hands were still outside, shoveling away the snow. All young men – one could not be older than fourteen – they were throwing snow at each other and laughing despite their cold-reddened faces and chapped hands. Rees stepped onto the shoveled but already snow-covered path and walked toward the street.

Although he had intended to walk to the Painted Pig, he realized that would be impossible. Rees saw only one wagon struggling to drive on the street. In the distance, a lone pedestrian fought through the snow toward him.

Rees turned around and walked up the drive. As he neared the top, someone shouted after him. 'Hey. Sir.' Rees turned. The young walker approached the end of the drive. 'I have a note . . .'

Rees walked back down to the end and took the missive from the youth's hand. 'Bad walk?'

'Terrible. But Mr Bartlett couldn't get the carriage out.'

Rees looked down at the paper in his hand. It was addressed to M Farrell in such flowing copperplate Rees struggled to read it. But E Bartlett was inscribed in the upper left corner. So, Edward had tried to reach Cordelia. 'Thank you,' Rees said. 'I will give this to her.' He knew she would be happy to receive it. 'Do you want a hot drink before you go?'

The young man, really little more than a boy, nodded his head enthusiastically. Rees guided the messenger to the kitchen door. Snow had already piled up over the step and Rees had a difficult time pulling the door open. When he stepped inside, he could hear the clatter of pots and pans and the cook's voice raised in reproof inside the kitchen. Poking his head inside, Rees called attention to the young man, and sent him in. The cook bustled forward and brought the young man into the steamy and fragrant interior.

Rees continued on to the servants' staircase but before he made the climb, he carefully broke the seal and unfolded the paper.

'*My love*,' he read, '*the problem is solved and we are safe once more. The weather prohibited last night's meeting but I eagerly anticipate the next. Your loving Eddy.*'

'Hmmm,' Rees thought, not quite sure what to make of this. He would have to share the contents with Lydia.

Folding the paper once again and mashing the seal down with his thumb – he didn't want his invasion to be too noticeable – he climbed the twisty servants' stairs and tapped on Cordelia's door.

'Who is it?'

'Rees.'

'Go away.'

'I have a note from Mr Bartlett—' The door was flung open and Cordelia's tear-stained face peered out. He held up the cream-colored square. Cordelia snatched it from his fingers and ripped it open so quickly she could not have seen the broken seal. Rees had taken no more than a few steps when he heard Cordy screaming with excited joy.

FORTY-FOUR

Although Rees had planned to descend the stairs and join the others in the breakfast room, he hesitated at the top. Other than Mrs Farrell's bedchamber, the one room he had not entered was James Farrell's boyhood den. With the memory of James talking about pawning his possessions, Rees walked quickly to the door. With a quick glance around, he stepped inside.

The interior smelled of dust and mice. Because the drapes were closed over the windows, the room was dim. Rees crossed the floor to throw open the curtains. The gray light from the snowy world outside did not illuminate the space very well. And since the fire had not been lit for many months, the room was very cold. He was glad he had worn his coat.

Rees looked around.

A regiment of lead soldiers, some with painted red coats, some with blue, were lined up on a shelf. A large bag of marbles was neatly placed against the wall. When Rees flung open the door to the clothes press, he saw a few pairs of white breeches, one with dirt on the knees, and two jackets, one brown, the other black. The left cuff of the latter coat was torn. The other shelves were empty, and he realized James had taken everything else to sell. As he closed the door, Rees glanced again at the lead soldiers. They would bring in some money, quite a bit, he thought. He guessed James could not bear to part with them, not yet anyway. Sheet music for violin was stacked upon his desk but Rees saw no violin or violin case. Since a violin was an expensive item, that had probably been one of the first possessions to be sold.

Everything in this room spoke to a childhood of privilege. It could not have been easy for James to leave this behind when he refused to participate in his father's 'filthy trade'. Although James did not appear to be particularly brave or heroic, Rees thought the young man, if he had told the truth, was showing more courage than many. James was risking starvation for his principles. What a contrast with Mr Hutchinson, who appeared to have few ethics at all.

Rees glanced around once again before withdrawing from the chamber. But, before he went into the hall outside, he thought of something. He returned to the clothes press. He pulled out the knee breeches. They were quite small. Rees guessed these were from James's childhood; they certainly would not fit the young man now. But they would fit Cordelia when she sneaked out of the house to meet her young man.

Would Cordelia look like the young man seen running from the tavern?

He inspected the stains on the knees for some time, even carrying the breeches to the window to hold up to the daylight. But the dirt told him nothing and finally he returned the breeches to the clothes press.

He pulled out the black jacket. Although well-made and of expensive super-fine, James had not taken this to sell yet. The coat's left cuff had been caught on something and torn, a three-cornered tear that would be difficult to mend. Returning this jacket to the press, he took out the brown coat. At first glance, this garment appeared in perfect condition. But when Rees examined it more closely, holding up the sleeves, his fingers went over a stiff patch on the right sleeve. This time, when he held the garment to the light, he noticed dark stains on the right cuff. Only slightly darker than the coat itself, the substance had stiffened the cloth. Rees spread out the coat on the windowsill and examined it very closely, detecting additional spots spattering the right chest.

He sniffed at the stains marring the right cuff although he was already certain he knew what these blots were and was unsurprised to smell the faint coppery stink of blood.

Without a doubt, this was the dark coat worn by the murderer when he shot – she shot, for Rees no longer doubted Cordelia had been wearing this jacket – Benicio.

Rees stared at the sleeve for a long time. He did not understand why Cordelia would murder the man she thought was Roark. Did she even know of her father's long-ago interaction with Roark's father? She had certainly never mentioned it.

Finally, as no answer presented itself, Rees returned the jacket to the press and withdrew from the chamber. He would have to share this with Lydia, although he did not want to. She had demonstrated a continuing protectiveness for her sister and he knew she would fight his interpretation with all of her strength.

He knocked lightly on Lydia's door before entering. She was seated in front of the fire with a cup of tea. Today she wore one of her new gowns, cut in the new fashion so it disguised her growing belly, but made of finely woven wool instead of cotton or linen. The golden hue picked out the highlights in her hair and flattered her coloring. 'Where have you been?' she asked. And then, seeing his coat, she added, 'What have you been doing?'

'I took a walk,' Rees said, removing his coat. 'It is nasty outside.' He sat down in the chair across from her. 'Although your father managed to walk to his office, the rest of us will not be going anywhere today.'

She nodded and lifted her teacup to her lips. Returning the cup to the table with a little clink, she said in a tightly controlled voice, 'I daresay we will be leaving Boston soon. Now that we know my father conspired with Mr Hutchinson . . .' She could not go on.

'We may be returning home soon,' Rees agreed. He missed his family, his small town, and his friends more than he would have thought possible. What was the constable doing now, without Rees to help him? 'But I am persuaded your father is not guilty.'

'What? Why not?' Lydia regarded him unhappily. 'We know his reasons for wanting both Roark and Julian dead. I do not doubt he suspected the inn-keeper's wife of witnessing Benicio's murder.'

Rees nodded. He did not like Marcus Farrell and did not believe him to be a good man. He also thought Lydia's father was fully capable of murder – just not necessarily these murders.

'I admit, there is quite a bit of evidence against him,' Rees said. 'But there are a number of arguments against him as well.' He paused. He knew Lydia would not want to hear the evidence he had found against her sister. 'I need you . . .' He hesitated. How could he word this? He tended to speak bluntly, and he did not want to, not in this case. He wanted Lydia to think. 'Because several of the suspects are your family, you are too close.'

'But my intimate knowledge is also a help,' she argued.

'That's true. Up to a point. But I think you will be able to view the murders and the people we suspect if you step back from them. Pretend these people are not your family – with all the history you and they share. Consider them strangers and look at all the facts as though you were not related to any of them at all.'

She eyed him. 'But I am related to them,' she said. 'I can't pretend otherwise.'

'Please, try,' Rees said, his voice rising in frustration. Lydia stared at him in surprise. He took a deep breath and exhaled slowly. 'The connection you share with them is affecting your ability to think logically. Do you see that? And right now, I need you to examine the murders, and everything that has happened here, dispassionately. I need you to cut through the surface to the heart of the investigation, as you have done so often before. I need you to do that. Do you think you can?'

She stared at him for several seconds. 'I don't know,' she said at last. 'But I'll try.' She straightened up. 'Very well. What do we know? And why do you doubt my father's—' She caught herself. 'Mr Farrell's guilt?'

'Do we believe he bore an animus toward Benicio?' Rees answered with a question of his own. She shook her head. 'I agree. We don't know that Mr Farrell ever met Benicio. But we do know your father had met Roark. That is well documented. So why would he shoot Benicio? The murderer thought he was shooting Roark.'

'As we have discussed,' Lydia said, inclining her head in agreement.

'Yes.'

'But Mr Hutchinson, who we know serves as Mr Farrell's instrument, could have met Benicio in my father's stead and shot him, believing he was Roark.'

'True enough,' Rees agreed. He added gently, 'But that argument could as equally apply to Cordelia. Not James, he knew both Roark and Benicio.'

Rees watched his wife bite her lip. Although they had discussed her siblings as possibilities previously, she did not want to consider either as serious suspects, but especially not Cordy. Finally, Lydia spoke.

'Cordelia is a young girl and I fail to see what conceivable reason she could have for murdering not only two people she did not know but an uncle she loved dearly. However, she does own a muff pistol. She told us that. But I refuse to believe she shot Uncle Julian.'

'Perhaps that wasn't her,' Rees said. 'Perhaps it was James. He lives close by to the distillery so it would have been easy for him to have met your uncle there. He and Cordy could be working together.'

'For what purpose?' Lydia shook her head. 'I find it very hard to believe Cordelia could dissemble so.'

'And James?'

'I know him less well than I once did. I suppose it is possible he had some reason . . .' She hesitated once again. Rees remained silent as she fought through the tangle of her affections. She stopped again and forced a crooked smile. 'I vow, I would have been more suspicious of James if my father was the victim.'

'Yes,' Rees agreed. 'That is so.'

'James did claim he was poisoned in this house.'

'But James could be lying to deflect our suspicion from him,' Rees said. He now doubted this but felt he should keep an open mind.

Lydia nodded reluctantly. 'If James was not my brother, that is exactly what I would think as well. But I do know James and he is not a liar.'

'You *did* know James,' Rees pointed out. 'You knew him as a boy. You have not known him for many years.'

Lydia stared at her husband. After a moment, she slowly nodded. 'That is true.'

'In fact,' Rees said, 'you have not known any of your family for many years. They are almost strangers to you.'

Lydia did not speak for several seconds. 'I did not think of it that way,' she said at last. And then, leaning forward and putting her hand over his, she said, 'What are you not telling me? What have you discovered?'

FORTY-FIVE

R ees stared at her for several seconds. When he did not reply – he had hoped to lead up to his discovery more gradually – Lydia spoke with unusual sharpness. 'I know you are keeping something from me. Tell me now.'

He hesitated.

'I think it is best if I show you what I found,' he said at last.

He rose to his feet and held out his hand. She took it although she did not need help rising from her seat. They went into the hall. She looked at him in astonishment when he paused in front of her brother's door. He opened it and ushered her inside.

She stopped in the center and surveyed the carefully made bed, the soldiers on the shelf and the desk. 'I haven't been in here for years,' she murmured. 'There is a lot missing.'

'James has taken out and sold most of his possessions,' Rees said. He crossed to the floor and threw open the door to the clothes press. Lydia stared at the few garments inside and then turned to him with her eyebrows raised. 'I understand there is a market for used clothing,' he added, pulling out the dirty knee breeches. She took them from Rees and examined the dirt on the knees.

'So, these are the clothes my sister has been using to sneak out of the house,' she murmured. Rees nodded. Taking a deep breath, he pulled out the brown jacket.

'Inspect this coat closely,' he said. She put down the breeches and took the jacket. She studied it but saw nothing and turned a puzzled glance on her husband. He picked up the right sleeve and held it out to her. 'Feel the cuff,' he said. As instructed, she ran her fingers over the linen. Rees could see when she realized what the material stiffening the sleeve was; her cheeks paled.

'Is it blood?' she asked.

'It is,' Rees said. She clutched the coat and, closing her eyes, inhaled several times. He could see her resisting the harsh reality suggested by this jacket.

'Maybe she had a bloody nose,' she said finally, opening her eyes. Rees shook his head at her. Lydia sighed and put the coat on the bed. 'It might not be Cordy. Maybe James . . .' Her voice trailed away. She didn't like that choice any better.

'Lydia,' Rees said gently, 'look at the size. This coat is from James's youth. Do you think it would fit him now?'

'Maybe,' she said hopefully.

'Besides, James left this house . . . what, three months ago? And if he is the murderer, why would he hide his bloody clothing here?'

'Because he thought no one would ever look here?' Lydia suggested.

'The first time he visited this house in several months was for Julian's funeral,' Rees said.

Lydia hesitated. Finally, she shook her head, accepting the inevitable. 'All right. We must speak with Cordelia then,' she said at last.

Rees did not agree. He expected Cordelia to deny any involvement, whether she was innocent or guilty, so they would be no farther forward. But when Lydia looked at him, her lips were pressed together into a thin determined line. He could see she was prepared to fight him on this. 'Very well,' he said.

Lydia picked up the brown jacket. 'We might need this,' she said as she started for the door. 'Come on,' she added, turning to look behind her. 'We should talk to Cordelia now.'

Lydia continued out of the door, leaving Rees to scurry after her. They located Cordelia and Jerusha in their shared bedchamber. Lydia tapped on the door and, before anyone invited her to enter, she stepped inside. Rees followed, although he felt awkward stepping into Cordelia's space.

Jerusha, wrapped in her cloak, was sitting by the window with a book in her hands. She may have wanted to read but with Cordelia here as well, and talking at a high volume, she was finding reading impossible. Cordelia had her embroidery hoop in her lap but she was far too busy complaining about the unfairness of her life to ply her needle.

'What do you want?' she asked ungraciously.

Lydia held out the brown jacket. 'What is that?' Cordelia asked, mystified.

'How can you explain this?' Lydia demanded, thrusting the brown jacket at her sister.

'I don't know what that is,' Cordelia said.

'It is the jacket you borrowed from James's room,' Lydia said.

'But I never—'

'There is blood on the sleeve, blood from the man you shot with your muff pistol.'

'Shot? I haven't shot anyone. I have never ever used my muff pistol. When would I, when I am trapped in this house like Saint Barbara in a tower?' For a moment her sense of grievance overwhelmed her.

'You are not exactly trapped here if you are slipping out to meet your beau,' Rees put in sternly.

'But it was only a few times,' she wailed.

'Once is more than enough,' Lydia said, a knot forming on her forehead. 'At the very least you should have a care for your good name.'

'And what did you expect me to do? Eddy's parents don't want him to see me and my parents, my own parents, want me to marry an old man.'

If the situation wasn't so dire, Rees would have chuckled at that. In his eyes, Mr Hutchinson was still a young man. Lydia wisely ignored Cordelia's digression.

'Did you meet Benicio?' Lydia asked, holding up the jacket.

'I don't know who that is,' Cordelia replied sullenly.

'Benicio was shot in place of Roark,' Rees said.

Cordelia stared at him, her eyes widening.

'Of course not.'

'You did not leave this house and meet him?' Lydia asked, leaning forward. Even Rees found her intensity a little frightening.

'No. Why would I?' Cordelia gripped her hands together so tightly her knuckles went white. The embroidery hoop fell to the floor. 'I don't know him.'

'You swear you did not shoot him?'

'N-no.' Cordelia now looked frightened. 'Why would I?' she repeated.

'You swear you did not shoot your Uncle Julian?'

'Of course not.' Tears flooded her eyes. 'I loved him. Why are you saying these things to me?'

'I – we – suspect you wore your brother's jacket to shoot Benicio and your Uncle Julian,' Rees said with a quick glance at Lydia. 'As well as the tavern-keeper's wife at the Painted Pig.'

'I didn't. I don't know— I've never been to that tavern. I don't even know where it is,' Cordelia cried. She broke down into sobs. Lydia hesitated, torn between her desire to comfort her sister and the necessity to uncover the truth. Her affection won. She handed Rees the coat and put her arms around her sister. Jerusha, weeping in sympathy, glared at her father.

Rees sighed in frustration. 'I'd like to look at your muff pistol,' he said.

'It's in there,' Cordelia said, gesturing at her clothes press. When none of the women moved, Rees went to the unit and opened the door. He did not like pawing through all of Cordy's rose-scented gowns, but he steeled himself. He found the pistol in the back, wrapped in a cloth. It appeared unused and he smelled no gunpowder. But, he thought, the gun could also have been recently cleaned.

'I swear I did not murder anyone,' Cordelia said. Rees shut the door and turned to look at the young woman. 'I would swear it on the Bible.' Sobbing noisily, she leaned into Lydia's arms. 'I want to marry Eddy and I know he is making plans for us to run away. He said so in his note.'

Lydia glanced at Rees in perplexity, and he realized he'd forgotten to tell her about Bartlett's message. Sorry, he mouthed at her. She shook her head at him.

Rees thought sourly that this was exactly the result he'd expected. Everyone was upset and they had learned nothing new at all.

FORTY-SIX

Leaving the emotional women behind, Rees carried the jacket out into the hall. He intended to return it to the clothes press in James's bedroom. But before he had taken more than a few steps, he met Mrs Farrell ascending the stairs.

'What do you have there?' she asked, her gaze fixing on the coat in Rees's arms. 'That appears to be James's.'

'Yes,' Rees began.

'Why do you have this?' Mrs Farrell asked.

'Cordy . . .' Rees stopped, not wanting to accuse Cordelia to her mother.

'Did my daughter ask for it? I thought she'd grown out of wishing to wear his clothes. I'll take it.' She held out her hand for it. As Rees surrendered it to her, she added, 'I'll return it to his chamber.'

She turned and carried it away. Rees retraced his steps and went into Lydia's room. Feeling unaccountably tired, he sat down in one of the chairs before the fire. He wondered if Lydia would forgive him for accusing her sister. Lydia may have tried to separate her affection for her sister from her rational mind but in Rees's opinion she had not succeeded.

He hoped everything would go back to normal when they returned home to Maine. Once Lydia was removed from the fevered passions in her family, surely her own emotions would settle, and she would revert to her usual calm and well-ordered self.

Reflecting on home brought Rees's thoughts to his friends and children. How he missed them! He decided he would go to the nursery this morning and spend some time with Sharon. He smiled as he imagined her using the baby dolls as soldiers.

A soft tap sounded on the door. Rees opened it to reveal a maid carrying a large tea tray. Rees stared at her in surprise. 'Madame said you looked tired and distraught and she thought you might appreciate something to eat and drink.'

That was Lydia, Rees thought appreciatively. Always thinking of others. He gestured to the small table before the fire. The maid obediently arranged the teapot, the matching flowered cup and a platter of small cakes and biscuits on the table. The sugar bowl and a pitcher of cream followed.

Rees poured a little of the beverage in his cup, expecting tea. Instead it was coffee. Quite strong coffee by the fragrance. Rees took a cautious sip. It had been heavily sweetened, but he could still taste the bitterness underneath. Nonetheless, he drank half the cup in a couple of gulps. He considered drinking the entire cup; it felt like such a long time since he'd enjoyed a cup of coffee with sugar and cream, doctored the way he liked it. But sugar? How many men, women and children had toiled in the cane fields to produce this sugar? With a little shudder, Rees pushed the cup away. He loved sugared coffee but he couldn't allow himself to drink it.

Taking a biscuit, he nibbled it. Cinnamon exploded in his mouth. The cook in the Farrell household was truly a great baker. Rees settled back to ponder the murders. There were so many little things, inconsistencies that meant nothing by themselves. Added together, they could lead him to an unequivocal solution.

The door opened and Lydia came inside. Although she did not appear surprised to see him, she looked askance at the food on the table. 'The biscuits are delicious,' Rees said, gesturing at the plate in invitation. 'Thank you for this.'

Lydia helped herself to several of the small treats. She took a large bite and swallowed before speaking.

'I am very hungry.'

'You always are,' Rees said affectionately. Three or so months left before his new child made an appearance. 'You won't want to drink this; it is coffee. Not tea.'

Nodding, she wiped her mouth on her handkerchief. 'Cordy swears she had nothing to do with the murders,' she said. 'She is quite vehement.'

'Do you believe her?' Rees asked.

'I want to,' Lydia admitted. She took a nervous bite from her cake. Rees understood her reluctance; he wanted to believe Cordy as well. 'What did the note from Edward Bartlett say?'

'"The problem is solved and we are safe once more. The weather prohibited last night's meeting but I eagerly anticipate the next. Signed, Your loving Eddy."'

'What does that mean?' Lydia asked, her forehead wrinkling. 'What problem? Running away together?'

Rees nodded. 'Most likely. I would if I had killed someone.' Lydia shook her head. 'Here are the facts,' he said. 'We know she's been sneaking out of the house to meet her young man. And there's blood on the cuff of James's jacket.'

'James would have a hard time squeezing his shoulders into the bloody coat,' she agreed unhappily. 'What about Isabeau? She could fit into this jacket.'

Rees eyed her sympathetically. 'But it was Cordelia I saw last night,' he said gently. 'Not Isabeau. Besides, what reason would she have?' He knew Lydia would rather almost anyone be guilty other than Cordelia.

'I just can't imagine my small and feminine sister possessing the strength of will to shoot not just one man and then a woman she did not know, but her beloved uncle as well,' Lydia said miserably.

Rees took another biscuit and ate it while he pondered the bloody jacket. Was it possible James wore this jacket to kill Benicio? Like his sisters, James had a slim build and he might have lost enough weight recently to wear his old garment. He would not have expected a guest in his childhood home – Rees – to have the temerity to search his room and examine the clothing remaining in the press. Unconsciously, he shook his head. 'The most telling fact for me,' he said, 'is that James knows the difference between Benicio and Roark.'

Lydia stared at her husband for several seconds. Almost absently, she took another cake. 'That is true.'

'And, as you have said before, James has always been the most truthful of your siblings,' Rees continued.

Lydia stared at Rees, her eyes widening in anguish. 'But that doesn't mean . . .'

'No,' Rees agreed quickly. 'That doesn't mean the reverse isn't true now. James could be lying and relying on his past as a truth-teller. It does not mean Cordelia is lying.' He hesitated, not wanting to distress Lydia any further, but he felt he had to continue. 'James has no connection with Mr Hutchinson.'

'That we know of,' Lydia said quickly.

Rees nodded. It was a fair point. 'We know Cordelia does. He is courting her; they see each other regularly. Perhaps her expressed loathing is a lie, meant to hide their true connection. I believe we must still keep that young man under consideration.'

'That is so,' Lydia agreed. 'Is it unworthy of me to hope he is the guilty man?'

'Of course not,' Rees replied, so quickly Lydia knew he had meant only to comfort her. She sighed.

FORTY-SEVEN

It was a quiet group that assembled in the drawing room for luncheon. Cordy still looked tear-stained and upset and Mrs Farrell, after one surprised glance at Rees, focused her attention on her daughter. 'Has something happened, darling?' she asked. Cordelia shook her head and declared herself perfectly fine. Rees, whose stomach was a little upset, had hesitated before accompanying Lydia downstairs. He was not sure he would be able to eat.

As they prepared to enter the dining room, they heard voices in the hall. When Rees went to the front of the house, he saw both Farrell and Hutchinson removing their outer garments at the front door. Both were white with snow and as they divested themselves of their coats and scarves, snow drifted to the floor.

'Are you here for dinner?' Rees asked in surprise.

'For luncheon,' corrected Mr Farrell. 'Yes. Everything is quiet today. Many merchants could not make it through the snow.'

'The street outside is barely passable,' Mr Hutchinson added.

'And the snow is coming down so rapidly the servants can't keep up with it,' Mr Farrell said.

As the two men crossed the wet and slippery floor, Morris gathered the maids to wipe away the melting snow.

Rees waited for the two men to join him and they all walked together toward the dining room. Mrs Farrell regarded her husband in shock. 'I did not expect you until this evening,' she said.

'Everything is quiet,' her husband said. 'I invited Mr Hutchinson to join us. He can't make it home; the snow is too deep.'

'Two more places will have to be laid. I will see to it.' She hastened away. Rees heard her raise her voice as she directed Morris. When she returned, and saw everyone standing awkwardly by the dining room, she said briskly, 'There is no reason for us to wait in the hall. Let's return to the drawing room, shall we? It should still be warm in there.'

The drawing room was warm. The maid who had come in to stir up the fire looked over her shoulder at the group descending on the room and jumped to her feet and fled.

'Please sit down,' Mrs Farrell said, with a gesture of invitation. 'It will take but a moment for the maids to finish in the dining room.'

No one obeyed, instead choosing to stand around in an awkward half-circle. Cordy kept her gaze firmly fixed on the floor, her mouth drooping in a sullen curve. Jerusha also kept her eyes on the floor, but Rees thought she was shy rather than sulky. No one knew quite what to say. Finally, Mrs Farrell turned with a smile and said to Mr Hutchinson, 'And how do you like Boston, Mr Hutchinson, now that you've seen the worst of our weather?'

Surely she must have asked him that question previously, Rees thought. But he had to admire Mrs Farrell's efforts to make this uneasy situation seem perfectly normal.

'I like it very well,' Mr Hutchinson said easily. 'Except for this weather. I confess I have never seen anything quite like this.' He gestured at the whirling snow outside.

Mrs Farrell laughed. 'Indeed. Even in Boston most of us do not commonly see such weather.'

'I remember a few winters in my youth that would equal this one,' Mr Farrell commented. Neither Mr Hutchinson nor Mrs Farrell paid him the slightest attention.

'I am already longing for spring,' Mrs Farrell said. 'This is quite different from what I experienced as a girl.'

'You grew up in Saint-Domingue, didn't you?' Mr Hutchinson said. 'A beautiful – and warm – country.'

'Yes. The Pearl of the Antilles. Although I did spend several years in Jamaica,' Mrs Farrell said. 'I still long for the flowers of the islands.'

'I enjoyed my time there,' Mr Hutchinson said.

'Isabeau taught my brother and me how to distill rum from sugar cane,' Mr Farrell put in. 'She learned there . . .'

'I am eager to return, especially on days such as this,' Mrs Farrell said.

Rees looked at her blond curls bent close to Mr Hutchinson's dark head and realized with a jolt that Mr Farrell and Cordelia were not the only ones close to Hutchinson or had influence over him. He turned to look at Lydia.

'It could have been you,' she said to her stepmother in a wondering voice.

Mrs Farrell continued talking as though her good manners prevented her noticing this unseemly interruption.

'You could have persuaded Mr Hutchinson to commit the murders,' Lydia continued.

'What?' Mr Farrell shouted.

Cordelia began screaming.

'Really, Lydia,' Mrs Farrell said with a lazy smile. 'How silly.' Her quiet voice could barely be heard over the shouting.

'Everyone, please be quiet,' Rees said. 'And sit down.'

'To what purpose?' Mrs Farrell asked. 'I do not want to listen to this farrago of nonsense.'

'Quite right,' Mr Farrell agreed.

Rees looked at him.

'Don't you want to know the identity of the person who murdered Roark and left you to take the blame? The one who murdered your brother? And the one who tried to poison James? And had a go at me,' Rees added, recalling that bitter coffee.

For a few seconds the two men locked gazes and then Farrell surrendered. 'Very well then. Speak.'

But Mr and Mrs Farrell waited until everyone else had found seats. As Mrs Farrell finally lowered herself into her chair, Rees said to her, 'You thought I was getting too close, didn't you? When you saw me carrying James's jacket?'

She shook her head and did not reply.

'Show me your proof,' Mr Farrell said in a chilly voice. 'Let's finish this.'

'As everyone knows,' Rees began, 'my wife and I came to Boston on Cordelia's invitation. Mr Farrell had been accused of the murder of a young man, Roark Bustamonte, with whom he had been seen arguing. Cordy wanted us to prove her father's innocence.'

'I didn't expect you to accuse my mother,' Cordy said loudly.

'And why would she ask you to do this?' Mr Hutchinson asked condescendingly at the same time.

'Cordy and I have been regular correspondents,' Lydia said with a small tight smile.

'We've investigated and solved a number of crimes,' Rees added. 'Cordy knew about our successes. It made perfect sense for her to ask us for our help.'

Hutchinson settled back in his chair with a frown.

'Get on with this,' Mr Farrell said shortly.

Rees looked at him. 'Cordelia was convinced you were innocent of the murders. Her faith in you never wavered.'

Farrell turned to his daughter with a smile, the first sign of true affection Rees had seen him express.

Rees continued. 'Unfortunately, everything Lydia and I turned up only made you appear more guilty.'

'But I— You never said anything,' Farrell said, half-rising from his chair.

'Because we weren't persuaded you were the guilty man,' Rees said.

'Of course I'm not,' Farrell huffed.

'He was seen arguing with Mr Roark and accused of murder on the basis of gossip and innuendo,' Mr Hutchinson said.

'Exactly,' Mrs Farrell agreed as she waved away the maid who peeped into the drawing room. Luncheon would have to wait.

Rees looked at Mr Hutchinson. 'Do you know what Mr Farrell and Mr Bustamonte were arguing over? No? Does anyone here know? No?' Rees swept his gaze over the assemblage. No one knew – or was willing to admit he knew. 'Twenty years ago, Marcus Farrell and his brother visited the West Indies, and not for the first time. They'd made that journey several times seeking their fortunes. But this time was different. Marcus was now a widower. He had two children so he was also looking for a second wife.' He nodded at Isabeau. 'A woman he married.'

'Ancient history,' Marcus Farrell said angrily. 'No one needs to know any of this.'

'Not so ancient, I think. During that trip, they defrauded Roark's father of a sugar plantation. And worse. Roark believes Marcus Farrell murdered his father.'

'I did not,' Farrell blustered. Rees regarded his father-in-law thoughtfully. He believed Marcus Farrell was guilty of the murder of Roark's father. But he also knew there was no way to discover the truth or find justice now.

'Be that as it may,' Rees continued, 'last autumn, Roark Bustamonte came to Boston. With proof, I might add, of his right to that plantation.'

'Forgeries,' Mr Farrell said.

'Of course they are,' agreed Mrs Farrell.

Lydia turned to look at her stepmother.

'You knew about Mr Bustamonte and his papers?' Lydia asked.

Isabeau hesitated, trying to decide how to respond. Finally, she nodded. 'I'm his wife. He told me everything.'

'You shot him,' Lydia accused her.

'Why would I murder a boy I did not know?' Isabeau argued.

'Roark's arrival threatened Mr Farrell's wealth, and probably his reputation as well,' Rees replied. 'So he had to die.'

'This is nothing but supposition,' Hutchinson interrupted. Rees eyed the young man for several seconds.

'Perhaps. I thought you might be the murderer. You had opportunity. And no family feeling as well to prevent you from shooting Julian.'

'Why would I do that?' Hutchinson cried, horrified.

'Several reasons.' Rees allowed his gaze to rest on Mrs Farrell. 'Love, for one. You share an intimate connection.'

Cordelia looked confused but Marcus Farrell understood.

'Is this true?' he demanded.

Almost, Rees thought, as though Marcus had suspected something.

When neither Hutchinson nor Isabeau denied the accusation, Marcus jumped from his chair. He crossed the floor in two steps and put his hands around Mr Hutchinson's throat. 'Tell the truth. Were you sleeping with my wife?'

Caught by surprise, Rees stood frozen for a few seconds. Cordy and Lydia began screaming. Then Rees leaped forward, banging his knee on Lydia's chair as he hurried around it.

He pushed Farrell away with his left hand as he wrenched those grasping fingers away with his right. Several minutes passed before Rees managed to separate the combatants, and even then Morris had to be called in to help. After further struggle, in which Rees received a punch to the chest and a clout on the jaw, Farrell and Hutchinson were finally completely separated. The latter put his hands around his throat and struggled to catch his breath. Mr Farrell's nose was bleeding.

'It was only once,' Isabeau said defiantly. 'I realized it was a mistake.' She turned to Hutchinson. 'Why did you murder Julian? Not for me.'

'I didn't—' Hutchinson stared at her in horror. 'Isabeau . . .'

His fury undiminished, Marcus moved to a seat as far from his wife as he could get. Morris hastened to put a linen napkin into Farrell's hands.

'May I resume?' Rees asked in some annoyance.

'I did not murder anyone,' Hutchinson cried hoarsely. 'I had no reason.'

'Isabeau,' Lydia said tersely.

'And money,' Rees said. 'Once Roark was eliminated and Julian and James were out of the way, your marriage to Cordy would almost guarantee you inherited the entirety of Marcus Farrell's estate. Plantation, shipping business and all.'

Hutchinson, his face white, stared at Rees. 'But I didn't . . . I couldn't.'

'Wait. That can't be,' Marcus Farrell said, almost reluctantly. 'He cannot have murdered my brother. Hutchinson arrived that morning just after eight. He would not have had time . . .'

FORTY-EIGHT

'**N**o,' Rees said, turning to stare at Mrs Farrell. She was smiling slightly, as though this was all too ridiculous to contemplate. 'It was your wife. Julian recognized you, Isabeau. He tried to tell me it was Jarre. As in Isabeau Jarre. That was your maiden name, was it not?'

'She did not do it,' Farrell said, his voice muffled by the napkin he held against his bleeding nose. 'She could not have. It is possible she, or Hutchinson, murdered Benicio, believing he was Roark Bustamonte. I was out that night so I would not know that. But not

Julian. She arose early that morning and joined me just after nine for breakfast. The three of us were together.'

'Yes. But she had plenty of time to shoot Julian and return home before nine,' Rees said sadly.

'Benicio too,' Lydia said, turning to her stepmother. 'It was you the witness saw running away. You wearing James' discarded clothing. But you shot the wrong man.'

'It would have been dark then,' Hutchinson said in a hoarse voice. 'There is no way anyone could have seen anything.'

Mrs Farrell smiled at him in approval.

'Yes. I was told the murder occurred at night; a few hours after midnight,' she agreed, sounding bored.

'Sensibly,' Rees said, turning to look at her, 'you carried a lantern. That provided enough light for our witness to see the white breeches you wore with the silver buttons at the knee. James's old breeches.'

'It was Cordelia who was sneaking out,' Mrs Farrell said. 'Not me.'

'You knew I was meeting Eddy?' Cordy asked in shock.

'You weren't as careful as you thought you were,' Isabeau said critically.

'The note Eddy gave you at Faneuil Hall was meant for your stepmother,' Rees said.

'Is that true?' Marcus Farrell cried in anguish. 'You knew Cordy—' He could not continue.

'Why didn't you say something if you knew?' Lydia asked Isabeau angrily.

'Because it gave her cover,' Rees said. Mrs Farrell only smiled. 'But Cordelia wasn't wearing James' old clothes. I saw Cordy on one of her midnight excursions. She wore her prettiest and newest gown. In the middle of a snowstorm. And she stood at the bottom of the drive waiting for a carriage that never came.' He looked at Cordelia, who was staring at her mother in horror. 'Isn't that right, Cordy?'

She nodded.

'I wanted to be beautiful for Eddy.' She could scarcely force out the words.

'Of course you did. But Edward did not come.'

'Because of the weather,' she replied quickly.

'Not because of the weather,' Lydia said softly. 'That note was not meant for you.' She glanced at her husband. 'That line, the problem is solved, puzzled me. What problem? And then I realized we had bumped into Edward Bartlett several times, supposedly by accident. Isabeau always spoke to him privately. She called him Eddy by mistake several times. And she was quick to recover Edward Bartlett's missive from Cordelia. What if both messages were meant for Isabeau and Cordelia was simply a diversion?'

'And the problem Bartlett referred to was the death of the tavern-keeper's wife?' Rees guessed. 'Who he thought was the witness.'

Lydia nodded.

'No, this isn't true,' Cordelia screamed. 'Eddy is my beau.'

'But wait,' Mr Hutchinson said. 'Roark, or whoever that young man was, was shot. Isabeau could not have done that.'

'Why not?' Rees asked. 'Cordelia has a muff pistol that was given her by her father. To keep us safe, she told me. *Us.* I suggest that Mr Farrell gave one to his wife as well.'

'I did,' Mr Farrell gasped, pale with shock.

'Is this true?' Mr Hutchinson turned to stare at Isabeau.

'I have a muff pistol,' Mrs Farrell said dismissively. 'Many women do. It means nothing.'

'You used it to shoot Benicio and Julian,' Rees said.

'This is absurd,' Mrs Farrell said. 'I do not have to listen to any more of this.' She made as if to rise but her husband put his hand on hers.

'Let's hear the rest,' he said grimly.

'Julian knew what had happened all those years ago, about the fraud and the murder of Roark's father,' Lydia said. 'You rose early that morning, shot Julian, and then came home, changed clothes and breakfasted with my father to give yourself an alibi.'

Rees nodded in agreement, remembering the foreman describing the young man who visited Julian.

'You overheard Lydia and I discussing the tavern, and the witness, didn't you?' he asked.

She tossed her head. 'I was home then.'

'We know. You furnished Edward Bartlett with the muff pistol and he took care of it.'

'But why?' Cordelia asked, tears streaming down her cheeks. 'Why?'

'Maybe Cordy and Jerusha should leave,' Lydia suggested, turning to look at the girls.

'No! Don't treat me like a child,' Cordelia snapped. 'I'm staying, and that's final.'

Rees paused but when neither of Cordy's parents objected, he continued. 'Your father and his brother were quarreling over the distillery.'

'I needed money,' Farrell admitted reluctantly.

'You were threatening to sell the distillery,' Lydia said coldly. 'Uncle Julian did not want to.'

'In fact, Julian threatened to testify on Roark's behalf. We saw his letter to you,' Rees continued.

'My father would never hurt . . .' Cordy began. Her sobs prevented her from continuing.

'No. But Isabeau wanted to protect the distillery and all the money it brought in. Julian had to go.'

'A thinner tissue of lies I have never heard,' Mrs Farrell said vehemently. 'Although you've accused me and given absurd reasons for my motives, you have not told me how I supposedly accomplished these crimes.' She laughed. 'Marcus was out all night on November 15th, the night Roark – or whoever it was – was murdered. He just confessed it.'

'You remember that date well,' Rees murmured. 'And, as it happens, we did know that. We also know where he was. He could not have murdered Benicio. He was on the other side of town. In fact, he was seen by several influential men. Including a judge.' Silenced by surprise, Mrs Farrell stared at Rees in disbelief. 'They quashed the investigation.'

'How did you discover where—' Mrs Farrell began incredulously.

'That is not important,' Rees said.

'She could not have done it,' Mr Hutchinson said into the silence. 'I know that. She was with me.'

'I told you,' Mrs Farrell said spitefully.

'We know,' Rees said to them both, 'that Mr Hutchinson arrived home in the early hours of the morning. There is a witness to your movements,' he said, staring at Mr Hutchinson. 'Do you wish us to call her?'

Gaping at Rees, Mr Hutchinson shook his head.

'My, you have been busy, Mr Rees,' Mrs Farrell said softly.

'The Painted Pig is only half an hour or so walk away. It would have been a simple matter to change clothes after Hutchinson left you and hurry out. By the time your maid brought you your morning hot chocolate, you would have been back in bed. Unfortunately, you were seen running away.'

'You sent Edward to remove the woman who saw you. He murdered the tavern-keeper's wife,' Lydia said. 'By mistake.'

'But she was not the witness.' Rees's voice broke and, closing his eyes he took several breaths. 'I shall always blame myself for her death. She knew nothing.'

'This is nonsense,' Mrs Farrell said.

'And my son?' Farrell said. 'You mentioned James? You said James was poisoned?' His voice was shaking.

'Yes. James told me that. His fear of poisoning, even more than his estrangement from you, encouraged him to leave.' Rees turned his gaze onto Mrs Farrell. 'I don't know if you meant to kill him, but you achieved one end; he left, leaving you as the sole influence on his father. I didn't believe it until you served me that bitter coffee. You dosed it, and the food you served to James, with quinine, didn't you?'

'Of course not,' Mrs Farrell said. But her husband turned a horrified and appalled stare on his wife.

'My only son. How could you? And why? I gave you everything.'

What had Roark told Rees? That Farrell needed money because he wanted to wed a woman who desired many things.

'She committed the murders to protect your wealth,' Rees said. 'She didn't want you to gamble away everything. In fact, I suspect she hoped you would be charged and executed for the murders.'

Marcus Farrell's gaze moved to Mr Hutchinson and then to his wife.

'Was I to be your next victim?' he asked her. He lifted the bloody napkin to his face. Since the blood dripping from his nose had mostly stopped, Rees suspected he was hiding his tears.

'He was, wasn't he?' Lydia said. 'You were tired of my father, but you wished to keep his money.'

'Clearly, I cannot remain here after suffering these groundless accusations,' Mrs Farrell said. 'I would like to return to the West Indies.'

'We will go to Jamaica together,' Mr Hutchinson said to Mrs Farrell as he reached for her hand. She did not take it and when she did not speak, his smile faded and he gazed at her in dismay.

'You are a fool if you believe she wishes you to accompany her,' Lydia said. 'It is her partner in these crimes she wants. Edward Bartlett.'

'No, that can't be true,' Cordy shouted. 'No.'

Jerusha leaned forward and put her arm around Cordy's shaking shoulders.

'You were the goat,' Rees told Hutchinson bluntly. 'She chose you to perform double duty. You were her alibi, her defense if someone questioned her whereabouts at the time of Benicio's murder.'

'And, if my father escaped the noose and experienced an unfortunate accident that resulted in his death, why, you'd make a perfectly reasonable accused murderer,' Lydia said, not without compassion.

'Is – is that true, Isabeau?' Hutchinson stammered. When she did not reply, Mr Hutchinson's face twisted in agony. Rees saw the young man's devastation and realized he had never seen the woman behind Isabeau's beautiful and flirtatious exterior.

'I wouldn't sleep easily next to her,' Rees said sympathetically.

'This is quite a ridiculous tale,' Mrs Farrell said sharply. 'Of course I am innocent of these charges. Anyway, there is not one shred of proof to support any of these allegations.'

'There's the blood on the jacket,' Rees said. 'There's your own admission you were committing adultery with Mr Hutchinson. There is the note from Edward Bartlett, addressed no doubt to Mrs Farrell. Not Miss.' Cordelia uttered a quickly suppressed scream. 'There is your knowledge of your husband's past as well as your own birth and upbringing in the West Indies. The poisoning of James and myself. Oh yes,' he added, nodding his head, 'I am familiar with the bark. Too much and it is a poison. Fortunately, it is quite bitter. It is difficult to mask even with a great deal of sugar.'

'I believe him,' said Mr Farrell.

'So do I,' Mr Hutchinson agreed, his voice breaking. 'Oh, Isabeau.'

Mrs Farrell rose to her feet. 'I will not listen to this anymore.' She looked from her husband to Mr Hutchinson. 'I am glad neither of you will be accompanying me.' Turning to her daughter, she said, 'I am sorry, Cordelia. I truly am. But I want to be happy too.'

As Mrs Farrell approached the door, Cordelia, her face a chalky white, stumbled to her feet.

'I will always hate you.' She would have fallen if not for Jerusha, who leaped up and grabbed Cordy's arm. 'And I will never forgive you, never, for pushing me to marry Mr Hutchinson, your leavings, and for taking my Eddy away.'

'He's my Eddy. We are alike, he and I. In his eyes, you are just a child.'

As Mrs Farrell stalked from the room, her head held high, Cordelia collapsed, sobbing.

'Congratulations,' Mr Farrell said to Rees and Lydia. 'I asked you to let Roa— Benicio's murder go. Now look what you've done.'

He left the drawing room as well and was quickly followed by Mr Hutchinson. A few moments later, the front door slammed.

'I guess Mr Hutchinson will struggle home after all,' Rees said. He could only imagine how terrible the walk across Boston would be. Uncertainly, he turned to look at Lydia. Would she be unhappy with him? Doing as Cordelia wished and uncovering the identity of the real murderers had been a bit like throwing a lighted brand into kindling. The Farrell family had ignited and would probably never recover.

Lydia smiled at him, a faint smile but a genuine one, nonetheless.

'Thank you for not blaming me,' Rees said.

'For what? Telling the truth? My father will forgive us,' Lydia said as she linked arms with him. 'Especially after he remembers we identified his brother's murderer. And saved his life, and probably Cordy's as well.'

Rees didn't care as long as Lydia did not blame him.

FORTY-NINE

Although both Rees and Lydia were eager to quit the Farrell home, two awkward days passed before they could. The snowstorm did not blow itself out until later that evening. Rees and Lydia were packed and ready by the following afternoon, but the roads were still barely passable. The atmosphere in the house was so thick with tension that if any method of leaving this house had presented itself, Rees would have taken it, up to and including putting his wife's trunk on his back and carrying it to the coach stop.

Cordelia spent the entirety of the first day in her room weeping. Jerusha, who always saw the bright side of life, tried to console her. Rees did not think that was possible. Isabeau's betrayal would hurt Cordelia until the end of her days. And, although they would say nothing about Mrs Farrell's crimes, her abandonment of the family would be so scandalous that Cordy's life in Boston was over. Marcus planned to send his daughter away to a distant school.

Rees did not see Mrs Farrell once. She too remained in her bedchamber, taking her meals on trays brought up the stairs by the maids. Rather than feeling distressed, she was packing her newest gowns and anticipating her future. Clearly, she did not plan to make even a show of remorse. Very early on the second morning, after the worst of the storm had passed, she slipped out of the house. Bridget saw the Bartlett coach outside and Mrs Farrell's boxes atop, driving away.

Marcus Farrell made an occasional appearance at supper, usually when James joined them. Without Mrs Farrell, the meal was much more informal. Still, no one knew quite what to say so supper – all the meals in fact – passed in a succession of awkward silences. But although father and son would never agree, Rees saw a thawing in their relationship.

The sun did not begin to peek out from behind the clouds until late afternoon of the second day. Rees started to hear the sound of wheels in the street. Boston was waking up.

'Tomorrow, first thing,' he said, turning joyfully to his family, 'we will leave for home.'

Jerusha picked up Sharon and began to whirl her around the room until both were screaming with laughter.

By eight o'clock the following morning, the carriage was waiting in the drive. All the trunks and other parcels were downstairs waiting to be packed inside the vehicle. As Rees and his family ate breakfast, the tiger carried out the trunks and stowed them. Rees, who could barely sit still, kept rising to his feet and peering outside.

'Just making sure all of our possessions make it home,' he said to Lydia. She smiled knowingly.

'Are you going to drink your coffee?' she asked him. He shook his head. Maybe, when he arrived home once again, he would drink what had once been his favorite beverage again. But for now, he was still trying to learn to enjoy it without sugar.

He saw Lydia putting some of the biscuits in her pockets for the long journey home. Feeling almost as excited as a boy, Rees rose to his feet once again and peered out the window. He could feel the cold seeping in around the casement, but he thought it might not be as cold as it had been the day before.

By nightfall, they would be in Maine.

'We should go,' he said, moving to the door. Lydia nodded and rose to her feet. She moved a little awkwardly; although they had been in Boston only a few weeks she appeared much more pregnant than she had when they'd arrived. Rees hurried to her side but she brushed him off.

'I'm fine,' she assured him. Jerusha had already donned her outer clothing and when Rees and Lydia stepped into the hall they found Morris waiting for them with Lydia's winter cloak and Rees's greatcoat.

'May I say it was a pleasure to see you again,' Morris said to Lydia. 'And to meet your family.'

Etiquette be damned! Rees grasped Morris's hand and shook it.

'A pleasure,' Rees said. He thought Morris worked a far harder job than farming; Rees wouldn't serve as a butler for any price.

Lydia put on her cloak and tied her bonnet strings under her chin.

'I shall miss you,' Cordelia cried, hurtling down the hall towards her sister. 'Oh, I wish you and Jerusha could stay. Especially now.' She hugged Lydia with all her might, her enthusiastic embrace pushing Lydia's bonnet to one side. With one hand holding her hat, Lydia hugged her sister with the other. 'We will see you soon,' she promised.

'Thank you for visiting,' Marcus Farrell said, somewhat tentatively approaching the family at the front door. He stood a few feet from Lydia as though uncertain of her reaction. 'I appreciated it.'

Lydia nodded stiffly. 'Please give my love to James.'

'I will. He won't move back but, well, we are talking.' He hesitated and then said, 'I . . . you did a lot for us. For me. I will . . . there will be some changes made here. I am returning the plantation to Roark Bustamonte. It is only right.'

'And Isabeau?' Lydia asked.

'I don't know. I will offer her a settlement and from then on, I

will not be responsible for her bills. She . . . well, she is already
on her way south.' He hesitated again. 'Lydia. I just wanted to say,
I . . . uh—' Stumbling over his words, he reached out for her. He
could not force out any apology but 'I'm sorry.'

Lydia nodded and allowed him to peck her cheek.

He kissed both Sharon and Jerusha, making no distinction between
them as his granddaughters. Rees warmed to his father-in-law for
that and when Marcus Farrell held out his hand Rees took it readily.

'I am glad my daughter found a man who makes her happy,'
Farrell said. But he was still the same man he'd been when they'd
arrived and he had to continue on, tarnishing the tender moment.
'Isabeau was wrong. You are not a rustic,' he said. 'Lydia did far
better than I expected.'

'Very glad to meet my wife's family,' Rees said politely. Shaking
his head, for he could not conceive what possessed Marcus Farrell
to say such things, Rees went through the door and out to the
carriage waiting in the drive. He climbed in and sat next to Lydia.
The coachman called out to the matched four and Rees felt the
quiver of the wheels beginning to turn underneath him, skidding a
little in the snow.

They were going home.

AUTHOR'S NOTES

Boston

Since the birth of the United States, Boston has been one of the country's most important cities. It was settled by the Puritans in 1630 and quickly became a trading center and hub of commerce. In 1822, the citizens voted to change the name from the Town of Boston to the City of Boston. During Rees's visit, Boston would still have been a town.

Boston was also one of the first cities to adopt a metropolitan police force. In 1790, Boston's population was 43,000 and the ability of nightwatchmen and constables to keep order and protect lives and property was already strained. The rapid growth that occurred beginning in the early 1800s, and increased with the influx of foreign immigrants, further stressed the system. In 1837, Boston established a police force modeled on the London police.

Caleb Bingham

Although the description of the school in Boston is my own creation, Caleb Bingham was a real person. He was an early advocate of opening education to girls and set up a school in Boston, as described. This school was later taken over by the Boston public school system. Bingham also wrote a number of textbooks. His book *The Columbia Orator* is credited with helping noted abolitionist Frederick Douglass develop his public speaking style.

Charles Bullfinch

Charles Bullfinch is considered to be the first native-born American architect. The first building he designed was the Hollis Street Church. He went on to build the Massachusetts State House as well as a number of private homes and churches in Boston.

Faneuil Hall

The marketplace was opened in 1743. It was funded in part by the profits from the slave trade, and several early slave auctions took place nearby. It was built with a large open marketplace on the ground floor and assembly rooms above. Prior to the Revolution, speeches by such dignitaries as Sam Adams took place there, and so the hall is sometimes referred to as the Cradle of Liberty.

It was destroyed by fire in 1761 and rebuilt. In 1806 Charles Bullfinch expanded the hall, adding several galleries and more. It was rebuilt once again in 1898 of non-combustible materials.

Malaria and Quinine

Malaria is a microorganism transmitted by the Anopheles mosquito. Symptoms include fever, fatigue and vomiting. In extreme cases, it can cause seizures, coma and death. One of the hallmarks of the disease is reoccurrence; symptoms can return months and even years later. It is still endemic in Africa, Asia and Latin America.

Known for centuries in Europe and Africa (mal – bad, aria – air), it has been theorized malaria was carried to Latin America by the slaves brought from Africa to work on the plantations.

The first effective treatment for malaria came from the bark of the cinchona tree, which contains quinine. The cinchona tree grows in the Andes, primarily in Peru. The bark was brought to Europe in the mid-1600s. It remained the primary treatment until 1920 when other medicines were developed.

Quinine is toxic. Headache, sweating, nausea, hearing impairment, dizziness as well as more serious effects: vomiting, diarrhea, deafness, blindness can occur. Quinine is no longer a recommended treatment. There is one vaccine for malaria, but the most effective treatment remains mosquito control.

Taverns

Taverns were an important part of Colonial and Federalist life. All of the taverns mentioned in the book, with the exception of the Painted Pig, which is my own creation, existed in 1801. The Warren Tavern is still in use as a bar and restaurant. The Green Dragon, which was the Headquarters of the Sons of Liberty (and where much of the planning for the War of Independence occurred), was demolished in 1822.

Triangle Trade – Slavery and Rum

At its most basic, the triangle involved the New England merchants taking African slaves to the Southern United States and the West Indies for work on the plantations, especially the sugar plantations. The byproduct of making sugar, molasses, was shipped to New England for distillation into rum. The rum was exported to Great Britain and brought to Africa to purchase more slaves.

Saint-Domingue was the name for Haiti when it was under French control.

M   1-22

cl